EMINENT DOMAIN,
ALIEN STYLE

Sam restrained the urge to gulp his glass of whiskey. "They took her. The aliens—you must have read about them up here. They *appropriated* her, like losing your home to municipal construction. Sorry, railroad's coming through, we need your universe. No, not even that polite—I didn't even get the usual ten percent of market value and a token apology."

"Christ, Sam," Greg said, "I'm sorrier than I know how to say. Is she . . . I mean, how is she taking it?"

"Better than I would. She's still alive."

Greg's face took on the expression of a man who is not sure he should be saying what he is saying, but feels compelled to anyway. "Knowing you, the way you feel about such things, I'm surprised *you* didn't kill her yourself."

"I tried. I couldn't. You know, that may just be the worst part."

"Ah, Sam, Sam—"

"She begged me to. *And I couldn't!*"

BAEN BOOKS BY SPIDER ROBINSON

USER Friendly

SPIDER ROBINSON

BAEN

USER FRIENDLY

Copyright 1998 by Spider Robinson

Some of these stories and essays appeared in the magazines GALAXY, DESTINIES, ANALOG SCIENCE FACT/SCIENCE FICTION and OMNI; the original anthology TALES FROM THE PLANET EARTH, or the newspaper THE TORONTO GLOBE AND MAIL; or were commissioned by and read aloud on CBC Radio.

A Baen Books Original

Baen Publishing Enterprises
P.O. Box 1403
Riverdale, NY 10471

ISBN: 0-671-87864-6

First Printing, February 1998

Distributed by Simon & Schuster
1230 Avenue of the Americas
New York, NY 10020

Typeset by Windhaven Press, Auburn, NH

Printed in the United States of America

TABLE OF CONTENTS

USER FRIENDLY

When he saw the small, weatherbeaten sign which read, WELCOME TO CALAIS, MAINE, Sam Waterford smiled. It hurt his mouth, so he stopped.

He was tired and wired and as stiff as IRS penalties; he had been driving for . . . how long? He did not really know. There had been at least one entire night; he vividly remembered a succession of headlight beams coring his eyeballs at some time in the distant past. Another night was near, the sun low in the sky. It did not matter. In a few more minutes he would have reached an important point in his journey: the longest undefended border in the world. Once past it, he would start being safe again . . .

He retained enough of the man he had once been to stop when he saw the Duty-Free Store. Reflex politeness: a guest, especially an unexpected one, brings a gift. But the store was closed. It occurred to him distantly that in his half-dozen trips through these parts, no matter what time he arrived, that store had always been closed. The one on the Canadian side, on the other hand, was almost always open. Too weary to wonder why, he got back into his Imperial and drove on.

He had vaguely expected to find a long lineup at the border crossing, but there was none. The guards on the American side ignored him as he drove across the short bridge, and the guards on the Canadian side waved him through. He was too weary to wonder at that, too—and distracted by the mild surge of elation that came from leaving American soil, leaving the danger zone.

It was purely subjective, of course. As he drove slowly through the streets of St. Stephen, New Brunswick, the only external reminders that he was in Canada were the speed limit signs marked in metric and the very occasional bilingual sign (French, rather than the Spanish he was used to in New York.). Nonetheless, he felt as though the invisible band around his skull had been loosened a few notches. He found a Liquor Commission outlet and bought a bottle of Old Bushmill's for Greg and Alice. A Burger King next door reminded him that he had not eaten for . . . however long the trip had lasted so far, so he bought something squishy and ate it and threw most of it up again a few miles later.

He drove all the rest of that evening, and long into the night, through endless miles of tree-lined highway interrupted only seldomly by a village speed-trap, and once by the purely nominal border between the provinces of New Brunswick and Nova Scotia, and he reached the city of Halifax as the sun was coming up on his left. Dimly he realized that he would shortly be drinking Old Bushmill's and talking, and he expected both to be equally devastating to his system, so he took the trouble to find the only all-night restaurant in Halifax and tried eating again, and this time it worked. He'd had no chance to change his money, but of course the waitress was more than happy to accept Yankee currency: even allowing him a 130% exchange rate, she was making thirty-seven cents profit on each dollar. The food lifted his spirits just enough that he was able to idly admire Halifax as he drove through it, straining to remember his way. It had been many years since any city in America had looked this pleasant—the smog was barely noticeable, and the worst wino he noticed had bathed this year. As he drove past Citadel Hill he could see the harbor, see pleasure craft dancing on the water (along with a couple of toothless Canadian Forces destroyers and a sleek black American nuclear sub), see birds riding the morning updrafts and hear their raucous calls. He was *not*, of course, in a good mood as he parked in front of Greg and Alice's house, but he was willing to concede, in theory, that the trick was possible.

He was still quite groggy; for some reason it seemed tremendously important to knock on the precise geometrical center of Greg's door, and maddeningly difficult to do so. When the door opened anyway it startled him. His plans stopped here; he had no idea what to do or say next.

"Sammy!" His old college buddy grinned and frowned simultaneously. "Jesus, man, it's good to see you—or it would be if you didn't look like death on a soda cracker! What the hell are you doing here, why didn't you—"

"They got her, Greg. They took *Marian*. There's nothing I—"

Suddenly Greg and the front of his house were gone, replaced by a ceiling, and Sam discovered that he was indoors and horizontal. "—can do," he finished reflexively, and then realized that he must have fainted. He reached for his head, probed for soft places.

"It's okay, Sam. I caught you as you went down. Relax."

Sam had forgotten what the last word meant; it came through as noise. He sat up, worked his arms and legs as if by remote control. The arms hurt worse than the legs. "Got a cigarette? I ran out—" He thought for a moment. "— yesterday, I think."

Greg handed him a twenty-five pack of Export A. "Fill your boots. Have you eaten more recently than that?"

"Yeah. Funny—I actually forgot I smoked. Now, that's weird." He fumbled the pack open and lit a cigarette; his first puff turned half an inch to ash and stained the filter. "Did I drop the bottle?"

"You left it in the car." Greg left the room, returned with two glasses of Irish whiskey. "You don't have to talk until you're ready."

Sam restrained the urge to gulp. If you got too drunk, you had *less* control of your thoughts sometimes. "They took her. The aliens—you must have read about them up here. They *appropriated* her, like losing your home to municipal construction. Sorry, railroad's coming through, we need your universe. No, not even that polite— I didn't even get the usual ten percent of market value and a token apology."

"Christ, Sam, I'm sorrier than I know how to say. Is she . . . I mean, how is she taking it?"

"Better than I would. She's still alive."

Greg's face took on the expression of a man who is not sure he should be saying what he is saying, but feels compelled to anyway. "Knowing you, the way you feel about such things, I'm surprised *you* didn't kill her yourself."

"I tried. I couldn't. You know, that may just be the worst part."

"Ah, Sam, Sam—"

"She begged me to. *And I couldn't!*"

They waited together until he could speak again. "Damn," he said finally, "it's good to see you." And it would be even better to see Alice. She must be at work, designing new software to deadline.

Greg looked like he'd been missing some sleep himself. Novelists often did. "You might as well get it all out," he said. "How did it happen?"

Sam nodded slowly, reluctantly. "Get it over with. Not a lot to tell. We were laying in bed together, watching TV. We'd . . . we'd just finished making love. Funny, it was better than usual. I was feeling blessed. Maybe that should have warned me or something. All of a sudden, in the middle of David Letterman's show—do you get him up here?"

"We get all the American shows; these days, it's about all we get. Go on."

"Right in the middle of Stupid Pet Tricks, she just got up and left the room. I asked her to bring me back some ice water. She didn't say anything. A few moments later I heard the front door open and close. I didn't attach any significance to it. After five or ten minutes I called to her. I assumed she was peeing or something. When she didn't answer I got up and went to make sure she was all right. I couldn't find her.

"I could *not* figure it out. You know how it is when something just does not make sense? She wasn't anywhere in the apartment. I'd heard the door, but she *couldn't* have gone out—she was naked, barefoot, her coat and boots were still in the hall closet. I couldn't imagine her unlocking the door for anyone we didn't know, certainly not for someone who could snatch her out the door in two seconds without the slightest sound or struggle. I actually found myself looking under chairs for her.

"So eventually I phoned the police, and got all the satisfaction you'd expect, and called everyone we knew with no success at all, and finally I fell asleep at four A.M. hoping to God it was some kind of monstrous joke she was playing on me.

"Two government guys in suits came that night. They told me what had happened to her. 'Sir, your wife has been requisitioned by aliens.

Quite a few people's husbands and wives have been. And we wouldn't do anything about it if we could, which we can't.' They were good; I never laid a hand on them. When I calmed down enough they took me to the hospital to see her. She was in pretty good shape, all things considered. Her feet were a mess, of course, from walking the streets barefoot. Exposure, fatigue. After the aliens turned her loose, she was raped by four or five people before the police found her. You remember New York at night. But they didn't cut her up or anything, just raped her. She told me she almost didn't mind that. She said it was a relief to be only physically raped. To be able to struggle if she wanted, even if it didn't help. To at least have the power to protest." He stubbed his cigarette out and finished his drink. "Strange. She was just as naked while she was possessed, but no human tried to touch her until afterward. Like, *occupado*, you know?"

Greg gave him his own, untouched drink. "Go on."

"Well, God, we talked. You know, tried to talk. Mostly we cried. And then in the middle of a snuffle she chopped off short and got up out of the hospital bed and left the room. I was so mixed up it took me a good five seconds to catch on. When I did I went nuts. I tried to chase after her and catch her, and the two government guys stopped me. I broke the nose of one of them, and they wrestled me into somebody's room and gave me a shot. As it was taking hold I turned and looked sideways out the window, just in time to catch a glimpse of her, three flights down, walking through the parking lot. Silly little hospital gown, open at the back, paper slippers. Nobody got in her way. A doctor was walking in the same direction; he was a zombie too. Masked and gloved, blood on his gloves; I hope he finished his operation first . . .

"She came home the next day, and we had about six hours. Long enough to say everything there was to say five times, and a bunch of other things that maybe should never have been said. This time when she left, she left dressed, with an empty bladder and money to get home with when they let her go. We had accepted it, taken the first step in starting to plan around it. Only practical, right?" He shook his head, hearing his neck crack, and finished off the second drink. It had no more effect than had the first.

"What happened then?"

"I got in the car and drove here."

For the first time, Greg looked deeply shocked. "You *left* her there, to deal with it *alone?*"

Someone grasped Sam's heart in impersonal hands and wrung it out. Greg must have seen the pain, and some of the accusatory tone left his voice. "Jesus wept, Sam! Look, I know you. You've written three entire books on brainwashing and mind-control, 'the ultimate obscenity,' you call it: I know how uniquely horrible the whole thing must be to you, and for you. But you've been married to Marian for *ten years,* as long as I've been married to Alice—how could you possibly have left her?"

The words came out like projectile vomit. "*I had to, God damn it: I was scared!*"

"Scared? Of what?"

"Of *them*, for Christ's sake, what's the matter with you? Scared that the thing would look out of her eyes and notice *me*—and decide that I looked . . . *Useable*." He began to shudder, and found it extremely hard to stop. He lit another cigarette with shaking hands.

"Sam, it doesn't work that way—"

"I know, I know, they told me. Who said fear has to be logical?"

Greg sat back and sighed deeply, a mournful sound. There was a silence, then, which lasted for ten seconds or more. The worst was said, and there was nothing else to say.

Finally Sam tried to distract himself with mundane trivia. "Listen, I saw the 'No Parking' sign where I parked, I just didn't give a damn. If I give you my keys, will you move it for me? I don't think I can."

"Can't do it," Greg said absently. "I don't dare. They could fine me four hundred bucks if I get caught behind the wheel of an American-registered car, you know that."

The subject had come up on Sam's last visit, back in 1982. Marian had been with him, then. "Sorry. I forgot."

"Sam, what made you decide to come *here*?"

He discovered that he did not know. He tried to analyze it. "Well, part of it is that I needed to tell somebody the whole thing, and you and Alice are the only people on earth that love me enough. But there wasn't even that much logic to it. I was just terrified, and I needed to get to someplace safe, and Canada was the nearest place."

Greg burst out laughing.

Sam stared at him, scandalized. "What's so funny?"

It took Greg quite a while to stop laughing, but when he did—despite the smile that remained on his face—Sam could see that he was very angry.

"Americans, no kidding. You're amazing. I should be used to it by now, I guess."

"What are you talking about?"

"About you, you smug, arrogant bastard. There are nasty old aliens in the States, taking people over and using them to walk around and talk with, for mysterious purposes of their own—so what do you do? Take off for Canada, where it'll be safe. You just *assume*, totally unconsciously, that the aliens will think like you. That they'd never bother with a quaint, backward, jerkwater country like Canada, The Retarded Giant On Your Doorstep! Don't you read the papers?"

"I don't—"

"Excuse me. Stupid of me: it probably wouldn't make the Stateside papers, would it? You simple jackass, there are *three times* more Canadians hagridden than Americans! Even though you've got ten times the population. They came here *first.*"

"First? No, that can't be, I'd have heard—"

"Why? We barely heard about it ourselves, with two out of the sixteen channels Canadian-originated. It ain't news unless and until it happens in the friggin' United Snakes of America!" He had more to say, but suddenly he tilted his head as if he heard something. "Hell. Stay there." He got up and left the room hastily, muttering to himself.

Sam sat there, stunned by his old friend's inexplicable anger. He finished his cigarette and lit another while he tried to understand it. He heard a murmur of voices elsewhere in the house, and recognized the one that wasn't Greg's. Alice was home from work. Perhaps she would be more sympathetic. He got up and followed the sound of the voices, and it wasn't until he actually saw her that he remembered. Alice hadn't worked night shift in over a year—and she had a home terminal now anyway . . .

She was in pretty fair shape. Face drawn with fatigue, of course, and her hair in rats. She was fully dressed except for pants and panties; there was an oil or grease stain on the side of her blouse. She tried to smile when she saw Sam.

"He caught me sitting on the john," she said. "Hi, Sam." She burst into tears, still trying to smile.

He thought for a crazy second that she meant her husband. But no, of course, the "he" she referred to was not Greg, but her—

—her *rider*. Her User . . .

"Oh, my dear God," he said softly, still not quite believing. He had been so sure, so unthinkingly convinced that it would be safe here.

"Naturally the Users came here first," Greg said with cold, bitter anger, handing his wife the slacks she had kicked off on her way out the door some hours before. "We were meant for each other, them and Canadians. Strong, superior parasites from the sky? Who just move right in and take over without asking or apologizing?" His voice began to rise in pitch and volume. "Arrogant puppetmasters who show up and start pulling your strings for you, dump you like a stolen car when they're done with you, too powerful to fight and indifferent to your rage and shame? And your own government breaks its neck to help 'em do whatever they want, sells out without even stopping to ask the price in case it might offend 'em?" He was shouting at the top of his lungs. "Hell, man, we almost didn't even notice the Users. *We took 'em for Americans.*"

Alice was dressed again now. Her voice was soft and hoarse; someone had been doing a lot of talking with her vocal cords recently. "Greg, shut up."

"Well, dammit all, he—"

She put a hand over his mouth. "Please, my very beloved, shut your face. I can't talk louder than you this time, my throat hurts."

He shut up at once, put his own hand over hers and held it tightly against his face, screwing his eyes shut. She leaned against him and they put their free arms around each other; the sight made Sam want to weep like a child.

"Greg," she said huskily, "I love you. Part of me wants to cheer what you just said; many Canadians would. But you're wrong to say it."

"I know, baby, I know *exactly* the pain Sam's going through, don't I? That's why I got mad at him, thinking his pain was bigger 'cause it was American. I'm sorry, Sam—"

"That's only part of why you're wrong. This is more important than our friendship with Sam and Marian, my love. Pay attention: *you would never have said what you said if there'd been an Inuit in the room.* Or a MicMac, or a French Canadian, or a Pakistani. You'd never have said it if we were standing in North Preston, talking to someone who used to live in Africville till they moved all the darkies out to build a bridge approach. Don't you see, darling, *everybody is a Canadian now.* Everybody on Earth is now a Native People; a Frog; a Wog; a Paki; a Nigger— gradations of Niggerhood just don't seem all that important any more.

"Gregory, some of the Users wear a human body as though it ought to have flippers, or extra legs, or wings—I saw one try to make an arm work like a tentacle, and break it. There are a *lot* of different races and species and genuses of User—one of the things they seem to be using Earth for is a conference table at which to work out their own hierarchy of power and intelligence and wealth. I've heard a lot of the palaver; they don't bother to turn my ears off because they don't care if I hear or not. Most of it I don't understand even though they do use English a lot, but a few things I've noticed.

"If two neighboring races discover that one is vastly superior to the other in resources or wisdom or aggressiveness, they don't spend a lot of time whining about the inequity of it all. They figure out where it looks like the water is going to wind up when it's finished flowing downhill, and then they start looking for ways to live with that.

"I've never heard a User say the words, 'It's not fair.' Apparently, if you can form that thought, you don't reach the stars. The whole universe is a hierarchy of Users and Used, from the race that developed the long-distance telepathy that brought them all here, down to the cute little microorganisms that are ruthlessly butchered every day by a baby seal. We're part of that chain, and if we can't live with that, we'll die."

The three were silent for a time. Finally Sam cleared his throat. "If you two will excuse me," he said softly, "I have to be getting back home to my wife now."

Alice turned to him, and gave him a smile so sad and so brave that he thought his heart might break. "Sam," she said, "that's a storybook ending. I hope it works out that way for you. But don't blow your brains out if it doesn't, okay? Or hers. You write about mind-control and the institution of slavery because subversion of the human free will, loss of control, holds a special horror for you. You're the kind that dies fighting instead. Marian isn't. I'm not. Most humans aren't, even though they like to feel they would be if it came to it. Maybe that's why the Users came here.

"It may be that you and Marian can't live together any more; I don't know. I do know that you need twelve hours' sleep and a couple of good meals before it's safe to let you back on

the highway—and Greg and I badly need someone to talk to. My User won't be back for
another ten hours or so. What would you say to
some eggs and back bacon?"

Sam closed his eyes and took a deep breath.
"I guess I'd say, 'Hello there—do you mind if
I use you for twelve hours or so?'" *And turn you
into shit in the process*, he thought, but he found
that he was ashamed of the thought, and that
was something, at least. "Can I use your phone?"

"Only if you reverse the charges, you cheap
Yankee son of a bitch," Greg said at once, and
came and hugged him hard.

COPYRIGHT VIOLATION

I was singing along with John Lennon when she crowned me from behind: that's how the rape began.

I don't often sing along with jukeboxes; a fellow like me can get hurt that way. It's not just that I can't carry a tune. I seem to have one of those faces that stevedores and bikers and truckers—and even the odd minister in his cups—love to punch, just on general principles, I guess, so I tend to avoid drawing attention to myself when I'm in a bar.

No, I'll be more honest than that. I *can* be honest, you see—because it's *my* choice. I'll metaphorically strip myself for you, and then you'll see that it wasn't because she raped my body that I wanted to kill her, or even my mind, but because she raped my soul.

So, being honest: it isn't just for fear of

getting punched that I make myself inconspicuous in bars. Contrary to what you may have
heard, there aren't that many real bullies in the
world; most men looking for a fight will leave
me alone, the way a hunter with an elephant
gun will walk past a gerbil. What I'm really
avoiding when I make myself inconspicuous is
pity.

I mean, look at me. Most of the people who
ever have, failed to see me at all—the eye tends
to subtract me—but those who do notice usually feel sorry for me. My chin and my Adam's
apple are like twin brothers in bunk beds. I got
this nose. My dad used to say that my ears made
me look like a taxicab coming down the street
with the doors open. My glasses weigh more than
my shoes, and my shoes weigh more than the
rest of me.

I mean, I'll bet you think a prostitute will take
anybody, that any man with enough money can
get laid. It may be true. *I've* never had enough
money. Oh, once I got a woman to agree, for
three times the going rate . . . but the way she
went about it, I just couldn't do it—to her total
lack of surprise. I've never really given up hope
since, in my adolescence, I first heard the term
"mercy hump"—but so far, I haven't found that
much mercy in the world.

So when the jukebox clicked, and John Lennon
began to tell me that he was a loser, I just naturally chimed in on the second, "I'm a l-o-o-oser."

And felt something circular and weighty being
pressed down over my head—and heard the most
beautiful voice in the world, right behind my ear,

sing the next line of the song—and spun quickly around and saw her.

Oh my, it hurt to look at her. You're a normal man, friend, no doubt you've won some and lost some—but didn't you ever see one that you just *knew* on sight you'd trade your home and wife and children and hope of immortality and twenty years of your mortal life for ten minutes in bed with—and knew just as clearly that you'd never ever get her, even at that price? God, it's a sweet pain, that is, and I know a lot more about it than you do. Every man has in his mind an ideal of the Perfectly Beautiful Woman—she was better-looking than that, and better dressed.

"Forgive me, sir," she said.

I guess I should remember that those were the first words she said to me—if you don't count the song lyric. At the time I remember thinking that I was prepared to forgive her anything whatsoever. It shows you how wrong you can be.

To my gratified surprise, my voice worked. "Forgive you?"

"I just couldn't help myself."

With an effort I tore my attention from a close examination of her parts and perimeters, and tried to imagine why she could possibly feel a need to apologize to me. Oh yes—she had put something heavy on my head. I felt it with my fingertips. It felt like a crown. Reluctantly I took my eyes away from her and looked in the mirror behind the bar.

Yep, that was a crown on my head, all right. A simple, inch-wide band of gold around my forehead, elaborately chased but otherwise unadorned. It was so heavy, it had to be real gold or gilded lead.

Alongside the twin miracles of her existence and the fact that she was speaking to me (and calling me "sir"!), nothing was strange. "That's perfectly all right," I said, quite as though preternaturally beautiful women put thousands of dollars worth of gold on my brow every third Thursday, and I were becoming resigned to it. System crash of the brain.

She did something with her face that I don't have a word for. Deep in the shielded core of my heart, graphite rods slid up out of the fuel mass, and the pile temperature began climbing toward meltdown point. "It was unforgivable of me to intrude upon your privacy."

She had a faint, indefinable accent; I guessed Middle European of some kind. She was . . . well, I'd say she was beaming at me, but you'd think I only meant she was smiling. I mean she was *beaming* at me, the way an airport beams at an approaching plane to guide it. I realized with a start that she was looking at me just exactly the same way I was looking at her. Captivated, wistful, yearning—no, outright hungering and thirsting. I'd seen the look before, in movies starring Marilyn Chambers.

I ask you to believe that I am not a complete idiot. My first thought was that it had to be a mistake. But the light in the bar wasn't bad enough. So my second thought was that it had to be a trick, a trap of some kind.

That was absolutely fine with me. I tried to visualize the worst possible outcome. Say that, in exchange for being allowed to touch her, to put my hand somewhere on her skin—her shoulder, say—I were to be beaten, robbed and killed. Okay, fair enough; no problem there. A weird little phrase ran through my head: *I'll be her sucker if she'll be my succor*. (I seem now to hear a phantom Kingfish saying, "Boy, you is de suck*ee*.") Male black widow spiders obviously think they have a good deal going for them.

"It's uncanny," she repeated, and touched my hand. With hers.

"It certainly is," I said, referring to the astonishing discovery that knuckles can be erogenous zones.

"Would you mind standing up, sir?"

That kicked off an ambiguous reaction. If I stood up, the bulge in my trousers would become visible. Even more embarrassing, it might not become visible *enough*. Conflicting imperatives paralyzed me.

"I'm sorry," she said. "I'm being rude again. It's just that I dreamt about you last night. It was a *very* pleasant dream."

"I've dreamed about you all my life," I said, "and it has always been pleasant. You're very beautiful." A happy feeling was growing in me. First, because I had finally managed to say something intelligent and gallant. And second, because she had just named a barely plausible reason why a woman like her could be interested in a guy like me.

I mean, you have to understand that my father always insisted I wasn't his—until my sixteenth birthday, when he gave up and apologized to my mother. "It has to be some kind of mutation," he admitted. "You would *never* have cheated on me with someone who looked like that."

But anything can happen in a dream. Lord, who knows better than I? For the first time I was willing to—tentatively—believe that her obvious attraction signals might just be genuine. The possibilities were staggering.

"My mother was," she answered, dimpling, "the most beautiful Queen that Ragovia ever had."

"You're a princess." Well, of course. Dream logic.

"Only by courtesy. I'll never be queen—Ragovia became a democracy a few years ago."

"I'm *terribly* sorry to hear that."

"Oh, it was a bloodless coup. A telegram to our summer place in Barbados, and that was essentially it. Father moped for a week."

"Well, naturally."

"I can't get over how much you look like the man in my dream. He was wearing Father's crown. That's why I just had to put it on your head—to see if the resemblance could possibly be as complete as it seemed."

I threw caution to the winds and stood up. "And is it?"

Her eyes went down and then up me. On the way down they paused just where I had hoped/feared they would. When her eyes got back up to mine, she was smiling. "The resemblance is exact."

"Princess—uh—"

"Oh, forgive me again. My name is Marga."

"My name is Fleming, Princess Marga."

"Please, Marga alone is sufficient." And without the slightest hesitation or change of voice or manner, she went on, "Fleming, do you know of some quiet, private place nearby where we could be alone together?"

A man next to me made an odd swallowing sound. I dug a finger into my ear. "Too much noise in here. I could have sworn that you just asked me . . . " I could not repeat what I thought I had heard.

"I asked you if you have a place where we can be alone together. As we were in my dream last night."

I drew in a deep breath, and then could not remember what to do with it. "Why?" I croaked.

"So that I can screw you into a coma."

Exhale. That was what you did with deep breaths. No, too late now: I was paralyzed. That breath was going to have to last me the rest of my life.

"—" I said.

"If you have no place near," she went on, "we could find an alley. Or we could lock ourselves in the toilet here. But I am mad with lust for you and must have you as soon as possible."

People had been surreptitiously watching ever since Marga had sat down next to me, and now there were two small, musical explosions as the customers on either side of us dropped their drinks.

I decided that, while this was a splendid moment to die, even better ones might lie in the future; with an effort I got my breathing reflex started again.

"The feeling is mutual. That is, I hope it will be. That is—yes, I have a place near here."

"Let's *hurry*! In my dream we were *wonderful* together!"

A lot of people were watching now. I glanced around as I took her hand, the way I've seen it done in movies, and nothing in my life had ever tasted as good as the sight of all those gaping faces.

Understand, I knew perfectly well that something was going to go wrong. I would never get her to my place, or she'd change her mind, or I wouldn't get it up, or I wouldn't get it in, or I'd get in and it'd be disappointing, or she'd have AIDS, or a bonebreaker boyfriend—the exact nature of the doom was as yet unknown, but I knew in my heart that *some*thing was going to go wrong. (And of course, I was mistaken about that.) But I didn't care. The thrill of seeing all those stunned faces watching *her* leave with *me*, rubbing up against me like a cat who's just heard the can opener, was—I firmly believed—worth any disappointment. (And you know, perhaps I was nearly right about that.) As we reached the door, she opened it for me with her left hand, and her right hand settled firmly and unmistakably on my ass to guide me out into the night. There was an audible collective gasp from behind us.

Once we were on the street I flung up my arm to hail a cab. Cabs *never* stop for me, even when I wave large bills at them. I was operating on dream logic.

And a cab pulled up with a squeal of brakes, and the cabbie jumped out and *opened the door for us.*

It was her, of course, not me. I knew just how the cabbie felt. I could sense his astonishment that she was with me, and I agreed with him, and gave him a smile that tried to say, "It's a dream, pal, go with it. For God's sake, go with it!"

When he got back behind the wheel, he adjusted the rearview mirror and I met his baffled gaze. I gave my address, Marga added "—and *hurry!*" in a voice thick with lust, and his eyes widened even further. We started up with a roar and a lurch, and the moment we were up to speed she opened my fly.

The cab seemed to lock its brakes on ice, spin wildly and smash into a gasoline truck. She made a small sound of contentment and continued what she was doing. The phantom flames roared . . .

The cabdriver was so profoundly shocked he was actually driving at a safe legal speed, and took us to my place by the shortest, most direct route. Marga appeared to be totally engrossed in what she was doing, and God knows I was, but she sensed when we were approaching our destination somehow, and had me zipped back up as the cab came to a halt. She paid the driver before he or I could think of it. I had just enough presence of mind to hold the door for her as she got out. A group of leathered teens were monopolizing the stoop of my brownstone, as usual. They turned to brown stone at the sight of us, and did not even turn to watch as we walked up past them and into the building.

As the elevator door closed behind us, she shut off the light, leaned back against the wall and pulled me against her. She tucked my face against her neck and hugged me so tightly, with both arms and one leg, that I could move only a single muscle. But she seemed to be under no such constraint: she *rippled*, in several directions at once, and if I lived one floor higher I'd have disgraced myself. But the elevator door slid back and light burst in on us, and reluctantly she released me.

Standing outside the elevator, waiting to board, was Hal Grimsby, the slickest stud in my building, a jock type who had been bringing home a different girl every night for the four years I'd been living there, each girl prettier than the last. He was making no move to get on the elevator. You could have put one of his handballs into his mouth without touching his lips.

Marga straightarmed him out of the way and led me past him. "Hurry, darling," she said clearly. "I'm *dripping*."

Behind us, Hal made a faint gargling sound. The elevator closed and left without him.

And *still* it wasn't perfect yet. As we approached my apartment, the door across the hall opened and Mary Zanfardino stepped out.

For the past four years, Mary Zanfardino had been the leading lady in an endless series of fantasies much like the one I was now living— save that I didn't have this good an imagination. I had never succeeded in starting a conversation with her, but I knew that she was perfectly aware of my attraction to her, and deeply revolted by it. Now she was thunderstruck. I'd never seen pupils that large.

I turned to look at Marga. I found the sight of her as devastating as everyone else did. Her hair was disheveled. Her nipples were prominent beneath her silk dress. She smelled like Tina Turner's panties after a concert. Her eyes were heavy-lidded, and her smile would have looked just like the Mona Lisa's except for the smeared lipstick . . .

I turned back to Mary, former girl of my dreams. She looked like a mud simulacrum of a woman, fashioned by a primitive and dressed by a small child.

This was no time for introductions. I nodded curtly to Mary, brushed past her, and unlocked my door. As Marga came toward me (utterly ignoring Mary) she was unbuttoning her dress, and before I could get the door closed behind me she was out of it entirely. I caught one last flash-glimpse of Mary that made me want to giggle, but I knew intuitively that if I started I might never stop, and this once in my life I did not want to remind myself of Jerry Lewis. Then the latch slid home and Marga and I were alone. I knew that my bedroom was a mess, but I also knew we were not going to get that far.

I can see it in my mind, even now, but I can't describe it. Just say that, even displayed to the best possible advantage—that is, even if Marga were wearing it—there is nothing in the

Frederick's of Hollywood catalogue that could ever look half as lovely, as provocative, as inflammatory, as what Marga was wearing under that dress. Enchanted elves had made it. My mouth had gone drier than a user's manual, and I knew why: some helpful internal resource-dispatcher was rerouting all the moisture in my body to where it was most needed.

"Which one of us shall undress you, my king?" she asked.

We took turns. She left the crown on my head and I didn't argue.

* * * * *

No, I'm not going to cheat you; that was not a discreet fade to black. Those asterisks are there because what she and I did deserves to be set off by itself. It merits special ceremony.

I will admit that part of me wants to take refuge in those asterisks, to leave the lurid details in the limbo which is symbolized by the six-pointed star. I never learned to enjoy locker-room boasting; it never came up, so to speak. But if I don't tell you just how it was, you'll never understand how I felt afterward.

Besides, it won't be a *real* invasion of my privacy. I mean, it's only me *telling* you, and telling you *my* version of things, and only the parts that can be fit into words at that. Not even all of them. I'm trying to make the point that what she did to me was *worse* than anything I could do to myself.

So you want to know, was it good, eh friend?

* * * * *

As I've said, I *knew* going in that it would be
a fiasco of some kind; we'd be interrupted, or
I'd Fail To Perform and nothing would happen.
Probably that's what you're expecting, and I can't
blame you.

But then to my vast astonishment our clothes
seemed to melt away and we were naked and
touching and she was warm and slippery and it
was just sort of happening. No: it was not sort
of anything. It was most emphatically happening.

And happening.

The Physical Aspect:

I have no frame of reference except for what
I've read, and the accounts all conflict. You tell
me: is it normal for a twenty-five-year-old male
losing his virginity to experience eight orgasms
in four hours, without ever completely losing the
original erection? Does a woman's tenth orgasm
in half an hour usually trigger an hour-long
continuous climax? I'd always assumed those
Penthouse letters were fantasy. And is it always
that *noisy*? And wet? And glorious?

For the record, we did everything I've ever
heard of that can be done without additional cast
or esoteric equipment and doesn't involve former
food, former people, or animals. We *did* make
use, from time to time, of candles, neckties,
scarves, shoelaces, a little water-color paintbrush,
her hairbrush, butter, whipped cream, strawberry
jam, Johnson's Baby Oil, my Swedish hand

vibrator, a fascinating bead necklace she had, miscellaneous other common household items, and every molecule of flesh that was exposed to the air or could be located with strenuous search.

The Mental Aspect:

So that's what it's like to feel virile! Fascinating. Heady. As sweet as it's cracked up to be. Potentially addictive. Primitively stirring. Part of me wanted to go punch some son of a bitch—in a little while . . .

Part of me wanted to dedicate my remaining life to thanking her, even though—perhaps *because*—she was making it clear that she wanted no more thanks than she was getting. Hyperalert for pretense as only a virgin can be, I was certain I was genuinely pleasing her.

We *knew* each other, in more than the purely Biblical sense. At least, I seemed to come to know her more intimately, more quickly, than I have ever known anyone, not excepting my parents, and she, being more experienced than I, surely learned more than I did. She learned things about me that no one else had ever cared to, things that I didn't know. My grandmother's heirloom rocking chair collapsed under us and we howled with laughter together.

We *touched* each other.

The Spiritual Aspect:

Oh my God I'm not alone anymore! Even if I never see her again after tonight, I'm not alone anymore. Trillions of my cells, stamped with my identity, have left my shores and established colonies in another being—and it doesn't even matter *if all the colonies end up as dead as Jamestown or Jonestown: I'm not alone anymore! This isn't another test shot, another dummy run targeted for a handful of Kleenex, this is a genuine launch. My sperm have achieved spaceflight.* God, *they cry, dying on Mars, we made it!*

Thank you, God, for this crazy stranger, for granting me these memories to cherish; I never really believed in You before . . .

And inevitably there was an ending. I think that in my last round I finally lost the last shred of fear—the subconscious suspicion that any minute I was going to wake up from a coma or a jealous husband was going to kick in the door or some other slapstick disaster would spoil it—and was able to fully relax and enjoy myself. To lose myself, to throw myself away, to expand to the size of the universe and trust that there would still be someone to be when I recondensed.

Perhaps, indeed, I became someone else in that timeless time—or perhaps it was the glorious hours that led up to it which worked some kind of change on me, developing, or maybe only tapping, wells of unsuspected strength.

Because I'm fairly sure the man I had been when I'd walked into that apartment would have concluded such stupifying carnal excess with a deep sleep of hours, if not days . . .

Whereas I returned to something resembling normal consciousness, to a vastly changed but basically recognizable reality, only a few minutes after the last generation ship left the launch pad. I waited until my breathing slowed, and lifted myself up onto an elbow which was missing considerable skin, and said, "Tell me about yourself, Marga; what do you do with your life?"

Something infinitely subtle changed in her face, and even without my glasses I sensed she was unhappy with the question. The man I had been would have sprained his tongue changing the subject. I waited, forcing her to make some reply, and the wait was just long enough for me to notice that the silly crown she had insisted I leave on was heavy enough to strain my neck; I reached up to remove it.

"Don't!" she blurted. "It's still saving—"

There was no pause at all; I'm breaking the sentence only to indicate a barely perceptible alteration in the tone of her voice as she finished, "—the sweat from running into your eyes, my love."

A moment before I'd have been prepared to cut my throat if she wished it. But she herself had recently and repeatedly wakened in me the primitive male essence, the killer-ape ancestry I had always thought to be purely theoretical. The old ape is paranoid.

I removed the crown.

"Darling," she said, her lighthearted tone perfectly plausible, "don't spoil it, now. You look so handsome with it on—come, let me put it back on and I'll tell you anything about me you want to know. How I lost my virginity, perhaps . . . ?"

As she reached coyly for it I pulled it away and sat up. "Just a second, Marga." I switched on the table lamp—we were on the floor at the time—and turned fractionally away from her to study the crown. She made a grab for my elbow, aborted it quickly.

The light was just a little better than it had been in the bar. I held the crown close to my eyes, tilted it so the light picked out a portion of its interior surface in high relief. Most of the intricate engraving was unfamiliar to me, seemingly purely artistic in design, like the elaborate chasings on the outer surface, but a portion of it I recognized. Rotating the crown slightly I made out another such portion, extrapolated a total of three. It reminded me of a mouse I knew . . .

"I was afraid the sweat might be tarnishing the gold. It is pure gold, isn't it?"

"Yes, Fleming, but it's sealed against corrosion. Please put it back on? To please me?" She sat up beside me and tugged playfully at one of my nipples.

I pondered for a half second. "Anything to please you, Marga." I swept back my damp hair and put the crown back on my head, allowed her to adjust its position slightly. "Now if you'll excuse me for just one second, my . . . bladder is bursting."

I got up and padded toward the bathroom. Everybody has some cliché they use: my back teeth are floating, or, my eyes are turning yellow, or, my cup runneth over. My own customary euphemism is, "my buffer needs purging," and I was glad I had caught myself. It might have warned her.

I have never been a decisive, quick-thinking quick-responding kind of guy. It's easy to play practical jokes on me; I'm slow to catch on and even slower—days slower, usually—to figure out what to do about it. Maybe a dozen times in my life I've had one of those flashes of satori, those moments of insight in which a whole, long logic chain appears at once before the mind's eye— and each time it came in my work rather than my social life.

So maybe it helped that this one was work-related. Maybe it helped that I had just had the best confidence boosting of my life. Maybe there is a kind of preternatural clarity of thought that comes with total physical satisfaction . . . and how in Hell would *I* know?

It just seemed so simple, so obvious. So inescapable—

"Don't bang your elbow on that chair behind you, darling," I called back over my shoulder, and as she turned to look I bent down.

Just as I had guessed, the time machine was in her purse. It wasn't hard to recognize. It looked like a bulky watch with no band. I was interested to find that there was a weapon along with it, an unfamiliar but unmistakable handgun. I spun and leaped, whipping my head to shake off the crown, and the distance was short; as she was turning back toward me I cannoned into her and we went over in a heap, my cheek against hers and my arms tight around her. For perhaps a second she mistook it for clumsy erotic play, and that was enough time in the lamplight for me to read the little word QUIT and thumbnail the tiny recessed button which it labeled on her "watch."

The light changed drastically, became laboratory bright. Appropriate, as we were now in a laboratory.

So was an astonished man in a white smock of odd design, and a shorter, weasel-faced man in red high heels, pink patterned stockings, and a loudly-clashing maroon kilt. Marga and I looked down on them slightly from a railing-encircled platform whose height must have been calibrated to a high degree of precision.

Weasel-face was the loudest of the pair in more ways than one, and slowest on the uptake; as the other man gaped, he was booming cheerily, "Welcome back, pixel, did you get a good—*crash*, Marga! What did you bring the mark *back* for?" His face curled reflexively on itself. "The frotter wants points, eh?"

"*Jimby, help!*" Marga screamed, and he stepped back a pace, high heels clattering on the lab floor. She tried to break my embrace, and should have succeeded, but now I was as strong as a normal man. I not only held her, I got my thumbnail back on that button.

The lights dimmed again suddenly, and my rug prickled once again on my bare skin. I let her go and rolled convulsively clear, sprang to my feet clutching her time machine. She started to rise too. Halfway up she saw her gun in my other hand, and sank back down. I must have been holding it correctly.

I knew that if I said anything my voice would crack, so I waited until I was sure I had control.

"Did you ever think to wonder," I asked at last, "what a guy like me would do for a living?"

"Do you want me to guess?" she asked sullenly. "All right. A janitor? An accountant? A fast-food cook? A painter? A writer?"

I nodded. "You wouldn't know, would you? This is too good an apartment for any of those. But that aside, even in those professions you have to be . . . more impressive-looking than I am."

"I can believe it," she said. "All right, surprise me."

"I write software, for a mouse-driven computer called the Macintosh. Independents can't make a lot at it, but no one ever has to see your face."

"Frot," she said. It was some kind of obscenity where she came from.

"You may have heard of hackers. A vanguard subculture of today, like the beatniks and the hippies of earlier days. Just like with them, some expressions that will be common idiom in another ten or twenty years are familiar to me now. When you said the word 'save,' I heard it the way you would."

"Frot," she said again, a little more forcefully.

"Yeah. As in 'saving the changes to disk.' The inside of that crown thing looks a lot like the ball-cavity of the mouse on my Mac, two little phototransistors and a reference point. Yours wouldn't be optical, though, would they? Other than that, the analogy is pretty good: you . . .

'turn the head around,' and the sensors translate it into data. That's ROM circuitry around the sensors, sure as hell. The rest of the crown is storage space, right? Hell's own data capacity, from the size.

"So the rest was logic. The only thing you could possibly be recording from my head that required that kind of byte room was . . . my memories, my *thoughts*. My feelings. That told me you had to be from the future: even the Japanese don't have brain interface *yet*. You had to have a way to get back to your own time, and I was certain you were not wearing it, externally or internally. But you wouldn't go far from it, so it had to be in the purse. The only thing I don't understand is why your brain-robbing Peeping ROM takes so infernally long to write the data."

She looked up at me. There was none of the new respect in her eyes that I had earned. "Fool. We cannot get at *short*-term memory; Heisenberg effect. If we could we'd have effective telepathy, wouldn't we?"

I was feeling telepathic. I sensed her thinking about trying to take the time machine from me; with great pleasure I felt her decide against it. "And mind-control," I agreed. "I'd never have reached the purse. You have to wait for the memories to seep from short-term to long-term storage—and I came out of the fog too soon." I grinned. "Taking off that crown must have been like yanking a disk out of the drive while it's spinning, huh?"

Her eyes flashed. "I could have killed you. After all I did for you—"

Give me this much credit. I did not kill her then.

When I had myself back in control, I spoke very softly. "Recorded memories must have beat out most other artforms and recreations. I'll bet the pornography is sensational by my standards. But even my primitive pornography has taught me something interesting, and you confirmed it earlier tonight: *there is a finite limit to the possibilities*. There are only so many ways to do it for the camera: at some point even you people must get jaded. So you'll pay extra for the candid-camera kick, for the memories of someone who *doesn't know you're watching*, somebody with no copy protection on his head.

"More: for recordings of someone who's given up all hope of ecstasy, falling suddenly into the middle of his wildest wet dreams. For recordings of the ending of despair, the ending of a solitude such as none of you must ever have known. Heightened dramatic effect. Casanova may be happy, skillfully plundering his hundredth willing wench, but not a fraction as happy as I was tonight. Your world must not have pain like mine any more—you had to come back here to find it."

I shifted my weight, and my foot touched something cold. I glanced down and saw the crown.

Suddenly I was roaring in a voice I had never known I had. "Do you know that the moment a pain is first relieved is the moment you learn how large it truly was? Agony is *defined* by relief! I learned tonight just what a horrible joke my life

has been and will be—*and I didn't even mind*!
I was *grateful* to you for calibrating my misery!
For showing me *exactly* what I'd been missing!"

I crouched and came up with my ultimate wet
dream in my fist. I was dimly astonished to
realize that I was not crying. Rage had always
made me cry. "This *is* solid gold you've got here,"
I said, brandishing the crown. "You're very good
at what you do. Not hard, I suppose, when you
can rent—or more likely, copy—all the tricks
there are."

She scowled.

I looked at it for a while. "Can this thing play
back by itself," I asked huskily, "or do you need
other equipment?"

She looked me in the eye. For the first time
since I'd gotten up to pee, a smile touched the
corners of her mouth. "There's a thumbnail
toggle inside. Once to stop, twice to rewind,
three times to play back. You'll get the whole
thing in six seconds of realtime."

"Slick."

I tore my eyes from the crown, and made a
small gasping sound. In the soft lamplight, without my glasses, her naked body was the most
beautiful thing I had ever seen. Even more
beautiful, perhaps, than that same body had been
four hours ago. She did that thing that women
have been able to do since Eve. There are no
discernible gross muscle movements, but the
whole body seems to rearrange itself . . . to
beckon to you, somehow.

I didn't want to ask. The words were torn out
of me. "It was all faked, wasn't it, Marga?"

"In the sense that all performance art is faked."

A graceful out. I wouldn't take it. "You know what I mean. As the cliché goes . . . *was it good for you, too?*"

I saw a flicker of pity in her eyes, I know that one real well, and I saw it die in the instant it was born. She knew I couldn't be conned any more. She glanced down briefly to my groin, and back up. "You notice I didn't wear a crown myself," she muttered.

Again I didn't kill her. I didn't do anything at all, as far as I know. I'm sure I stopped breathing. I remember hearing the fan in the next room in the sudden silence. How long did I stare at her in the stillness, feeling the metal crown cool against one palm, the time machine and gun faintly warm against the other? My medulla kicked in finally, and I sucked in a deep breath.

And she said, clear as a bell and twice as pretty, "But you *were* sweet, and you're taking it like a man. All right: nine percent of the net, my final offer. Jimby will be furious—that's a point over the going rate."

In that instant I became, not merely a functional male animal, but a man.

I put the time machine gently down on the couch. "All right," I said, "you got me good. I guess the joke's on me. And as long as you're prepared to give me a whore's usual cut, I guess I really have no kick coming, have I? Oh, I admit, I'm tempted to give you a good spanking—"

Her eyes showed genuine interest for the first time.

"—but why give you more good material for free? Tell you what: make my end *ten* percent— why should I pay an agent's commission?—and you can have your time machine and gun and crown back."

She relaxed. "Fleming, you're a sport."

"Damn right." I smiled. "A contact sport, as clumsy and laughable as professional wrestling. But at least I'm well-paid."

And I gave her back her time machine and gun and crown, and she went back home to her boss Jimby. I'm still waiting to hear back from her, but I assume the check is in the mail.

Perhaps the delay has something to do with what I did *before* I gave her back her things. While I still held the gun trained on her lovely face, I took that crown and crushed it flat in my hands, and ripped it into pieces, and hammered the pieces into gold leaves with a ball-peen hammer, and made multiple passes over each leaf with my tape-head demagnetizer, and scrubbed them with steel wool, and heated them just to melting point with a blowtorch, and I really *had* had to pee for quite some time so I cooled the pieces the way they used to temper swords, and finally I wrapped the damp and sizzling shards up in her dress and handed her the whole bundle with my compliments—

—yes, now that I come to think of it, I *do* seem to recall a rather unhappy expression on her face as she winked out of existence for the last time.

I don't see why. I let her live . . .

There was a whole lot of tedious low comedy then, which lasted several days. Too many people had the vivid memory of Marga coming home with me indelibly engraved on their brains, in persuasive detail; too many neighbors had heard our frenzied athletics and shouted quarrel and the sound of repeated hammering; no one had seen her leave. No clothing or ID was found. I had not cleaned up the suggestive clutter in the apartment. I flatly refused to hear any questions whatsoever concerning her, let alone answer them. I declined a lawyer. I ignored the third degree treatment, the good cop/bad cop and the threats and all that.

What kept it from mattering was that they lacked a corpse and they lacked a missing person from which to infer one. All witnesses were unanimous and emphatic in describing the kind of woman who could not conceivably disappear from the world (by any means known) without being missed. There was no Marga missing. The bartender and two patrons remembered the name "Ragovia," and of course there is no such country. The only people who were *certain* where she had gone had, in all likelihood, not been born yet. The police, growing more indifferent as they sensed a conviction receding out of probability, finally stopped bothering me.

Mary Zanfardino knocked on my door a few days after that, and a few days later she became my girlfriend. She has never once asked me about Marga, and she has no complaints about my lovemaking, and all things considered we are reasonably happy. One of these days perhaps we'll come to know each other so well that we'll be inside each other's skull—and since she'll be there *by invitation*, I don't plan to charge her.

I know *exactly* how happy we are, and exactly how happy we are not. And she and I are the only persons anywhere in space and time who know that . . . and that suits me fine.

THE MAGNIFICENT CONSPIRACY

1.

By the time I had pulled in and put her in park, alarm bells were going off all over my subconscious so I just stayed put and looked around.

After a minute and a half, I gave up. *Everything* about the place was wrong.

Even the staff. Reserved used-car salesmen are about as common as affable hangmen—but I had the whole minute and a half to myself, and as much longer as I wanted. The man semivisible through the dusty office window was clearly aware of my arrival, but he failed to get up from his chair.

So I shut off the ignition and climbed out into un-air-conditioned July, and by God even the music was wrong. It wasn't Muzak at all; it was an old Peter, Paul and Mary album. How can you psych someone into buying a clunker with music like that? Even when I began wandering around kicking tires and glancing under hoods he stayed in the office. He seemed to be reading. I was determined to get a reaction now, so I picked out the classiest car I could see (easily worth three times as much as my Dodge), hotwired her and started her up. As I'd expected, it fetched him—but he didn't hurry. Except for that, he was standard-issue salesman—which is like saying, "Except for the sun porch, it was a standard issue fighter jet."

"Sorry, mister. That one ain't for sale."

I looked disappointed.

"Already spoken for, huh?"

"Nope. But you don't want her."

I listened to the smooth, steady rumble of the engine. "Oh, yeah? Why not? She sounds beautiful."

He nodded. "Runs beautiful, too—now. Feller sold it to us gimmicked 'er with them pellets you get from the Whitney catalog. Inside o' five hundred miles you wouldn't have no more rings than a spinster."

I let my jaw drop.

"She wouldn't even be sittin' out here, except the garage is full up. Could show you a pretty good Chev, you got your heart set on a convertible."

"Hey, listen," I broke in. "Do you realize you could've kept your mouth shut and sold me this car for two thousand flat?"

He wiped his forehead with a red handkerchief. "Yep. Couple year ago, I would've." He hitched his glasses higher on his nose and grinned suddenly. "Couple year ago I had an ulcer."

I had the same disquieting sensation you get in an earthquake when the ground refuses to behave properly. I shut the engine off. "There isn't a single sign about the wonderful bargains you've got," I complained. "The word 'honest' does not appear anywhere on your lot. You don't hurry. I've been here for three minutes and you haven't shaken my hand and you haven't tried to sell me a thing and you *don't hurry.* What the hell kind of used-car lot is this?"

He looked like he was trying hard to explain, but he only said, "Couple of year ago I had an ulcer," again, which explained nothing. I gave up and got out of the convertible. As I did so, I noticed for the first time an index card on the dashboard which read $100. "That can't be the price," I said flatly. "Without an *engine* she's worth more than that."

"Oh, no," he said, looking scandalized. "That ain't the price. Couldn't be: price ain't fixed."

Oh. "What determines the price?"

"The customer. What he needs, how bad he needs it, how much he's got."

This of course is classic sales doctrine—but you're not supposed to *tell* the customer. You're supposed to go through the quaint charade of an asking price, then knock off a hastily computed amount because "I can see you're in a jam and I like your face."

"Well then," I said, trying to get this script back on the track, "maybe I'd better tell you about my situation."

"Sure," he agreed. "Come on in the office. More comfortable there. Got the air conditioning."

I saw him notice my purple sneakers as I got out of the convertible—which pleased me. You can't buy them that garish—you have to dye them yourself.

And halfway to the office, my subconscious identified the specific tape being played over the sound system. Just a hair too late; the song hit me before I was braced for it. I barely had time to put my legs on automatic pilot. Fortunately, the salesman was walking ahead of me, and could not see my face. *Album 1700*, side one, track six: "The Great Mandella (The Wheel of Life)."

"So I told him

"That he'd better

"Shut his mouth And do his job like a man And he answered Listen (*father didn't even come to the funeral and the face in the coffin was my own but oh God so thin and drawn like collapsed around the skull and the skin like gray paper and the eyes dear Jesus Christ the eyes he looked so content so hideously* content *didn't he understand that he'd blown it blown it bl*)own it very long, Mr. Uh?"

He was standing, no, squatting by my Dodge, peering up the tailpipe. The hood was up.

If you're good enough, you can put face and mouth on automatic pilot, too. I told him I was Bob Campbell and that I had owned the Dodge for three years. I told him I was a clerk in a supermarket. I told him I had a wife and two children and an MA in Business Administration.

I told him I needed a newer model car to try for a better job. It was a plausible story; he didn't seem to find anything odd about my facial expressions, and I'm sure he believed every word. By the time I had finished sketching my income and outgo, we were in the office and the door was closing on the song:

"Take your place on
"The Great Mandala
"As it moves through your brief moment of (*click*) time that Dodge of yours had a ring job, too, Bob."

I came fully aware again, remembered my purpose.

"Ring job? Look, uh . . . " We seated ourselves.

"Arden Larsen."

"Look, Arden, that car had a complete engine overhaul not five thousand miles ago. It's—"

"Stow it, Bob. From the inside of your exhaust pipe alone my best professional estimate is that you are getting about forty or fifty miles to a quart of oil. Nobody can overhaul a slant-six that bad." I began to protest. "If that engine was even so much as steam cleaned less'n ten thousand mile ago I'll eat my socks."

"Just a damned minute, Larsen—"

"Don't ever try to bamboozle a used-car man my age, son—it just humiliates the both of us. Now, it's hard to tell for sure without jackin' up the front end or drivin' her, but I'd guess the actual value of that Dodge to be about a hundred dollars. That's half of what it'd cost you to rent a car for as long as the Dodge is liable to last."

"Well, of all the colossal . . . I don't have to listen to this crap!" I got up and headed for the door, which was corny and a serious mistake, because when I was halfway to the door he hadn't said a word and when I was upon it he still hadn't said a word and I was so puzzled at how I could have overplayed it so badly that I actually had the door open before I remembered what lay outside it.

"Tell the jailer

"Not to bother

"With his meal of bread and water today

"He is fasting till the killing's over here and I'll get you some ice water, Bob. Must be ninety-five in the shade out there. You'll be okay in a minute."

"Yeah. Sure." I stumbled back to my seat and gratefully accepted the ice water he brought from the refrigerator in a corner of the office. I remembered to keep my back very straight. *Get a hold of yourself, boy. It's just a song. Just some noise . . .*

"Now as I was sayin', Bob . . . figure your car's worth a hundred. Okay. So figure the Dutchman up the road'd offer you two hundred, and then sell it to some sorry son of a bitch for four. Okay. Figure if you twisted his arm, he'd go three— Mid-City Motors in town'd go that high, just to get you offa the lot quick. Okay. So I'll give you four and a quarter."

I sprayed ice water and nearly choked. "Huh?"

"And I'll throw in that fancy convertible for three hundred, if you really want her—but you'll have to let us do the ring job first. Won't cost

you anything, and I could let you have a loaner
'til we get to it. Oh yeah, an' that $100 tag you
was askin' about is our best estimate of monthly
gas, oil and maintenance outlay. I'd recommend
a different car for a man in your situation myself,
but it's up to you."

I didn't have to pretend surprise, I was flabbergasted. "Are you out of your mind?" Apparently my employer was given to understatement.

He didn't have the right set of wrinkles for
a smile like that; he must have just learned how.
"Feels like I get saner every day."

"But . . . but you can't be serious. This is a
rib, right?"

Still smiling, he pulled out a wallet the size
of a paperback dictionary, and counted out one
hundred and twenty-five dollars in twenties and
fives. He held it out in a hand so gnarled it
looked like weathered maple. "What do you say?
Deal?"

"I say, 'You're getting reindeer shit all over my
roof, fatso.' What's the catch?"

"No catch."

"Oh, no. You're offering me a free lunch, and
I'm supposed to just fasten the bib and open my
mouth, right? Is that convertible hot, or what?"

He sighed, scratched behind his glasses. "Bob,
your attitude makes sense, in a world like this.
That's why I don't much like a world like this,
and that's why I'm working here. Now I understand how you feel. I've seen ten dozen varia-
tions of the same reaction since I started working
for Mr. Cardwell, and it makes me a little sad-
der every time. That convertible ain't hot and

there ain't no other catch neither. I'm offerin' you the car for what she's honestly worth, and if you can't believe that, why, you just go down the line and see the Dutchman. He'll skin you alive, but he won't upset you any."

I know when people are angry at me. He was angry, but not at me. So I probed. "Larsen, you've got to be completely crazy."

He blew up.

"You're damn right I am! Crazy means out o' step with the world, and accordin' to the rules o' the world, I'm supposed to cheat you out of every dime I smell on ya plus ten percent an' if you like that world so much that you wanna subsidize it then you get yer ass outa here an' go see the Dutchman but *whatever* you do *don't* you tell him we sent ya you got that?"

Nothing in the world makes a voice as harsh as the shortness of breath caused by a run-on sentence. I waited until he had fed his starving lungs and then said, "I want to see the manager," and he emptied them again very slowly and evenly, so that when he closed his eyes I knew he was close to hyperventilating. He clenched his fingers on the desk between us as though he were trying to pull it toward him, and when he opened his eyes the anger was gone from them.

"Okay, Bob. Maybe Mr. Cardwell can explain it to you. I ain't got the right words."

I nodded and got up.

"Bob . . . " He was embarrassed now. "I didn't have no call to bark at you thataway. I can't blame you for bein' suspicious. Sometimes I miss my ulcers myself. It's—well, it's a lot easier to live in a world of mud if you tell yourself there ain't no such thing as dry land."

It was the first sensible thing he'd said.

"What I mean, I'm sorry."

"Thanks for the ice water," I said.

He relaxed and smiled again. "Mr. Cardwell's in the garage out back. You take it easy in that heat."

I knew that I'd stalled long enough for the cassette or record or whatever it was to have ended, but I treated the doorknob like an angry rattlesnake just the same. But when I opened it, the only thing that hit me in the face was the hot dry air I'd expected. I left.

2.

I went through an arched gate in the plank fence that abutted the office's rear wall, and followed a wide strip of blacktop through weedy flats to the garage.

It was a four-bay job, a big windowless wood building surrounded with the usual clutter of handtrucks, engine blocks, transmissions, gas cans, fenders, drive trains, and rusted oil drums. All four bays were closed, in spite of the heat. It was set back about five hundred yards from the office, and the field behind it was lushly overgrown with dead cars, a classic White Elephant's Graveyard that seemed better tended than most. As I got closer I realized the field was actually organized: a section for GM products, one for Chryslers, one for Fords and so on, each marked with a sign and subdivided by model and, apparently, year. A huge Massey-Ferguson sat by one of three access roads, ready to haul the next clunker in to its appointed resting place. There was big money in this operation, very impressive money, and I just couldn't square that with Arden Larsen's crackpot pricing policy.

Arden seemed to have flipped the cassette to side two of *Album 1700*. I passed beneath a speaker that said it dug rock and roll music, and entered the garage through a door to the right of the four closed bays. Inside, I stopped short. Whoever heard of an air- conditioned garage? Especially one this size. *Big* money.

Over on the far side of the room, just in front of a Rambler, the floor grew a man, like the Wicked Witch melting in reverse. It startled the hell out of me—until I realized he had only climbed out of one of those rectangular pits the better garages have for jobs where a lift might get in the way. With the help of unusually efficient lighting, I studied him as he approached me. Late fifties, snow-white hair and goatee, strong jaw and incongruously soft mouth. A big man, reminding me strongly of Burl Ives, but less bulky, whipcord fit. An impression of enormous energy, but used only by volition—he walked slowly, clearly because he saw no need to hurry. Paradoxical hands: thin-fingered and aristocratic, but with the ground-in grime which is the unmistakable trademark of the professional or dedicated-amateur mechanic. The right one held a pipe wrench. His overalls were oily and torn, but he wore them like a not-rented tux.

I absorbed and stored all these details automatically, however, while most of my attention was taken up by the utter *peacefulness* of his face, of his eyes, of his expression and carriage and manner. I had never seen a man so manifestly content with his lot. It showed in the purely decorative way in which the wrinkles of his years lay upon his face; it showed in the easy swing of his big shoulders and the purposeful but carefree stride; it showed in the eager yet unhurried way that his eyes measured me: not as a cat sizes up another cat, but as a happy baby investigates a new person—with delighted interest. My purple sneakers *pleased* him. He was plainly a man who drank of his life with an unquenchable thirst, and it annoyed the hell out of me, because I knew good and goddam well when was the last time I had seen a man possessed of such peace and because nothing on earth was going to make me consciously acknowledge it.

But I am not a man whose emotions are wired into his control circuits. I smiled as he neared, and my body language said I was confused, but amiably so.

"Mr. Cardwell?"

"That's right. What can I do for you?" The way he asked it, it was not a conversational convention.

"My name's Bob Campbell. I . . . uh . . . "

His eyes twinkled. "Of course. You want to know if Arden's crazy, or me, or the both of us." His lips smiled, then got pried apart by his teeth into a full-blown grin.

"Well . . . something like that. He offered to buy my car for, uh, more than it's worth, and then he offered to sell me the classiest-looking car on the lot for . . . "

"Mr. Campbell, I'll stand behind whatever prices Arden made you."

"But you don't know what they are yet."

"I don't need to," he said, still grinning. "I know Arden."

"But he offered to do a free ring job on the car, for Chrissake."

"Oh, that convertible. Mr. Campbell, he didn't do that 'for Chrissake'—Arden's not a church-going man. He did it for his sake, and for mine and for yours. That car isn't worth a thing without that ring job—the aggravation it'd give you would use up more energy than walking."

"But—but," I sputtered, "how can you possibly survive doing that kind of business?"

His grin disappeared. "How long can any of us survive, Mr. Campbell, doing business any other way? I sell cars for what I believe them to be genuinely worth, and I pay much more than that for them so that people will sell them to me. What's wrong with that?"

"But how can you make a profit?"

"I can't."

I was shocked speechless. When he saw this, Cardwell smiled again—but this time it was a smile underlain with sadness. "Money, young man, is a symbol representing the life energy of those who subscribe to it. It is a useful and even necessary symbol—but because it is only a symbol, it is possible to amass on paper more profit than there actually is to be made. The more people who insist on making a profit, all the time, in every dealing, the more people who will be required to go bankrupt—to pour their life-energy into the system and get nothing back—in order to keep the machine running. A profit is without honor, save in its own country—there is certainly nothing sacred about one. Especially if you don't need it."

I continued to gape.

"Perhaps I should explain," he went on, "that I was born with a golden spoon in my mouth. My family has been unspeakably wealthy for twelve generations, controlling one of the oldest and most respected fortunes in existence— the kind that calls for battalions of tax lawyers in every country in the world. My personal worth is so absurdly enormous that if I were to set a hundred dollar bill on fire every minute of my waking life I would never succeed in getting out of the highest income tax bracket."

"You . . . " My system flooded with adrenaline. "You *can't* be *that* Cardwell."

BIG money.

"There are times when I almost wish I wasn't. But since I have no choice at all in the matter, I'm trying to make the best of it."

"By throwing money away?" I yelped, and fought for control.

"No. By putting it back where it belongs. I inherited control of a stupendous age-old leech— and I'm forcing it to regurgitate."

"I don't understand." I shook my head vigorously and rubbed a temple with my thumb. "I just don't understand."

He smiled the sad smile again, and the pipe wrench loosened in his grip for the first time. "You don't have to, you know. You can take your money from Arden and drive home in a loaner and pick up your convertible in a few days and then put it all out of your mind. All I'm selling is used cars."

He was asking me a question.

I shook my head again, more slowly. "No . . . no, I'd like to understand, I think. Will you explain?"

He put the wrench down on an oil drum. "Let's sit down."

There were a pair of splendidly comfortable chairs in the rear of the garage, with foldaway armrests that let you select for comfort or elbow room at need. Beyond them stood an expensive (but not frost-free) refrigerator, from which Cardwell produced two frosty bottles of Dos Equis. I accepted one and sat in the nearer chair. Cardwell sprawled back in his and put his feet up on a beheaded slant six engine, and when he drank he gave the beer his full attention.

I regret to say I did not. *Despite* all the evidence, I could not make myself believe that this grease-stained mechanic with his sneakers on an engine block was actually *the* Raymond Sinclair Cardwell. If it was true, my fee was going to quintuple, and Hakluyt was fucking well going to pay it. Send a man after a cat, and forget to mention that it's a black panther . . . *Jesus*.

Cardwell's chair had a beverage holder built into the armrest; he set his beer in it and folded his arms easily. He spoke slowly, thoughtfully; and he had that knack of observing you as he spoke, modifying his word choice by feedback. I have the knack myself; but I wondered why a man in his situation would have troubled to acquire it. I found myself trying as hard to understand him as he was trying to be understood.

I don't know [he said] if I can convey what it's like to be born preposterously wealthy, Mr. Campbell, so I won't try. It presents one with an incredible view of reality that cannot be imagined by a normal human being. The world of the very rich is only tangentially connected with the real world, for all that their destinies are intertwined. I lived totally in that other world and that world view for thirty-six years, happily moving around mountains of money with a golden bulldozer, stoking the fires of progress. I rather feel I was a typical multibillionaire, if that conveys anything to you. My only eccentricity was a passion for working on cars, which I had absorbed in my youth from a chauffeur I admired. I had access to the finest assistance and education the world had to offer, and became rather handy. As good as I was with international finance and real estate and arbitrage and interlocking cartels and all the other avenues through which a really enormous fortune is interconnected with the world, I enjoyed manipulating my fortune, *using* it—in some obscure way I believe I felt a duty to do so. And I *always* made a profit.

It was in London that it changed.

I had gone there to personally oversee a large

and complex merger involving seven nations. The limousine had just left the airport when the first shot killed my driver. He was the man who taught me how to align-bore a block and his name was Ted. The window was down; he just hurled sideways and soiled his pants. I think I figured it out as the second shot got my personal bodyguard, but by then we were under the wheels of the semi. I woke up eight weeks later, and one of the first things I learned is that no one is ever truly unconscious. I woke up speaking in a soft but pronounced British accent precisely like that of my private nurses, and it persisted for two days.

I discovered that Phillip, the bodyguard, had died. So had Lisa, a lady who meant entirely too little to me. So had Teal, the London regional director who had met my plane, and the driver of the semi. The rifleman had been apprehended: a common laborer, driven mad by his poverty. He had taken a gun to traffic in the same way that a consistently mistreated Doberman will attack anyone who approaches, because it seemed to him the only honorable and proper response to the world.

[Cardwell drank deep from his beer.]

My convalescence was long. The physical crisis was severe, but the spiritual trauma was infinitely greater. Like Saint Paul, I had been smashed from my horse, changed at once from a mover and shaper to a terrified man who hurt terribly in many places. The best drugs in the world cannot truly kill pain—they blunt its edge without removing it, or its terrible reminder of mortality. I had nearly died, and I suddenly had a tremendous need to explain to myself why that would have been such a tragedy. I could not but wonder who would have mourned for me, and how much, and I had a partial answer in the shallow extent of my own mourning for Ted and Phillip and Teal and Lisa. The world I had lived my life in was one in which there was little love, in which the glue of social relationships was not feelings, but common interests. I had narrowly, by the most costly of medical miracles, avoided inconveniencing many hundreds of people, and not a damn thing else.

And, of course, I could not deal with this consciously or otherwise. My world view lacked the "spiritual vocabulary" with which to frame these concepts: I desperately needed to resolve a conflict I could not even express. It delayed my effective recovery for weeks beyond the time when I was technically "on my feet"—I was simply unable to reenter the lists of life, unable to see why living was worth the terrible danger of dying. And so my body healed slowly, by the same instinctive wisdom with which it had kept my forebrain in a coma until it could cope with the extent of my injuries.

And then I met John Smiley.

[Cardwell paused for so long that I had begun to search for a prompting remark when he continued.]

❅   ✖   ❅

John was an institution at that hospital. He had been there longer than any of the staff or patients. He had not left the bed he was in for twelve years. Between his ribcage and his knees he was mostly plastic bags and tubes and things that are to a colostomy bag what a Rolls-Royce is to a dogcart. He needed one and sometimes two operations every year, and his refusal to die was an insult to medical science, and he was the happiest man I have ever met in my life.

My life had taught me all the nuances of pleasure; joy, however, was something I had only dimly sensed in occasional others and failed to really recognize. Being presented with a pure distillate of the thing forced me to learn what it was—and from there it was only a short step to realizing that I lacked it. You only begin to perceive where you itch when you learn how to scratch.

John Smiley received the best imaginable care, far better than he was entitled to. His only financial asset was an insurance company which grudgingly disbursed enough to keep him alive, but he got the kind of service and personal attention usually given only to a man of my wealth. This puzzled me greatly when I first got to know him, the more so when I learned that he could not explain it himself. But I soon understood.

Virtually every doctor, nurse, and long-term patient in the hospital worshipped him. The rare, sad few who would have blackly hated him were identified by the rest and kept from him. The more common ones who desperately needed to meet him were also identified, and sent *to* him, subtly or directly as indicated.

Mr. Campbell, John Smiley was simply a fountain of the human spirit, a healer of souls. Utterly wrecked in body, his whole life telescoped down to a bed he didn't rate and a TV he couldn't afford and the books scrounged for him by nurses and interns and the Pall Malls that appeared magically on his bedside table every morning—and the people who chanced to come through his door. John made of life a magnificent thing. He listened to the social and sexual and financial and emotional woes of anyone who came into his room, drawing their troubles out of them with his great gray eyes, and he sent them away lighter in their hearts, with a share of the immeasurable joy he had somehow found within himself. He had helped the charge nurse when her marriage failed, and he had helped the head custodian find the strength to raise his mongoloid son alone, and he had helped the director of the hospital to kick Demerol. And while I knew him, he helped a girl of eighteen die with grace and dignity. In that hospital, they sent the tough ones around, on one pretext or another, to see John Smiley—and that was simply all it took.

He had worked for the police as a plainclothesman, and one day as he and his partner were driving his own car into the police garage, a two-ton door had given way and come down on them. Ackroyd, his partner, had been killed outright, and so Mrs. Ackroyd received an award equivalent to half a million dollars. John's wife was less fortunate—his life was saved. They explained to her that under the law she would not collect a cent until he was dead. Then they added softly that they gave him a month at the outside. Twelve years later he was still chain-smoking Pall Malls and bantering with his wife's boyfriend when they came to visit him, which was frequently.

I wandered into John Smiley's room one day, sick in my heart and desperately thirsty for something more than thirty-six years had taught me of life, seeking a reason to go on living. Like many others before and since, I drank from John Smiley, drank from his seemingly inexhaustible well of joy in living—and in the process, I acquired the taste. I learned some things. Mostly, I think, I learned the difference between pleasure and joy. I suppose I had already made the distinction, subconsciously, but I considered the latter a fraud, an illusion overlaid upon the former to lend it respectability. John Smiley proved me wrong. His pleasures were as restricted as mine had been unrestricted—and his joy was so incandescently superior to mine that on the night of the day I met him I found myself humming the last verse of "Richard Corey" in my mind.

Cardwell paused, and his voice softened.

He forgave me my ignorance. He forgave me my money and my outlook and my arrogance and *treated me as an equal*, and most amazing of all, he made me forgive myself. The word "forgive" is interesting. Someone robs you of your wallet, and they find him down the line and bring him back to you, saying, "We found your wallet on this man," and you say, "That's all right. He can have—can have had—it; I fore-give it to him."

To preserve his sanity, John Smiley had been forced to "fore-give" virtually everything God had given him. In his presence you could not do less yourself.

And so I even gave up mourning a "lost innocence" I had never had, and put the shame he inspired in me to positive use. I began designing my ethics.

[I interrupted for the first and last time.

"A rich man who would design his own ethics is a dangerous thing," I said.]

Damn right [he said, with the delight of one who sees that his friend really *understands*]. A profit is without honor except in its own country—but that's a hell of a lot of territory. The economic system reacts, with the full power of the racial unconscious, to preserve itself—and I had no wish to tilt at the windmill. I confess that my first thought was of simply giving my money away, in a stupendous orgy of charity, and taking a job in a garage. But John was wise enough to be able to show me that that would have been as practical as disposing of a warehouse full of high explosive by setting fire to it with a match. You may have read in newspapers, some years back, of a young man who attempted to give away an inheritance, a *much* smaller fortune than mine. He is now hopelessly insane, shattered by the power that was thrust upon him. *He did not do it to himself.*

So I started small, and very slowly. The first thing I did was to heal the ulcers of the hospital's accounting department. They had been juggling desperately to cover the cost of the care that John Smiley was getting, so I bought the hospital and told them to juggle away, whenever they felt they should. That habit was hard to break; I bought forty-seven hospitals in the next two years, and quietly instructed them to run whatever loss they had to, to provide maximum care and comfort for their patients. I spent the next six years working in them, a month or two each, as a janitor. This helped me to assess their management, replacing entire staffs down to the bedpan level when necessary. It also added considerably to my education. There are many hospitals in the world, Mr. Campbell, some good, some bad, but I know for certain that forty-seven of them are wonderful places in which to hurt.

The janitor habit was hard to break, too. Over the next ten years I toured my empire, like a king traveling incognito to learn the *flavor* of his land. I held many and varied jobs, for my empire is an octopus, but they all amounted to janitor. I spent ten years toiling anonymously at the very borders of my fortune, at the last interface between it and the people it involved, the communities it affected. And without me at the helm, for *ten years*, the nature and operation of my fortune changed in no way whatsoever, and when I realized that, it shook me. I gave up my tour of inspection and went to my estate in British Columbia and holed up for a few years, thinking it through. Then I began effecting changes. This used-car lot is only one of them. It's my favorite, though, so it's the first one I've implemented and it's where I choose to spend my personal working hours.

But there are many other changes planned.

ξ

The silence stretched like a spring, but when at last I spoke my voice was soft, quiet, casual, quite calm. "And you expect me to believe that none of these changes will make a profit?" He blinked and started, precisely as if a tape recorder had started talking back to him.

"My dear Mr. Campbell," he said with a trace of sadness, "I frankly don't expect you to believe a word I've said."

My voice was still calm. "Then why tell me all this?"

"I'm not at all sure. But I believe it has much to do with the fact that you are the first person to *ask* me about it since I opened this shop."

Calm gone. "Bullshit," I roared, much too loud. "Bullfuckingshit, I mean a king-size meadow muffin! Do you goddammit," I was nearly incoherent, "think I was fucking born yesterday? Sell *me* a free lunch? You simple sonofabitch I *am not that stupid!*"

This silence did not stretch; it lay there like a bludgeoned dove. I wondered whether all garages echoed like this and I'd never noticed. *The hell with control, I don't need control, control is garbage, it's just me and him.* My spine was very straight.

"I'm sorry," he said at last, as sorrowfully as though my anger were truly his fault. "I humbly apologize, Mr. Campbell. I took you for a different kind of man. But I can see now that you're no fool."

His voice was infinitely sad.

"I don't mind a con, but this is stupid. You're giving away cars and you and Larsen are plenty to handle the traffic. I'm your only customer—what do you take me for?"

"The first wave has passed," he said. "There are only so many fools in any community, only a few naive or desperate enough to turn out for a free lunch. It was quite busy here for six months or so, but now all the fools have been accommodated. It will be weeks, months, before word-of-mouth gets around, before people learn that the cars I've sold them are good cars, that my guarantees are genuine. Dozens will have to return, scream for service, promptly receive it and numbly wander home before the news begins to spread. It will get quite busy again then, for a while, and probably very noisy, too—but at the moment I'm not even a Silly Season filler in the local paper. The editor killed it, as any good editor would. He's no fool, either.

"I'm recruiting fools, Mr. Campbell. There was bound to be a lull after the first wave hit. But I believe that the second will be a tsunami."

My voice was a whip. "And this is how you're going to save the world? By doing lube jobs and fixing mufflers?"

"This is one of the ways, yes. It's not surgery, but it should help comfort the patient until surgery can be undertaken. It's hard to concentrate on anything when you have a boil on your ass."

"*What?*"

"Sorry. A metaphor I borrowed from John Smiley, at the same time I borrowed the idea itself. 'Ray,' he said to me, 'you're talking about using your money to make folks more comfortable, to remove some of the pointless distractions so they have the energy to sit down and think. Well, the one boil on everybody's ass is his vehicle—everybody that has to have one, which is most everybody.' Everywhere I went over the next decade, I heard people bitterly complaining about their cars, pouring energy and money into them, losing jobs because of them, going broke because of them, being killed because of them. So I'm lancing the boil—in this area anyway.

"It makes an excellent test operation, too. If people object too strongly to having their boils lanced, then I'll have to be *extremely* circumspect in approaching their cancers. Time will tell."

"And no one's tried to stop you from giving away cars?"

"I don't give away cars. I sell them at a fair price. But the effect is similar, and yes, there have been several attempts to stop me by various legal means. But there has never been a year of my life when I was being sued for less than a million dollars.

"Then there were the illegal attempts. For a while this lot was heavily, and unobtrusively, guarded, and twice those guards found it necessary to break a few arms. I've dismissed them all for the duration of the lull between waves, but there'll be an army here if and when I need it.

"But until the next wave of customers hits, the only violence I'm expecting is a contract assassination or two."

"Oh?"

The anger drained from my voice as professional control switched in again. I noted that his right hand was out of sight behind his chair—on the side I had not yet seen. I sat bolt upright.

"Yes, the first one is due any time now. He'll probably show up with a plausible identity and an excellent cover story, and he'll probably demand to see the manager on the obvious pretext. He'll wear strikingly gaudy shoes to draw the attention of casual witnesses from his face, and his shirt will have a high collar, and he'll hold his spine very straight. He'll be completely untraceable, expensive, and probably good at his work, but his employers will almost certainly have kept him largely in the dark, and so he'll underestimate his opposition until it is too late. Only then will he realize that I could have come out of that pit with an M-16 as easily as with a pipe wrench if the situation had seemed to warrant it. What *is* that thing, anyway? It's too slim for a blowgun."

If you've lost any other hope of misdirecting the enemy, try candor. I sighed, relaxed my features in a gesture of surrender, and very slowly reached up and over my shoulder. Gripping the handle that nestled against my last few vertebrae, I pulled straight up and out, watching the muscles of his right arm tense where they disappeared behind the chair and wishing mightily that I knew what his hand was doing. I pointedly held the weapon in a virtually useless overhand grip, but I was unsettled to see him pick up on that—he was altogether too alert for my taste. *Hang on, dammit, you can still pull this off if you just hang on.*

"Stiffened piano wire," I said, meeting his eyes, "embedded in a hardwood grip and filed sharp. You put it between the correct two ribs and shove. Ruptures the heart, and the pericardial sac self-seals on the way out. Pressure builds. If you do it properly, the victim himself thinks it's a heart attack, and the entry wound is virtually undetectable. A full-scale autopsy would pick it up—but when an overweight car dealer in his fifties has a heart attack, pathologists don't generally get up on their toes."

"Unless he happens to be a multibillionaire," Cardwell noted.

"My employers will regret leaving me in ignorance. Fluoroscope in the fence gate?"

"The same kind they use in airports. If that weapon hadn't been so damned interesting, you'd never have reached the garage."

"I wanted to do the research, but they were paying double for a rush job." I sighed. "I knew better. Or should have. Now what?"

"Now let go of that thing and kick it far away."

I did so at once.

"Now you can have another beer and tell me some things."

"Sorry, Cardwell. No names. They sent me in blind, and I'll speak to them about that one day, but I don't give names. It's bad for business. Go ahead and call the man."

"You misunderstand me, sir. I already know Hakluyt's name quite well, and I have no intention of calling police of any description."

I knew the location of every scrap of cover for twenty yards in any direction, and I favored the welding tanks behind me and to my left—he looked alert enough not to shoot at them at such close range, and they were on wheels facing him. If I could tip my chair backwards and come at him from behind the tank . . .

" . . . and I'd rather not kill you unless you force me to, so please unbunch those muscles."

There was no way he was going to let me walk away from this, and there was no way I was going to sit there and let him pot me at his leisure, so there was no question of sitting still, and so no one was more surprised than me when the muscles of my calves and thighs unbunched and I sat still.

Perhaps I believed him.

"Ask your questions," I said.

"Why did you take this job?"

I broke up. "Oh, my God," I whooped, "how did a nice girl like me wind up in such a profession, you mean?" The ancient gag was suddenly very hilarious, and I roared with laughter as I gave the punchline. "Just lucky, I guess."

Pure tension release, of course. But damned if he didn't laugh at the old chestnut, too—or at himself for all I know. We laughed together until I was done, and then he said, "But why?" and I sobered up.

"For the money, of course."

He shook his head. "I don't believe you."

What's in your right hand, old man? I only shrugged. "It's the truth."

He shook his head again. "Some of your colleagues, perhaps. But I watched your face while I told you my story, and *your* empathic faculty seems to be functioning quite nicely. You're personally involved in this, involved with me. You're too damn mad at me, and it's confusing you as you sit there, spoiling your judgment. Oh no, son, you can't fool me. You're *some* kind of idealist. But *what brand?*"

There isn't a policeman in the world who knows my name, none of my hits have so much as come to the attention of Homicide, and the reason for it is that my control is flawless, I am an unflappable killing machine, like I said, my emotions aren't even in circuit, and well yes, I had gotten hot under the collar a couple of times this afternoon for reasons I would certainly think about when I got a chance, but now of course it was killing floor time and I was in total command, and so I was again surprised and shocked to find myself springing up from my chair and, not diving behind the welding tanks, or even leaping for his right hand, but simply running flat out full tilt in plain sight for the door. It was the most foolish imaginable move and half of my mind screamed, *Fool! Fool! At least run broken field your back is a fucking perfect target you'll never get halfway to the door* with every step until I was halfway to the door and then it shut up until I had reached the door and then the other half said quietly *I knew he wouldn't shoot* but then I had the door open and both halves screamed. It hadn't occurred to any of us that the sound system might be antiquated enough to use those miserable eight-track tapes.

Eight-tracks break down frequently, they provide mediocre sound quality under the best playback, their four-program format often leaves as much as ten minutes of dead air between programs, and you can't rewind or cue them. And they don't shut themselves off when they're done. They repeat indefinitely.

> **Hunger stopped him**
> **He lies still in his cell**
> **Death has gagged his accusations**
> **We are free now**
> **We can kill now**
> **We can hate now**
> **Now we can end the world**
> **We're not guilty**
> **He was crazy**
> **And it's been going on for**
> **ten thousand years!**

It is possible for an unrestrained man to kill himself with his hands. I moved to do so, and Cardwell hit me from behind like a bag of cement. One wrist broke as I landed, and he grabbed the other. He shouted things at me, but not loud enough to be heard over the final chorus:

"Take your place on the Great Mandala

"As it moves through your brief moment of time

"Win or lose now: you must choose now

"And if you lose you've only wasted your

(life is what it really was even if they called it five years he never came out the front door again so it was life imprisonment, right? and maybe the Cong would've killed him just as dead but they wouldn't have raped him first and they wouldn't have starved him not literally we could have been heroes together if only he hadn't been a fucking coward coward coward . . .)

"Who was a coward?" Cardwell asked distantly, and I took it the wrong way and screamed, *"Him!* Not me! HIM!" and then I realized that the song had ended and it was very very silent out, only the distant murmuring of highway traffic and the power hum from the speakers and the echo of my words; and I thought about what I had just said, and seven years' worth of the best rationalizations I ever built came thundering down around my ears. The largest chunk came down on my skull and smashed it flat.

Gil, I'm sorry!

4.

Ever since Nam I've been accustomed to coming awake instantly—sometimes with a weapon in my hand. I had forgotten what a luxurious pleasure it can be to let awareness and alertness seep back in at their own pace, to be truly *relaxed.* I lay still for some time, aware of my surroundings only in terms of their peacefulness, before it occurred to me to identify them. Nor did I feel, then, the slightest surprise or alarm at the defection of my subconscious sentries. It was as though in some back corner of my mind a dozen yammering voices had, for the first time within memory, shut up. All decisions were made . . .

I was in the same chair I'd left so hastily. It was tilted and reshaped into something more closely resembling the acceleration cradles astronauts take off in, only more comfortable. My left wrist was set and efficiently splinted, and hurt surprisingly little. Above me girders played geometric games across the high curved ceiling, interspersed with diffused-light fixtures that did not hurt to look at. Somewhere to my left, work was being done. It produced sound, but sound is divided into music and noise and somehow this clattering wasn't noise. I waited until it stopped, with infinite patience, in no hurry at all.

When there had been no sound for a while I got up and turned and saw Cardwell again emerging from the pit beneath the Rambler, with a thick streak of grease across his forehead and a skinned knuckle. He beamed. "I love ball joints. Your wrist okay?"

"Yes, thanks."

He came over, turned my chair back into a chair, and sank into his own. He produced cigarettes and gave me one. I noticed a wooden stool, obviously handmade, lying crippled near a workbench. I realized that Cardwell had sawed off and split two of its legs to make the splints on my wrist. The stool was quite old, and all at once I felt more guilt and shame for its destruction than I did for having come to murder its owner. This amused me sourly. I took my cigarette to the front of the garage, where one of the great bay doors now stood open, and watched night sky and listened to crickets and bull frogs while I smoked. Shop closed, Arden gone home. After a while Cardwell got up and came to the door, too, and we stepped out into the darkness. The traffic, too, had mostly gone home for the night, and there was no moon. The dark suited me fine.

"My name," I said softly, "is Bill Maeder."

From out of the black Cardwell's voice was serene. "Pleased to meet you," was all he said.

We walked on.

"I used to be a twin," I said, flicking the cigarette butt beneath my walking feet. "My brother's name was Gil, and we were identical twins. After enough people have called your twin your Other Half, you begin to believe it. I guess we allowed ourselves to become polarized, because that suited everyone's sense of symmetry or some damned thing. Yin and Yang Maeder, they called us. All our lives we disagreed on everything, and we loved each other deeply.

"Then they called us in for our draft physical. I showed up and he didn't and so they sent me to Nam and Gil to Leavenworth. I walked through the jungles and came out a hero. Gil died in his cell at the end of a protracted hunger strike. A man who is starving to death smells like fresh-baked bread, did you know that? I spent my whole first furlough practically living in his cell, arguing with him and screaming at him, and he just sat there the whole time smelling like whole wheat right out of the oven."

Cardwell said nothing. For a while we kept strolling. Then I stopped in my tracks and said, "For seven years I told myself that *he* was the coward, that he was the chump, that he had failed the final test of survival. My father is a drunk now. My mother is a Guru Maharaj Ji premie." I started walking again, and still Cardwell was silent. "I was the coward, of course. Rather than admit I was wrong to let them make me into a killer, I gloried in it. I went freelance." We had reached my Dodge, and I stopped for the last time by the passenger-side door. "Goodness, sharing, caring about other people, ethics and morals and all that—as long as I believed that they were just a shuck, lies to keep the sheep in line, I could function, my choice made sense. If there is no such thing as hope, despair can be no sin. If there is no truth, one lie is no worse than another. Come to think of it, your Arden said something like that." I sighed. "But I hated that God-damned mandala song, the one about the draft resister who dies in jail. It came out just before I was shipped out to Nam." I reached through the open car window and took the Magnum from the glove compartment. "Right after the funeral." I put the barrel between my teeth and aimed for the roof of my mouth.

Cardwell was near, but he stood stock-still. All he said was, "Some people never learn."

My finger paused on the trigger.

"Gil will be glad to see you. You two tragic

expiators will get on just fine. While the rest of us clean up the mess you left behind you. Go ahead. We'll manage."

I let my hand fall. "What are you talking about?"

All at once he was blazing mad, and a multi-billionaire's rage is a terrible thing to behold. "You simple egocentric bastard, did it ever occur to you that you might be *needed?* That the brains and skills and talent you've been using to kill strangers, to play head-games with yourself, are scarce resources? Trust an assassin to be arrogant; you colossal jackass, *do you think Arden Larsens grow on trees?* A man in my kind of business can't recruit through the want ads. I need people with *guts!*"

"To do what?" I said, and threw the pistol into the darkness.

MY MENTORS

(READ ALOUD ON CBC-RADIO, MARCH 1987)

I have been influenced by three people so heavily that I consider each to be a "mentor," in the precise meaning of "one who teaches how to think." The first two are gone, now; only the third is in shape to play football. All three, however, are immortal.

I was born, physically, in 1948. But I was born as a thinking being in early 1955, at age 6, when a librarian whose name I do not know gave me the first book I ever read all by myself, with no pictures in it. It was called *Rocketship Galileo*, the first of the books written especially for young people by the already legendary Robert Anson Heinlein, the first Grand-Master of Science Fiction.

81

I don't think it's possible to overstate the influence that book had on my life and work. It was about three teenaged boys whose Uncle Don took them along on the first-ever flight to the Moon, where they found diehard Nazis plotting a Fourth Reich, and outsmarted them. I was entranced. When I had finished it I went back to the library and asked if they had any more by this guy. They took me to a section where all the books had the same sticker on the spine, showing a V–2 impaling an oxygen atom, and my life began. Valentine Michael Smith, the Man from Mars; Lazarus Long, the wise and ornery immortal; the nameless man who, thanks to a time machine and a sex change, was both of his own parents and his only child, a closed loop in time . . . When I had worked my way through all the Heinlein titles, enjoying them hugely, I tried some of the ones filed on either side . . . and while they weren't *quite* as good, they were all superior to anything else I could find in the building. (This was back when any sf novel which had been both published in hardcover and purchased by a library had to be *terrific*.)

It wasn't just the thrilling adventure, or even the far-out ideas—you could find those in comic books—but the meticulous care and thought with which the ideas were worked out and made plausible, related to the known facts of science. Almost incidentally, seemingly accidentally, Heinlein's sf taught me facts of science, and the love of science—taught me that in science could lie adventure and excitement and hope. I still remember my confusion and dismay at the way all my schoolteachers conspired to make science seem dry and dull and impenetrable. It was my first science teacher who told me flatly that manned spaceflight was nonsense. How many young minds did he ruin?

Three years ago I visited my cousin Clare at her office in New York. As we chatted, my eyes kept inexplicably slipping from her, irresistibly drawn to a shelf at the edge of my peripheral vision. Finally they focused, and I understood. Clare is the children's book editor at Scribner's. I began to explain my rude inattention, and she cut me off. "I know," she said, "the Heinlein juveniles; happens all the time." Sure enough, there they were, the building blocks of my reason, arrayed in the same order they'd had on the shelf of the Plainview Public Library, all those years ago.

That Clare understood my problem at once suggests just how much influence Heinlein has had on the world, since he began writing in 1939. You can't copyright ideas, only arrangements of words . . . but if you *could* copyright ideas, every sf writer in the world would owe Heinlein a bundle. There can't be more than a handful of sf stories published in the last forty years that do not show his influence one way or another. He opened up most of science fiction's frontiers, wrote a great many definitive treatments of its classic themes, and in his spare time he helped design the spacesuit used by NASA, and invented the waterbed and the waldo (if you don't know what a waldo is, ask anyone who has to manipulate radioactives or other deadly substances).

But what I admire most about Heinlein is what he chose to teach me and other children in his famous sf juvenile novels: first, to make up my own mind, always; second, to think it through *before* making up my mind; and finally, to get as many facts as possible *before* thinking. Here are some brief quotes from his book *Time Enough for Love*, short extracts from the notebooks of a 2,500-year-old man:

God is omnipotent, omniscient, and omni-benevolent—it says so right here on the label. If you have a mind capable of believing all three of these divine attributes simultaneously, I have a wonderful bargain for you. No checks, please. Cash and in small bills. (and:)

If it can't be expressed in figures, it is not science; it is opinion. (and:)

Democracy is based on the assumption that a million men are wiser than one man. How's that again? I missed something.

Autocracy is based on the assumption that one man is wiser than a million men. Let's play that over again, too. Who decides? (and:)

It's amazing how much mature wisdom resembles being too tired. (And my own personal favorite:)

Writing is not necessarily something to be ashamed of—but do it in private, and wash your hands afterwards.

Just as Robert Heinlein used love of adventure to teach me the love of reason and science, Theodore Sturgeon used love of words, the beauty that could be found in words and their thoughtful esthetic arrangement, to teach me the love of . . . well, of love.

Not the kind of love found in Harlequin romances or bad movies, but the love which is the basis of courage, of hope, of simple human persistence. When I was sixteen—barely in time—I read a story of his called "A Saucer Full of Loneliness," and decided not to kill myself after all. Ten years later I read another Sturgeon story called "Suicide" aloud to a friend of mine who had made five progressively more serious attempts at self destruction, and she did not make a sixth. (Should you know anyone who needs them, the former appears in the collection *E Pluribus Unicorn*, and the latter in *Sturgeon is Alive and Well*.)

It has become something of a cliché to say that all of Ted's work was about love; he himself did not care for the description, perhaps because the word "love" begs too many questions. I know, because he told me once, that he accepted Robert Heinlein's limiting definition of love: "the condition in which the welfare of another becomes essential to your own." Ted wrote about that state, but about much more as well; about all the things which fuzzy-minded people *confuse* with love, but about much more than those things too. I think that if he must be distilled to some essential juice, it would perhaps be least inaccurate to say that he wrote about need, about all the different kinds of human need and the incredible things they drive us to, about *new* kinds of need that might come in the future and what *those* might make us do;

about unsuspected needs we might have *now* and what previously inexplicable things about human nature they might account for.

Or maybe what Ted wrote about was goodness, human goodness, and how often it turns out to derive, paradoxically, from need. I envision a mental equation with which I think he would have agreed: Need + Fear = Evil, and Need + Courage = Goodness.

One of Ted's finest stories, included in the collection *Beyond* and in my own anthology *The Best of All Possible Worlds*, is actually called "Need." It introduces one of the most bizarre and memorable characters in the history of literature, a nasty saint named Gorwing. How can a surly rat-faced runt with a streak of cruelty, a broad stripe of selfishness and a total absence of compassion be a saint? Because of an unusual form of limited telepathy. Gorwing perceives other people's needs, any sort of need, as an earsplitting roar inside his own skull, and does whatever is necessary to make the racket stop. Other people's pain hurts him, and so for utterly selfish reasons, he does things so saintly that even those few who understand why love him, and jump to do his bidding. Whenever possible Gorwing charges for his services, as high as the traffic will bear—because so many needs are expensive to fix, and so many folks *can't* pay— and he always drops people the moment their needs are met. Marvelous!

Ted's own worst need, I think, was to persuade me and others of the post-Hiroshima generation that there *is* a tomorrow, that there is a point to existence, a reason to keep struggling, that all of this comic confusion is *going* somewhere, *progressing toward* something—and although he believed in his heart that this something was literally unimaginable, he never stopped trying to imagine it, and with mere words to make it seem irresistibly beautiful. He persisted in trying to create a new code of survival for post-Theistic man, "a code," as he said, "which requires belief rather than obedience. It is called ethos . . . what it is really is a reverence for your sources and your posterity, a study of the main current which created you, and in which you will create still a greater thing when the time comes, reverencing those who bore you and the ones who bore them, back and back to the first wild creature who was different because his heart leaped when he saw a star."

Let me quote the closing paragraph of Ted's "The Man Who Lost The Sea," about a man who, as a boy, nearly died learning the lesson that you *always* spearfish with a buddy, even if you wanted the fish all to yourself—that "I" don't shoot a fish, "we" do. Now the sea sound he seems to hear is really earphone static from the spilled uranium which is killing him:

The sick man looks at the line of his own footprints, which testify that he is alone, and at the wreckage below, which states that there is no way back, and at the white east and the mottled west and the paling flecklike satellite above. Surf sounds in his ears. He hears his pumps. He hears what is left of his breathing.

The cold clamps down and folds him round past measuring, past all limit.

Then he speaks, cries out: then with joy he takes his triumph at the other side of death, as one takes a great fish, as one completes a skilled and mighty task, rebalances at the end of some great daring leap; and as he used to say "we shot a fish," he uses no "I":

"God," he cries, dying on Mars, "God, we made it!"

When the Halifax science fiction convention, Halcon, asked me to be their Guest of Honour, I agreed on the condition that they fly Ted Sturgeon in to be the Toastmaster, for I had long yearned to meet him. I will spare you the now-legendary story of the horrid duel of puns which Ted and I waged across the port city of Halifax (and the starboard city of Dartmouth), but I must tell of the Two Kinds of Hug.

A fan approached him and asked if she could give him a hug; he agreed. "Ah," he said gently as they disengaged, "that was a Letter A." "What do you mean?" I asked. "You hug me," he ordered, and I did. "Now that," he said, "was a Number One." A crowd had begun to form, as they so often did around Ted. He had various people hug, adjudging each hug as either a Letter A or a Number One.

At last we began to get it. Some of us hugged touching at the top, joined at the middle, and spread apart at the bottom, like a capital A. Others, unafraid to rub bellies, hugged so as to form a Number One. "There is really only one sense," Ted told us, "and that is touch; all the other senses are only other ways of touching. But if you can't touch with touch, you can't touch with much."

There came a time in my life when, for reasons too complicated to go into, I needed to make some money without working for it. Heinlein had taught me how to think; Sturgeon had taught me how to feel; but there was not much call for either of those skills. My schooling had taught me very little, and much of that was turning out to be false or worthless. My only assets were a vast collection of tattered sf paperbacks which I was unwilling to sell.

Suddenly I made the mental leap: perhaps *I* could write tattered sf paperbacks!

Well, the idea couldn't have been all bad: the first story I attempted sold, on first submission, to the highest paying market in sf, *Analog Science Fact/Science Fiction*. I quit my regular job and went freelance on the strength of that $300 check.

But everything I wrote *after* that bounced, not only at *Analog* but everywhere. A year after I went freelance I had a superb library of first-edition rejection slips, equalled only by my collection of Absolutely Final Notices from creditors.

What saved me from a life as a civil servant, or some other form of welfare, was the fact that the editor of *Analog* at the time (and subsequently of *Omni*) was Ben Bova.

Many editors regard writers as regrettably

unavoidable nuisances, and new writers as avoidable ones. The slush pile, as the heap of unsolicited manuscripts is called, is often seen as a source of comic relief for idle moments in the editorial day. But Ben always treated it as a treasure trove. He read every manuscript that came in the door—and when he found new writers he felt displayed promise, he cultivated them carefully.

Ben cultivated me in several ways. The first, of course, was to send me a check. But with the check came a letter inviting me to lunch at my convenience. (This is not as altruistic as it seems: when an editor dines alone, he pays for it; when he dines with the newest and greenest of writers, the publisher pays.) Over lunch he answered hundreds of my beginner's questions: how to prepare my manuscripts more professionally, why I didn't need an agent until I was ready to try a novel, how to join the Science Fiction Writers of America so my manuscripts wouldn't land in the slush pile, what a con was and how it could affect my income, what Heinlein and Sturgeon were like as people, the basics of plotting commercial fiction, hundreds of things I desperately yearned to know. I took pages of notes. He also stroked my ego, and demanded more stories.

So I went home and wrote more stories, and as I've said, Ben—and every other editor—bounced them all. But Ben didn't send rejection slips, he sent rejection *letters*. Brief ones, rarely more than two or three sentences explaining what specific errors made this story unpublishable . . . but those few sentences amounted to a condensed correspondence course in writing commercial fiction. "You're writing too many stories at once here, Spider." Or, "I don't give a damn about your hero." Or, "Nothing *happens* here; no problem gets solved, nobody learns anything." Things like that.

Most of these nuggets of wisdom horrified or infuriated me. Say, for example, that I had sweated blood for weeks, produced a 20,000-word masterpiece of adventure and irony, and gotten it back from Ben with the single sentence, "Cut it to 6,000 words." I would scream. Then I would examine my dwindling bank balance and try to cut the story, at least a little. Then I'd call Ben. "I *can't* cut 14,000 words, Ben, there isn't a spare word in there." "I know," he would say. "They're all gems. But just as an exercise, pretend that someone is going to give you a dime for every word you cut." I would thank him glumly and hang up, and then ignore his advice and send the manuscript to his competitors. When they had all bounced it, with form rejection slips, I'd shelve it.

After a year of this, I was desperate. So I'd dig out the dusty manuscript, look at it mournfully and, just as an exercise, see how much flesh I *could* slice from my baby before I cut into its spine. Howls of pain! A few days later I would call him again. "Ben, remember that story about the malfunctioning time machine? I've got it down to 10,000 words, and there's just nothing else I can cut, and I've already cut some terrific stuff."

"I know," he'd say. "But just as an exercise, pretend that a large man is going to come around with a maul and break one limb for every thousand words above six."

Cursing the Bova clan root and branch, weeping with fury, I would amputate a few more of my child's appendages, and when I had it down to 6,000 words I'd dry my eyes and reread it—

—and discover to my horror that it was now a much better story—

—and send it to Ben and get a check.

In addition to tutoring me, Ben made a point of introducing me to other writers, to artists and editors and other professionals, to influential fans. And when I had sold a half dozen stories, he sat me down at a convention and said, "It's time you started a novel and got an agent." Meanwhile, down the hall, a mutual friend was, at Ben's instigation, telling one of the best agents in the business that it was time he took on a few new clients—this guy Robinson, for instance. When I complained once that I couldn't think of any story ideas, Ben showed me an entire drawer full of ideas and invited me to help myself. On one memorable occasion, he returned a story I had submitted, saying, "This is *too good* for me to buy; *Playboy* will pay you three times as much as I can." (One of his few failures as a prophet, drat the luck. He bought the story two months later.)

But of all the things Ben did for me, one in particular stands out in my mind. During the year of apprenticeship I mentioned earlier, during which I sold no stories, it eventually became necessary to get a job. Luck was with me; I found employment as a journalist, and so continued to avoid honest work. I spent a year as Real Estate Editor for a Long Island newspaper: during the day I typed lies purporting to be the truth, while at night I tried to teach myself how to write truths purporting to be fiction for Ben. The newspaper job was dull, dishonest and demeaning—and quite lucrative: I had never made so much money in my life. At the end of my year of trial, I still had only the one original story sale under my belt . . . and then a horrid thing happened.

The publisher of the newspaper called me into his office and told me that he knew I was doing my job with half my attention—and doing it well; he was not complaining. But he offered to double my already high salary if I would give up this fiction nonsense and throw my full attention into the world of real estate, become an insider, socialize with realtors and join their clubs. Or, I could quit. He gave me a week to decide.

I called my friends for advice. But Ben was the only friend I had who was earning a good salary—in fact, the only one who was not on unemployment—and the only one who did not give me an immediate, knee-jerk answer. The night before I had to give my decision, he called me back. "I've been thinking all week about your problem," he said. "Spider, no one can pay you enough money to do what you don't want to do."

I thanked him and quit my job. A week later, I sold my second story (to another editor), and a few months after that I won the John W. Campbell Award for Best New Writer, and by the end of the year I was selling regularly and had been nominated for my first Hugo Award. And because I had to live on a writer's income, I moved to the woods of Nova Scotia, where I met my wife Jeanne.

And so in a sense it could be said that I owe everything I have in the world to Ben Bova.

Mind you, nobody's perfect. It was Ben who encouraged me to put puns in my stories. He is himself an excellent and accomplished writer, who once wrote about a robot policeman named "Brillo."

Metal fuzz . . .

These, then, are my three mentors: Robert Anson Heinlein, Theodore Sturgeon, and Ben Bova. All great writers, all great teachers. Generalizations are a nasty habit, but perhaps it would be least inaccurate to say that Robert taught me how to think, Ted taught me how to feel, and Ben taught me how to survive as a writer. I owe all three a debt I will never be able to repay.

TEDDY THE FISH

*In combined homage to two of my favorite
saints, I offer this rap. It is my interpretation
of what Lord Buckley might have said
about Theodore Sturgeon . . .*

M'lords and miladies of the Royal Court . .

Here ah is again, here's me, and there's you.
Now I heard all you cats talkin' 'bout who the
greatest cat in the *world* was, talkin' 'bout Dr. A
and Quarrelin' Harlan, and High Gee Wells, and
Admiral Bob, and Ten-Foot Pohl, and Herb Varley
on his Verb Harley, and the Lawd knows there
ain't a cat alive that can blow the way ol' Virile
Cyril Kornbluth used to do—but ah'mo' put a cat
on you . . . dat was the sweetest . . . gonest . . .

wailin'est . . . grooviest cat that ever stomped upon dis swingin' sphere! And they call dis-yar cat—

Teddy the Fish!

That's what they called him, Teddy the Fish, cuz he *swung* skiffy, he *wailed* skiffy, he *gassed* skiffy, he *grooved* skiffy and ah'mo' tell you why: you see, skiffy was bugged wit the *critic*. Ev'y time skiffy people wanna pass the jug to the neighbor, go up to a mundane, say, "Dig a taste of this, brother," WHAM, here come the critic, start puttin' it down: *Dat stuff is bad jazz, go further, it ain't no real jazz at all, fact, what it is is Top Forty.* And PFFFFT! TWEET! the mundane split the scene and there stand the skiffy cat stoneless: bugged 'em to death.

That was before Teddy the Fish blew in on the scene, you see—and the day the Fish *blew* in on the scene seemed to be that critic's big swingin' day, cuz he was into that highbrow bag up to his *shoulders,* wailin' up an *in-sane breeze.* Sayin': *them skiffy people is tone deaf, and they got no heart, and they got no soul, got no credentials, don't know no chords, they ain't no serious cats, and furthermore, whoever heard of 'em?* Then he look up—

—and here come the Fish—

—lookin' like the merriest goat you ever see, makin' the scene wid his bad buddy, Admiral Bob (but that's a whole other lick, tell ya 'bout Bad Bob 'nother time), and the Fish look at the critic, and he smile like a faun diggin' a nymph, an' the critic start to look away—

So the Fish back off about thirty-forty feet,

and he put out his arms, co-o-o-o-l-wise, and he take a runnin' broad jump and WHACKED on that critic's tail *so hard,* he got the cat's *attention*—

—and that gassed skiffy. *Gassed* 'em! People standin' round wid de eyes buggin' out, sayin', "Look what the Fish put on that boy!"

And the Fish say, TONE DEAF, IS WE? and he blew a lick God went home hummin' that night.

Fish say, NO CHOPS, HUH? an' he blew a sixteen-chorus solo in *i*ambic pen*tameter,* with two fingers of his lef' han'.

Fish say, NO HEART? an' he blew a chorus made the critic cry like a widowed woman.

Say, WE AIN'T NO SERIOUS CATS? an' blew a lick made the critic laugh like a chile.

Say, DON'T KNOW NO CHORDS? an' blew a chord with seventeen notes scared the critic wigless, had to send out for the wig-tappers to put it back on.

Fish say, NO CREDENTIALS? an' he sat in wid the *New York Times,* hippin the mundanes to skiffy till they all got straight.

Fish say, GOT NO SOUL, IS WE? an' he blew a stanza made the critic dance like a drunken monkey, sayin', "Lord, I see Yo' plan at last, an' it ain't such a bad deal after all."

And when the critic come down, he say, "O great, sweet, swingin', groovey, non-stop, high double-clutchin' pinetop *go* of all double-swings and beauty . . ." An' the Fish say, "WELL IF I AIN'T, I'M A GREAT BIG GROOVEY POLE ON A ROUGH HILL ON THE WAY THERE."

Critic say, "Tell me somethin'," (See, he was a very hip cat, the Fish was) said, "Tell me somethin', Yo' Sweet Hipness. Straighten me . . . cause I'm ready. Tell me: what in the world is you *smokin'*?"

An' the Fish look at him, an' the love-look come on his face, an' he say, "LOVE AND CURIOSITY, BABY. HEH HEH. DA'SS ALL, IT'S JUST LOVE, AND CURIOSITY."

Critic say, "Always *did* like that skiffy, and furthermo' I dig it *in front*, man, the first one hip." An' Admiral Bob outs wid a laser cannon an' shoot 'im through the wishbone, an' the skiffy people start to party down at last . . .

Pretty soon the fame o' the Fish is jumpin', an' the grapevine is shootin' off sparks forty feet long, talkin' bout how he laid it down for the critic, cat dug it: *didn't dig it*—put it down again, dug it: *didn't dig it*—put it down a third time, WHAM, critic dug it to death, next thing you know you got skiffy people playin' Carnegie *Hall!* And that *gassed* skiffy! Anybody blowin' skiffy for a livin' today got the Fish to thank that he ain't sellin' shoes on the side to keep some juice on the table. Anybody diggin' skiffy, they got the Fish to thank if the bag ain't no drag. Anybody *ain't* diggin' skiffy, it's their own damn fault, cause the Fish laid it down, and WHAM . . . it *stayed* there.

Now the Fish went down a couple o' verses back, joined the Hallelujah Chorus in the sky. His frame is cold, his tale is told, an' he can't come to the phone. But he left his eyes behind. See, Fish had them pretty eyes. He wanted ev'body to see out his eyes, so they could see how pretty it wuz . . . when you look with love, and curiosity . . . Well, dig what I tell you now: FISH LIVES!

The Fish can touch *you* any time you ready to get straight. All his best licks got recorded, baby, an' you can put 'em on any time you like and hear 'em again. Just put on his eyes, an' you can dig the world like he did, wid love, and curiosity.

The Sturgeon may be swimmin' somewhere else—but we still got the caviar . . .

—Halifax, 10 March 1986

LORD BUCKLEY facts:
—Born Stockton, CA, 1907.
—Died NYC, 1960.
—Beginning in 1925, he would get up on stage, fire up a big bowl of reefer, and start to rap, in free-associated jazzman's idiom, the vernacular of the hip.
—Sported a waxed mustache, evening dress, a monocle, and a pith helmet ("so necessary in a nightclub, dear boy").
—Owned a nightclub in Chicago in the thirties called Suzi Q, in which was held The Church of the Living Swing, substituting belly dancers for altar boys; this eventually got him run out of town by the Vice Squad.
—Once allegedly led an audience naked through the streets to crash a Frank Sinatra concert at the Waikiki Hilton.

—One friend characterizes him as " . . . a stone crazy, six and a half foot tall, half Cherokee ex-lumberjack who pretended to be an English aristocrat . . . by common consent an uncouth unreliability, forever on the con . . . who drank like he had a thirst you could photograph, guzzled pills like candy, and fucked anything with a handbag."

HIS OWN PETARD

"Steven, can you come over right away?" Ann's uncharacteristically flat, hollow voice asked.

Some people find it odd that a science fiction writer, in this day and age, should choose to live without a modem, a pager, or a fax machine. I'm of the opinion that modern technology has made it *too* easy for people to get in touch with each other. I concentrate for a living, or rather, I try my damnedest. But you *have* to have a phone—at least, if you want to make a living. Damn it.

Well, that's why God made answering machines. It was a cold night outside, and I had been hard at work when the phone rang. Ann was a friend: she knew I often turned off the speaker on the machine so I could concentrate on writing without interruption. She was a friend: she wouldn't be too disappointed if I didn't pick up the call.

She was a *good* friend, and she sounded like she needed help badly . . .

I hesitated with my hand an inch from the phone, thinking that the definition of "friend" should be, "someone you don't have to make excuses to."

"Rubin's dead," her voice said. "I was there."

Well, that would have been more than enough to fetch me—at any time of day or night, in any weather. But then she clinched it . . . by bursting into tears.

I picked up the handset, said, "Fifteen minutes," and hung up.

"Well," I said to my wife as I pulled on my shoes, "that was the most amazing call of the month."

"Who was it?" Mariko asked obligingly. A good straight man is welcome when you're in a hurry.

"Ann. She says Rubin is down."

Her jaw dropped. "Billy Rubin? Dead?"

"Brown bread," I agreed. "She says she saw it happen."

"Wow. That *is* amazing."

I shook my head. "That's not the amazing part. Get this: *she didn't sound happy about it.*"

I left Mariko looking as puzzled as I was, and drove to Ann's place.

Ann is a science fiction writer too, just starting out. Tall, willowy, blonde, pleasant-faced and good-natured, in her late twenties. She's had a few short stories in small-press anthologies and fanzines, one real sale to *Analog*, and has had a novel ostensibly sold to Charnel House for the last eighteen months, although they still haven't given her a firm pub date yet. She's pretty good—good enough that if she has incredible luck, and lives long enough, one day she might be as poor as I am. I like her as a person, too. More important, my wife, who possesses a very subtly calibrated Jerk Detector, also likes her.

She was in rotten shape when I arrived at her flat. Tear-tracked, half in the bag, spattered with blood—Rubin's blood!—an uncapped half-empty bottle of vodka next to an open bag of grass on the coffee table. She was wearing a swatch of yellow POLICE—CRIME SCENE tape around her forehead like a ninja headband, canted rakishly over one eye. Her eyes were dangerously bright, and her voice was higher in pitch than usual. I sat beside her on her sprung and faded couch while she told me the story.

"I know I shouldn't have," she said, "but I was desperate. Charnel House has had *The Cosmic Cabal* for almost three years now, and I haven't even been able to get that rat bastard down there to return a phone call or answer a query since he bought it—a year after I sent it to him. Any minute now, he'll get fired or move to another house, and my book will get published as an orphan . . . if it's ever published at all."

"Your contract specifies a date they have to publish by, right?"

"Sure. And if they don't, I can take the book back . . . and go tell other editors, 'I have a book here that someone else bought dirt-cheap and then decided not to bother printing after all—

want a look?' And my agent says there's no point even *trying* to sell a *second* book until the first one's been out long enough to have some kind of track record to judge by . . . Jesus, who'd have guessed you could bring your whole career to a shuddering halt by selling a book? I'm maxed out at Visa, the bank, and the credit union; even my parents are starting to tighten up. So I called Rubin."

"Jesus," I said, "that is desperate."

If you're new to science fiction, Billy Rubin was almost certainly the most influential critic in sf history, with a regular column in *Alternities*. He was also, in the nearly unanimous opinion of the membership of SFWA, a direct descendant of the Marquis de Sade. Almost any critic will pull the wings off a crippled fly, of course— it's part of the job description—but Rubin was the kind of guy who would stake out a pregnant female fly, slice her open without anesthesia, and pull the winglets off all her little fly feti in front of her eyes. Elegantly. It was he who called Pournelle "The King of The Cyber Rifles," accused Gibson of "reasoning incorrectly from data which he does not possess," dubbed Shepard "The Sultan of S.W.A.T.," summed up *The Jaws That Bite, The Claws That Catch* with "Beware the dub-dub book, and shun the four-and-a-quarter snatch," and reviewed a nonexistent book by Bradley called *Dragon Harass*. He's the one who created that whole resonant-sounding, ultimately meaningless and divisive dichotomy between the "anti-science" fiction writers and the "Aunty Science" fiction writers, which has had the whole field at each others' throats for a couple of years now. No matter how new to sf you are, this ought to convey something: *Harlan Ellison was polite to Rubin*.

In short, Rubin was to science fiction writers what Geraldo Rivera is to people of alternate lifestyles. No, worse, for the slimy bastard had a modicum of genuine wit, used a surgical scalpel rather than a clumsy bladder full of dung. He evinced a special fondness for flensing beginners. First novels were his favorite victims-of-choice: since few of his readers had actually read them, he was relieved of that onerous necessity himself, and the tyros had no cliques of friends to fight back for them. In a few famous cases he had actually succeeded in single-handedly aborting the publication of a first novel, by panning the galley proofs so savagely that the publisher changed his mind and decided to eat the advance.

In corollary, Rubin could also get a first novel published with a phone call, if he chose. Or hurry one along the pipeline. And he lived here in town . . .

"So I invited him out to dinner," Ann said.

"Ann, Ann," I said, shaking my head.

"Dammit, I was desperate! Don and Ev told me about a new restaurant in Chinatown where the owner was so green he hadn't learned to confirm plastic before accepting it yet, so I had Rubin meet me there and stuffed him full of Szechuan. He was actually pleasant, for Rubin. Ordered the most expensive stuff, naturally, and of course he eats twice as much as a human—"

She tripped over the present tense. "Well, he did, anyway. And had five rye and gingers. So I played it very cool, didn't say a word about the book or the business, just kept the talk general. I charmed the shit out of him, Steven."

"Sure you did," I said soothingly.

"So I wait until we're outside the restaurant, walking toward where I'm parked so I can drive him home, and then I casually mention that I've got this novel stuck in the pipe at Charnel House . . . " Her face went to pieces.

I took her hand and held it until she could continue.

"It sounds like something out of a cheap porno movie," she said finally, "but I swear to God the moment I said that sentence, he got an erection. Wham, like that. I thought his pants were going to rip. And he gave me this *look*—" She began crying again.

I hugged her with some awkwardness. "He certainly lived up to his pen name," I said savagely.

Even through her tears, her puzzlement was plain.

"It's got to be a pseudonym," I explained. "He probably thought nobody else was smart enough to get it. Medical students are usually too busy to read sf. Bilirubin is a primary component of bile."

She snorted, but was still too upset to giggle, so I went on. "It has special relevance here. All bilirubin is, really, is red blood cells that died and decomposed. Dark brown goo. The liver skims it out of the blood, and passes it on to

the intestines for disposal. It's why shit is brown
. . . and part of why it smells bad. Pretty appropriate name for him, huh?"

This time she did giggle—but only for a second, and then the giggle segued back into tears
again. I gave up and held her. She would tell
the rest of it when she was ready.

She had passed the point where further tears
could be any help: the only thing that might
make the nut now would be to get her to laugh
somehow. And I couldn't see any angle of
approach. I tried constructing something about
"Rubin on rye . . . can't cut the mustard," but
before it would jell she was speaking again and
it was too late. Her voice was harsh, strident,
full of self-disgust.

"I was going to do it. I knew what he was
going to say, and I was just making up my mind
to say yes. Can you understand that? I had time
enough to know that I was going to say yes, and
he had time to see it in my eyes. And then we
saw them."

I already had a rough idea where she was
going. "A gang."

"Yeah."

"What colors?"

She shook her head. "The cops wanted to
know that too. All I saw was eyes—and blades.
Generic Asian streetgang, that's all I can tell you.
Lots of eyes. Lots of blades. All sharp. You know
about the swords?"

I nodded grimly. This year the streetgangs all
seemed to realize at once that fighting with guns
uses up troops too fast, and has no element of

skill. But fighting with knives requires *too much* skill, gets in too close and nasty and personal, and also violates the "concealed weapon" statutes. So they began using swords. It started with Japanese kids wearing ceremonial samurai blades, for show—but the idea made so much sense from the streetgang point of view that before long, puzzled fencing supply outlets were sold out. It'll take the establishment at least another year to get the laws changed. Meanwhile the streetgangs all give each other Heidelberg scars—not that they'd understand the reference.

"Let me guess," I said. "Rubin ran away so fast his heart exploded."

She grimaced, as though she wanted to smile but was not entitled. "You know, that's *exactly* what I was expecting. I'm like: well, I better make sure I'm not in his way, wouldn't want to get trampled to death before I get a shot at being raped and cut. Or the other way around. You know: thinking how stupid I'd been to come to Chinatown without a man with me. And then he did it—or I guess I mean he was already doing it."

"Did what?"

"Nothing."

I sighed. "I see," I lied politely.

"No, I mean, he did nothing whatsoever to acknowledge their existence. He just kept right on walking. Like they weren't there. We're walking along, and these guys materialize in front of us, and I stop in my tracks so I can get mugged and killed like a decent citizen—and Rubin just keeps right on walking, and since he's just taken my arm, now I'm walking again too, and we walk right into the middle of them."

Making people laugh is a large part of what I do for a living . . . but I sure didn't have much to work with, here. "Jesus."

"So this real little guy is right smack in front of us, like, small, but the moment you see his eyes you know he's the meanest guy in the gang, okay? And he waves that big shiny sword, and he goes, 'You can motor, Fatty, if you leave the slut.' And the rest close in from both sides . . . "

She trailed off as the memory looped on her.

After a time, still hoping against hope for a way to get her laughing, I prompted, "So Billy died of happiness?"

She didn't even crack a smile. "He stopped, and he let go of my arm, and he walked right at that little snake. He just walked right at him, not even putting his hand out like he was going to push the guy out of his way, and he walked right onto the sword. He just kept walking until it came out his b-b-back, and . . . and then he just stood there, locking eyes with the little guy, squirting blood all over him, looking sort of puzzled, until finally he . . . he fell down and died. And the little guy just looked down at him—and then he walked away. Like, in tribute to his courage! Do you see? I owe my life to the heroism of *Billy Rubin*! I've lost even the luxury of hating him."

I began to laugh.

I couldn't help myself. Maybe it was the worst thing I could have done at that particular moment, as wrong as laughing can ever be—I knew I should be comforting my shocked and traumatized friend—but that just made it funnier. Unable to stop, unable to explain, I roared until the tears came.

Ann was nearly crying herself again by then—tears of anger this time, at me. And I couldn't blame her. But finally I got enough control to explain.

"Don't you get it?" I honked. "Jesus Christ, it's perfect! The son of a bitch was done in by the most ironic weapon imaginable: his own narrow mind. Woo ha hoo! What an appropriate fate for a critic: he died of his own preconceptions! Oh, haw haw haw . . ."

"What the hell are you talking about?" Ann demanded.

"Don't you see? Heroism, my left kidney! He literally didn't see that sword. Billy Rubin was a *science fiction critic*. He said it himself a hundred times in his column: he was fundamentally, constitutionally incapable of believing in a world that has *both* laser beams *and* sword fights!"

Her eyes widened . . . and at long last, thank God, she began to laugh too.

ADMIRAL BOB

Another eulogy for a departed saint,
again in the style of that most
immaculately hip aristocrat,
the sainted Lord Buckley . . .

Milords an' Ladies of the Royal Court . . .

Now we been swingin ourselves up a fine little jam session this weekend, got down tight an' right an' blew us some nice skiffy riffs—cause we all dig that skiffy—an' I heard all you cats talkin 'bout who the greatest cat in the *world* was, talkin' 'bout Dr. A the Robot Gasser, an' Compact Carlan Ellison, an' High Gee Wells, an' Teddy the Fish, an' Herb Varley on his Verb Harley, an' Steele-Drivin' Al, an' Freddy the Ten-Inch Pohl, an' Jaws, the Poul Shark, an' the Lawd knows these are all heavy cats—

—but ah'mo' put a cat on you . . . that was
the sweetest . . . gonest . . . *wailin'est* . . .
GROOVIEST cat that ever stomped upon this
swingin' sphere! He was the stone king of skiffy,
an' they call dis yar cat—

ADMIRAL BOB . . .

That's what they called him: Admiral Bob,
retired gob, he done the job an' stoned the mob.
(For a change, if you dig.) He didn't invent skiffy,
understand—but he's the cat that made skiffy
spiffy! An' if he never blew, I wouldn't be here
talkin' to you.

Like I say, he was a sailor cat in front, figured to drive the battleship, an' sure as God
made little green parkin' tickets he'd of made
it, too . . . but one day the Black Leather Angel
come swingin' on by, sayin', "TB, or not TB?"
an' Bob say, "Baby, that's a good question
(COUGH!)," an' *wham*, they put him on the
beach an' give him the walkin' paper: tell him
to buy a rowboat an' a cannon an' go into business for himself.

But it didn't bring him down. Cat just say, "My
problem is clear. I need somethin' *heavier* than
a battleship. Gotta have a *really* dangerous
weapon," an' he bought him a typewriter.

Now, cats an' kitties blew skiffy in them days,
we're talkin nineteen-thirty-an'-leapin'-nine, an'
there was some pretty heavy players in town:
studs like Julie the Frog, an' High Gee Wells, an'
Doc Smith, an' Cactus Jack, an' ©a funny little
cat named Binder that had two heads. They was
puttin' down some nice roots kinda riffs—dudes
had been blowin' skiffy ever since a stud named

I Owe Greenbacks opened up the first skiffy club,
but you still had to go over the tracks to dig it.

Now the joint that jumped the most was called
Astounding, on account of it was, an' the club
owner was a cat they called Heavy John Campbell: very heavy cat indeed. Had dudes hitchin'
a thousand miles for a chance to play for pass-
the-hat, had to beat 'em off the stand with a
club, an' if you couldn't blow for Heavy John,
you was Square an' Nowhere.

So one night it's Open Mike Night, an' cats
an' kitties are blowin' up an insane breeze, havin'
a cuttin' contest, you dig, an' Heavy John sayin'
(point) "Groovy," an' (point) "Later, Jackson," an'
the back door bang open, an'—

WHAM! There stand Admiral Bob . . .

. . . standin' there straight as a bass an' tall
as a tree, uniform got a crease on it that'd cut
like a killer review, gold braid an' a sword, an'
half the cats there saluted without even thinkin'.

An' he took out his ax an' begun to blow.

An' my Lords an' my Ladies, ahmo hip you:
you may have heard all kinda jam sessions
blowin' off, you may have heard New Orleans
licks, you may have heard it Chicago Style, you
may have the bebop version, you may have dug
all *kind* of musical insane flips, but you studs
an' stallions an' cats an' kitties never dug any
session like this cat *blew!* He wailed *so* hard, they
had to send out for the wig tappers: *every*body
flipped their wig, an' it took all night to get 'em
nailed back down again—people walkin' round
with the eyes buggin' out, askin' each other,
"Where do we go to surrender?"

An' when the last lick faded, ol' Heavy John fix Bob with the gimlet eyeball that turned so many sidemen to sushi, an' everybody get real quiet, an' Heavy John frown like a storm comin' off the water, an' he say:

"What are your orders, sir?"

Everybody *flipped*!

Admiral Bob had a miracle wig: he could work that miracle lick any time he took a notion. After he'd been blowin' over across the tracks awhile, they had to move the tracks, 'cause the trains couldn't get through the people. Cat put a man on the Moon with his own two hands, picked up plutonium in a pair of waldos, gave orgasms to computers, told a lie that was three thousand years Long, capital L, put a rap on the U.S. Congress . . . an' in his *spare* time, he thought up the water bed! Admiral Bob shot craps with the Devil four times, an' won three. An' if that ain't heavy enough, dig this, Jack: he kept the same chick smilin' for forty years!

He come from Squaresville, had a general for a brother, but he could love like his buddycat Teddy the Fish. Come from the Navy, but every boat *he* wrote had *chicks* on the bridge—an' the chicks wore pants. Come on like an atheist, but when the freezer cats wanted to put his frame on ice, he said, "How do I know it wouldn't interfere with rebirth?" an' sent 'em away frameless an' bugged. Come on like a tight cat with a shekel, but he had his ear open, an' any time a skiffy cat or kitty was scoffless an' hung, he straightened 'em, quiet an' cool. He was a science cat, but he could write a poem. He was a hip square. He was a cool straight. He was a saintly old stud you didn't want to mess with.

I mean, the *sphere* owes this cat—but skiffy? Baby, if Admiral Bob ever called in all his markers, he'd *own* the mother. All us skiffs'd be *riffless*. Every bag, every groove, Big Bad Bob been there first, an' maybe you could cut him, but you better bring your lip. You don't even have to dig him, but you ain't never gonna get around him, see? 'Cause when he put it down, *SHAZAM*: it stayed there!

Far as anybody know, the cat never smoked his second reefer . . . but I'll tell you this, baby: he was High'n Lyin' *all* the time!

WHEN NO MAN PURSUETH

"Yes indeed, m'boy," wheezed the old Colonel, "if you want to get yourself a real education before you get to Secundus, you've certainly picked the right way to go about it. Riding a tramp like this will teach you more about life with a capital *L* than all the seminars and professors on Secundus, I daresay."

"Precisely my thought," Fleming replied in what he hoped were mature tones. Although he faced the pot-bellied Colonel next to him at the bar, he was aware in every nerve ending of the impossibly beautiful girl in blue seated across the room, at whom he had been sneaking glances ever since her arrival. In point of fact, he had booked passage on the *I.V. This Train* because it represented a saving of over a hundred credits; but before this girl he wished very desperately to appear worldly—or, if he could not pull that

off, at least eager to be. The frequent glances
he stole at her were no help at all, either, for
she stared right back at him; and while she was
not staring him between the eyes, that rhymes
with what she was staring between. He racked
his brains in vain for a means of introduction,
even as he took the Colonel for two credits six.

"Not many realize what it's like out here," the
Colonel rumbled on in the fond belief that
Fleming was listening. "Fringe worlds. The
incredible diversity. Ultimate solution to the
minority opinion problem, actually. Anyone's got
a crackpot idea on how to run things, give him
a planet and let him try it out. Make for some
interesting planets. Why, over on Why Should
I they've actually done away with taxation. Except
on a voluntary basis, of course—but if a politi-
cian has some project he thinks should be done,
he has to convince people to pay for it—and any
project that people aren't willing to shell out cold
cash for is scrapped. Only time will tell if it's
viable, of course, but it certainly is one of the
more streamlined governments I've ever seen.
And for centuries it was only a crackpot idea.

"Yes, m'boy, there's room out here on the
fringe for just about any kind of society. You
don't see that sort of thing on the big passenger liners, non-stop jumps from Federation
Planet to Federation Planet with their bland,
homogenous 'culture' to make them identical.
Out here there's variety. You meet people who
think differently, who live differently than you.
Stimulating."

"Sometimes," said the girl in blue in a voice

like the mellowest of clarinets, "it can be very stimulating indeed."

This seemed to Fleming a clear-cut invitation to repartee, and he did not hesitate. "Huh?" he riposted, shuffling the cards gently.

She smiled, and both men shivered slightly. "Well, I do not quite understand it myself. But I have discovered that for some reason, many men find the customs of my planet extremely stimulating."

"What customs, my dear?" asked the old Colonel, clearly in better control than Fleming, though not by much.

"Well," she said demurely, "on Do It—my home planet—we have a society based on total sexual access. The theory is that if we can eliminate absolutely every sexual inhibition, we'll achieve a truly happy society."

Fleming put down the cards, got outside of a couple ounces of bourbon with considerable alacrity and dialed for more, mashing down savagely on the button marked TRIPLE "Does it work?" he croaked.

Her smile disappeared, and he hastily searched his assets for something that might bring it back again. "Well, we do have one little problem. One of the first inhibitions to go was the incest taboo, and there wasn't an awful lot of us to begin with. Father keeps saying something about our gene pool being too small—anyway, we started having a lot of babies that weren't . . . quite right, one way or another." She frowned, then smiled again, and Fleming turned his triple into a single with one gulp. "But we figured out the solution, and that's when we instituted the custom I was talking about.

"You see, Do It law requires any and all females to become impregnated by any off-worlder who offers them half a chance."

There came a sudden clatter as of dueling castanets, but it was only the sound of ice rattling furiously in two glasses at once.

The girl rose, traveled to the bar by a method that "walking" does not even begin to describe, and seated herself on the empty stool between Fleming and the Colonel, dialing a sombrero with a blood-red fingernail. Fleming essayed a gay smile, and produced a horrible grimace; the Colonel tried to clear his throat, and plainly failed.

"Why don't you gentlemen come and visit me in stateroom 4-C tonight, say about 2300? Perhaps I can show you more of the customs of my planet." She turned to Fleming and added softly, " . . . and I may have a business proposition for you, young man. If you are interested . . . "

Fleming allowed as how he might be interested. She rose, smiled at them both, and left.

Fleming and the Colonel looked at each other. As one they turned back to the bar and dialed fresh triples, bourbon and a stengah. Raising their glasses in silent toast, they drank deep, then smashed the glasses against the bulkhead.

"2300 hours, she said?" asked Fleming at last.

The Colonel looked pained. "I say, old boy. I mean . . . dash it, both of us? Together?"

"How do we know what her customs are?" Fleming reasoned. "It may be necessary. Or something."

"Yes, but . . . "

"You want to blow it?"

The Colonel closed his mouth, opened it, then closed it again.

"Come on. Let's get back to your poker lesson."

Curiously, Colonel Enderby-Thwaite had a run of beginner's luck after that. At the close of the lesson, Fleming was a little startled to realize that he was down about thirty credits, and what with one thing and another, he had much to preoccupy him as he made his way above-decks to the passenger level. But when his head cleared the hatchway of C-Deck and he saw a large, ferocious-looking Greenie tiptoeing down the corridor away from him with a blaster in its fist, he came instantly alert.

Greenies—natives of Sirius II—were the first and so far only alien race ever encountered by man; and the history of that encounter was not a happy one. Captured Greenies had been used as domestic animals for years before it was decided that they possessed intelligence, and even then it had taken a war with Sirius and several determined slave revolts before men learned to see the green humanoids as equals. Even now, a hundred years later, many Greenies were still a little surly about it, and college students like Fleming had learned not to mess with them. This Greenie was large even for his race, and he was armed in the bargain.

But Fleming was not an uncourageous lad— there was, in truth, a streak of romanticism in him that yearned for glory and danger, battle and sudden death. He silently eased himself the rest of the way through the hatch and began shadowing the Greenie.

From behind, a Greenie resembled nothing as much as the fabled, perhaps mythical Incredible Hulk, said to have walked the face of Old Terra centuries ago in the Age of Marvels—that is, roughly human, if one uses Hercules as a comparison. From the front, Fleming knew, its humanoid look would be somewhat modified by the long, gleaming fangs and trifurcate nose, but it was otherwise remarkably similar to a human. One of the problems that Greenies had faced in fighting for equality was that they turned out to be cross-fertile with human beings—and the males had enormous genitals.

This one wore native Syrian garb, shorts and a fringed doublet, with a curious armband around its right bicep. As he padded silently behind the alien, Fleming noted uneasily that the armband would have been too big around to serve him as a belt. He hoped this Greenie was not one of those thionite addicts. They were said to be violent and unpredictable.

The giant creature stopped before a stateroom door, and Fleming hastily ducked into an alcove. It placed an ear against the door and listened. Then it stepped back, brought up its blaster and burned the lock off the door, leaping quickly through the smoldering doorway as it burst open. Fleming scurried down the corridor to the doorway, but stopped outside.

"Did you think you'd be allowed to keep all

this money to yourself, Carmody?" he heard the Greenie boom within. "That's pretty selfish of you."

"You'll never get away with this," a human voice responded.

"You think not? You think perhaps you have friends on board? If so, they will be taken care of, Carmody. This is the end of the road for you." The human voice rose to a shriek, there was a harsh, metallic ZZZZZAP!, and then silence.

Fleming waited, paralyzed, in the corridor. From within the stateroom came the sounds of drawers being torn open, closets being ransacked. At last there was a triumphant exclamation, followed by a rattling noise.

Fleming remained hidden behind the open door, frozen with fear. It was too late now to think of flight—the Greenie had found whatever it was looking for and would exit at any moment. He cursed his curiosity.

The alien stepped out into the hallway and stopped, separated from Fleming only by three inches of bulkhead door. It paused there a moment, and Fleming's heart yammered mindlessly in his chest. Then it strode off down the corridor in the other direction without closing the door behind it.

Fleming realized all of a sudden that he had not breathed for some time, and debated soberly whether he ought to resume. He tried to move, discovered that he could, shrugged his broad shoulders and inhaled deeply.

It cleared his head somewhat; he stepped

round the bulky pressure door and entered the room that the fearsome Greenie had left.

A stocky, balding man lay on his back on the floor of the room, an expression of agonized despair frozen across his features. His tunic was of extremely expensive cut and fabric, and his outflung hands were uncalloused and well-manicured. He did not appear to be breathing.

Fleming slowly crossed the room, bent down and reached for the man's wrist, intending to take his pulse. He recoiled at the touch and stood up. Carmody's wrist was quite cold. *Omigod*, Fleming thought, *omigod what do I do now?* He was suddenly overcome with terror at the realization that the Greenie might return to the scene of the crime at any moment, and scrambled back to the doorway. Hearing nothing, he risked a look—no one there.

He fled.

Without taking time to reason it out, Fleming found himself making for Colonel Enderby-Thwaite's stateroom. He felt a desperateness to share his secret with someone, and the old gentleman had reminisced convincingly and at great length during the poker lesson about dangers and intrigues that he had known in his day. He modestly admitted a public career spanning three interplanetary wars and two revolutions, and hinted delicately of a familiarity with interstellar espionage, although of course he was "retired from all that now." Fleming had found him rather glamorous. Surely the Colonel would know what to do.

But as he reached the old man's stateroom,

Fleming paused, struck by a thought. Sooner or later, the Greenie was going to get around to realizing that its crime was not especially well-concealed. Perhaps it was skulking around right now, trying to see if anyone was behaving unusually. If he contacted the Colonel overtly, he might be inadvertently placing the old soldier in jeopardy. What would such a seasoned campaigner think of him if he did that?

No, he had to think like a pro, like the steely-eyed spies in the romantic fiction to which he was addicted. *Subtlety*, he told himself. Without so much as pausing at the Colonel's door, he strode on past to his own stateroom and went in.

Once inside he carefully locked the door, sighed with relief, and lit a filter-tip Grassmaster, inhaling deeply. *How can I do this cleverly*, he thought, *like the legendary Bond?* Inspiration came; he took out pencil and paper and wrote, "HAVE OBSERVED CRIME. THIS IS SERIOUS. MESSAGE TO CAPT. AT ONCE." He folded the note endwise, stood and looked round the room. Books lay scattered everywhere. He picked one up at random: *Captain Galaxy Meets His Match*. Inserting the note at page 134, he closed the book, walked to the door and opened it gingerly. Looking carefully up and down the corridor, he stepped out and strolled to the Colonel's door with maximum nonchalance, whistling a popular air just a bit too loudly. He knocked purposefully and waited.

Colonel Enderby-Thwaite *harrumph*ed into view, his jowls flapping like twin saddlebags from his lower lip. "What? What? Fleming, my boy, how are you? What do you want? Nothing gone wrong with the young lady I trust?"

"No, Colonel, nothing like that," Fleming said heartily. "Just thought you might enjoy a bit of light reading. I just finished this one, and it was awfully good. I'm sure you'll enjoy it." He thrust the volume at the Colonel with an elaborate wink.

The Colonel blinked back at him in astonishment and glanced at the book. "Captain Galaxy? My dear boy, this isn't exactly my cup of *chai*, you know. Grateful for the thought of course, but . . ."

"I'm certain you'll like this one, Colonel," Fleming broke in, winking furiously. "Very interesting battle scenes, *especially on page 134.* Be sure and check that one out, if nothing else."

"I say, Fleming, what the devil is the matter with your eye?"

"Eyestrain. I couldn't put that book down. Especially the part on page 134, be sure and read that chapter. In fact, start there. Look, I have to run back to my room, now, I just remembered I left a joint burning, I'll see you in 4-C at 2300, don't forget to read page 134." He turned and fled back to his own room, slamming the door behind him.

"Most extraordinary," breathed the Colonel, and looked down again at the gaudily-jacketed book. "*Captain Galaxy Meets His Match?*"

He shrugged, and closed his door.

Fleming passed the rest of the afternoon in an almost ecstatic state of anticipation. Glory was

certain to come from this! Perhaps the Captain
would decide to place the Greenie under arrest,
have the Galactic Patrol send a ship to rendezvous with *This Train* instead of waiting until
planetfall was reached. That would be lovely, as
then the girl in blue, not to mention whatever
passengers were on board, would know that he
was a hero, a witness to a serious crime and an
accomplished conspirator. The Captain might
even require his help in subduing the Greenie;
you could never tell. Fleming waited feverishly
to be recontacted by the Colonel.

But by suppertime he had heard nothing at
all—no cryptic messages under his door, no hue
and cry from without, nothing. Puzzled, but
determined to be patient, Fleming made his way
belowdecks to the lounge for the evening meal.
By the time he was halfway there, he had convinced himself that the Colonel was merely
waiting for a plausibly coincidental opportunity
to run into him, to avoid the appearance of
anything out of the ordinary. He decided that
the Colonel was a genius.

But although Fleming dawdled over his dinner for well over an hour, the old warhorse never
appeared. To his great consternation, the Greenie
did. It shouldered brazenly through the door
about halfway through Fleming's dessert, and
took a seat in a far corner, facing the room.

Fleming tried to become absorbed by his chair
and, failing, looked about wildly. At that moment
the girl in blue also entered the lounge, still in
blue and as desirable as ever. Fleming learned
the ancient truth that there is nothing like being

in immediate personal danger for hiking up that old biological urge.

Seeing him, she smiled, and made her way to his table, by the same preternatural means she had used once before, seating herself in a manner remarkably similar to a hummingbird coming to rest. With a major effort of will, he tore his gaze from her momentarily and looked over at the Greenie.

It was staring intently at the two of them, and it was frowning.

"Hello," she crooned, recapturing Fleming's eyes. "Where is your friend, the old gentleman? You're both coming tonight, aren't you?"

His mind raced. Fleming was not really an idiot, but the books he had read had instilled in him the notion that it was somehow *de rigeur* to spill deadly dangerous secrets to unarmed, helpless girls—besides, this conspiracy was getting intolerably lonely. "Look," he blurted, "something's come up."

"Well, you'll just have to save it until 2300," she said. "Right now I'm hungry." She slid the table's console open and dialed steak, extra rare, with everything.

"No, no," said Fleming, "You don't understand. Colonel Enderby-Thwaite has disappeared."

She made a face. "Your companion? Such a shame. He seemed like such a courageous old gentleman," she said wistfully. The table finished synthesizing steak and plate; she picked up the former and began tearing at it with even, white teeth. *Different Customs*, Fleming reminded himself wildly, and tried again.

"No, listen, uh . . . gosh, I don't know your name."

"Nandi."

"Listen, Nandi. There's been a serious crime committed on this ship. Migod, you've dropped your steak. Oh the hell with it, listen Nandi, will you please? Colonel Enderby-Thwaite may even now be in terrible danger. We've got to get word to the Captain at once." He described the day's events, blurring the outlines of the actual murder scene—and his personal reactions at the time—with all the skill of a darkroom wizard turning pornography into artistic statement. He allowed her to retain the impression that only concern for possible innocent bystanders had prevented him from taking on the Greenie there and then. Fleming understood Art.

For all that, Nandi appeared exceedingly skeptical throughout Fleming's tale. "What could the Captain do if we got word to him?" she asked when he was finished. "Would he start a panic, perhaps endanger his passengers by trying to arrest the demon?"

"Of course not," said Fleming, who favored this alternative himself. "He could call the Patrol and have them send a cruiser to match speed and course with *This Train*. Let them capture the Greenie; they'll have sleepy gas and hypnodrene and vibes by the case. And in the meantime, we concentrate on lulling the Greenie into a false sense of security by preserving an air of normalcy."

"Why not just wait until we ground on Forced Landing and have it picked up as it debarks?"

"No good. We don't reach Forced Landing for at least 72 hours. Somewhere in that time, it may remember that it left that damned airtight door open. Even if nobody happened to glance in, sooner or later a meteorite drill would make it pretty conspicuous indeed."

"Well, there goes your air of normalcy."

"Maybe; maybe not. That Greenie may be wasted on thionite, not thinking clearly. They often are. If we move fast . . . "

"Have you known many?" Nandi asked softly.

"Eh? Anyway, one way or another we've got to get word to the Captain before it decides to clean up after itself."

"I suppose you're right," the girl said grudgingly. She tossed cascades of lush brown hair casually back over one white shoulder and puffed a joint into life. "All right then. First, where is the Greenie now?"

Fleming had been waiting patiently for this line for fifteen minutes. Precisely as Humphrey Bogart would have done it, he deadpanned, "Ten feet behind you," and *rolled* a joint of his own.

Her eyebrows rose satisfactorily, and if the orbs below them twinkled, Fleming failed to notice.

"How then shall we communicate with the Captain without tipping it off?" she asked. "I don't even know how one gets to see the Captain. Are you certain we've got one? My travel agent was a trifle vague."

Still Humphrey Bogart, Fleming essayed a humorless grin, producing a hideous grimace. "Relax. It's a snap. I've already taken care of it."

"You have?" she asked with new respect. "How?"

"Wrote a message on one of my rolling papers just before you got here. I leave it in my plate, and the steward passes it up the chain of command to the Captain." In the ancient and bloody wars that had accompanied the birth of commercial space travel, the powerman's union had fared much better than the cooks. While cheap machinery was good enough to feed the passengers and crew, a human crewmember would feed the Converter with the leftovers, as well as the day's output of trash, performing valet duties in between to earn his keep.

Nandi's eyes widened, the increased candlepower melting the fillings in Fleming's teeth. "What a brilliant idea, Mister . . . what is your name?"

"Ayniss, Fleming Ayniss. My friends call me Flem."

"Listen, Phlegm, what do you suppose actually happened to Colonel . . . Benderby? Engleby?"

Fleming's deadpan acquired rigor mortis. "Enderby-Thwaite," he mumbled. "I don't know." He looked grimly across the room at the Greenie. "But that damned thionite-head was late for dinner."

"No no. I mean, how do you know that the Colonel simply hasn't been taken with indigestion?"

"I knocked on his door on the way here," explained Fleming, stung that she thought him jumping to conclusions like some romantic adolescent.

"Perhaps he has, diarrhea, then, and ignored you. Or . . . or suppose he's in conference with the Captain right now? Let's . . . "

"Let's go to his room and wait for him," said Fleming, fighting to retain control of the situation.

They rose and left together, brushing past the Greenie with utter aplomb. Behind them, on the table, gravy began dripping lethargically across a cigarette paper half-buried in mashed potatoes, that read, "THIEF ON BOARD. CAPTAIN MUST KNOW. WASTE NO TIME."

Although the pair waited vigilantly in a lounge across from the Colonel's stateroom, Enderby-Thwaite had not returned by the time the ship's computer darkened the corridor lights for evening. Fleming and Nandi sat silent and motionless in the reduced light for ten seconds, then spoke simultaneously.

"My place or yours?"

Both blushed, but the phenomenon looked much more natural on Fleming. To his credit, however, his gaze never trembled, and if his knees did somewhat, that seemed only natural. A man's knees were supposed to tremble around girls like Nandi, to incline one toward taking a load off one's feet.

They ended up in her stateroom by Hobson's choice—his was a mess. Hers was considerably neater; only the bedclothes were rumpled. Nandi flicked on the light and crossed the room to the bed, sliding a trunk from beneath it. "You'll find some pot on the dresser behind you," she said over her shoulder as she attacked the clasps of the trunk.

Fleming came back from a far place. "Er, no thanks."

"Oh, go ahead," she giggled. "It has to be all smoked up before we reached Forced Landing anyway. It's illegal there, remember? Go ahead and light up while I change into something more comfortable."

Eyes bulging at the sight of what and how little she considered comfortable, Fleming turned obediently and began puttering with an elaborate water pipe. When he turned back, she was just stooping out of the blue dress, humming ethereally. The narghile slipped from his nervous fingers and landed on the floor with a crash.

She looked up; dimpled. "Oh. I hope I haven't upset you. It's only that I have nowhere else to change. Do you mind?"

"Not . . . not at all," croaked Fleming. A grapefruit seemed to have become lodged in his larynx somehow, and he strove mightily to swallow it. "G-go right ahead."

"You're so understanding," she beamed, slipping gracefully into what Fleming instantly realized was the most comfortable-looking garment he had ever seen. Intangible as a promise, its surface rippled with changing colors, flesh being the predominant tone. Wax began running out of his ears. "There now, that's better." She lowered her gaze, drew in her breath suddenly. "Why Fleming. I've . . . I've aroused you, haven't I?"

"Er," he replied.

"Or is that a blaster in your pocket?"

"Well . . . yes. I mean, no, it's not. I mean, yes, you have . . . uh, yes," he stammered.

"Oh Fleming, how flattering," she grinned. "Do you know what I'm going to do to you?" She paused, looking thoughtful. "That reminds me, Fleming, I have a small favor to ask of you."

Fleming indicated a willingness to fetch a comet barehanded.

"No, nothing like that. I want you to keep something for me. My jewels." She returned to the bed, bent over the open trunk (kicking Fleming's adrenals into overdrive), and removed a large package about the size of a shoebox. Opening it, she spilled fire onto the bedspread: several dozen gems that blazed with an unquenchable inner brilliance.

"Why, those are Carezza Fire-Diamonds," gasped Fleming, who had thought himself already as awestruck as possible. That many Fire-Diamonds would suffice to buy a fair-sized planet; one of them would have purchased *This Train* with enough change to pay for the balance of Fleming's education.

"Yes, my brave one. The hope of my planet. I have been sent to convert them into credits for the planetary coffers of Do It, so that we can begin a massive galaxy-wide advertising campaign to encourage immigration. The gene pool, you know. Will you take care of them for me, until this inhuman thief has been disposed of?"

Fleming stood on one leg, opened his mouth, and made a gargling sound.

"I knew I could count on you," Nandi

bubbled. "Lock them away somewhere, as tight as the Fist of Venus.

"You don't know the Fist of Venus? A standard accomplishment among my people. Among the women, that is. Here, let me show you."

She swept the bedful of diamonds to the floor, let her negligee join them. The floor became a riot of pulsing color. Smiling, she beckoned.

Fleming actually paused for a second. "If we were going to do this all along, why did you go through that business of changing into something more comfortable?"

"I thought you might enjoy the show," Nandi giggled. "Was I wrong?"

Fleming demonstrated that she had not been wrong.

Morning brought no word from the Captain, no sign of Colonel Enderby-Thwaite, and no steward at breakfast. To Fleming, who had begun the day with no sleep, it seemed that a definite negative trend had been established. In less than twenty-four hours he had become involved in at least one and possibly three murders, had taken on the responsibility of guarding more wealth than he could comprehend, and had learned the most astonishing and disappointing of truths, that there is such a thing as an overdose of pleasure.

The sandy-haired youth had annihilated six eggs, half a pound of home fries and two quarts of coffee before he felt reasonably safe in attempting rational thought. Now he rather regretted the undertaking.

It seemed obvious that the Greenie knew Fleming had witnessed its crime—the disappearance of the only two men to whom he had imparted his secret had to be more than coincidence. But how had it found out, in spite of all his circumspection? Fleming buried his head in his hands, and the answer smacked him in the face. For his iridescent yellow boots, reportedly all the rage among the collegiate set on Secundus, gleamed up at him with a brilliance that was matched by no other footwear on the ship. At once Fleming remembered that stateroom doors stop four inches short of the deck, for a tighter airseal. The Greenie could scarcely have overlooked Fleming's toes—the mystery was that it hadn't murdered him there and then.

Well, that was that. Time to break cover and get to the Captain *fast*. Fleming had no idea where the Captain was to be found at this hour—his travel agent had been as vague about *This Train* as Nandi's—but he seemed to recall that anything above C-Deck was "officer's country." *This Train* had been a luxury liner before she was a freighter, before all but one of her passenger decks were ripped out for maximum cargo space, and she bore quarters for a far larger crew than any tramp needed or could support. Considerations of mass distribution made converting that cubic into cargo room impractical. Consequently, finding the Captain could take on some of the salient aspects of finding the proverbial football in the asteroid belt.

"Unless he's actually in the Control Room,"

Fleming mused aloud, putting down his eighteenth cup of coffee.

"Beg pardon?" said Nandi, who had been absorbing considerable fuel herself. "Who's in the Control Room?"

"The Captain, I hope," Fleming replied, then looked frantically round for the Greenie. It was not in sight. "Or one of the other officers," he finished in a whisper.

"Well, as I understand it, there's only one other *up* there," Nandi whispered back, "the Executive Officer."

"My God," gasped Fleming. "You mean they're the whole crew?"

"Well, there's the Chief Engineer, but I think he stays below with his converters and things. And the steward, of course, but we don't know where he is. The rest of the crew goes *clank* when you kick it."

"Well, how many passengers are there?"

"Aside from us, the Colonel and the Greenie are the only ones I've seen. The murdered man makes five."

Fleming had been counting on considerably more allies. He briefly considered stealing the Greenie's gun and blowing his own brains out with it. Being a hero was incredibly hard work.

But there was no help for it—no turning back. Resolutely he stood up, drawing Nandi to her feet. "Let's go," he said tersely, "before the Greenie shows up for breakfast."

They left and began climbing for officer country. Fleming paused when they reached C-Deck, frowning. "Look," he said, "the Captain or the

Exec could be in any one of a couple dozen staterooms—but either of them *might* be up in the Control Room. Why don't you pop up and check while I start searching here? That way we may save some time."

Nandi nodded. "All right, but be careful, my hero."

"My sentiments exactly."

He had tried about nine rooms unsuccessfully before it occurred to him that Nandi was a long time returning. Either she had found one of the officers, or . . . he sped back to the stairshaft, swarmed up three levels to the Control Room, and burst through the hatchway in classic unarmed-combat stance, ready to deal sudden death in any direction.

A mustached, competent-looking man in ship's uniform blinked amiably at him from one of the pilot's couches. "Sorry," he apologized, "I don't dance." He produced a green, odd-shaped bottle: three chambers hooked in parallel to a common spout. "Prepared to offer you a shot of Triple Ripple, though."

Fleming shook his head.

"Sure? Great stuff. Can't let the ingredients mix until you're ready to swallow, but when they do . . . oh boy! I'm the Executive Officer, by the way. Name's Exton." He put out his hand.

"Where's Nandi?"

"Never heard of it; must be Capella way. Check the navigational computer."

"No, dammit. Nandi, your female passenger. Hasn't she been here?"

"Nobody been here, no women for *damn* sure. Nandi? . . . don't believe I recall the lady."

"Then you've never met her," Fleming said positively. "Never mind, the important thing is that she's in deadly danger. Where's the Captain?"

"Aw now, the Captain wouldn't hurt no *passenger*. He's a gentleman."

Fleming gritted his teeth, then counted to ten and told Exton the whole story. The Exec listened attentively, tugging alternatively at the Triple Ripple and his mustache. When the youth had finished, he leaned back on the acceleration couch and slapped his thigh. "Old son, that's the craziest story I ever heard. No wonder you don't want any Triple Ripple—it'd just bring you down. Let me tell you one about my Uncle Jed—true story too."

"Dammit, Exton, I'm telling you the truth. We've got to find Nandi before it's too late— and we've got to have the Captain flash the Patrol, so they can send a cruiser to rendezvous with us." He broke off, distracted by a sudden indescribable sensation in his loins.

"Well now," drawled the Exec, "Captain Cavendish is something of an independent gent. Take a lot to make him call in the Patrol."

"You've lost sixty-nine percent of your passengers and twenty-five percent of your crew," Fleming barked, tugging unconsciously at his crotch. "What do you think the Captain would consider serious?"

The Exec blinked, looked thoughtful. "Well, your story certainly deserves checking, young fellow. Let's go below."

"Now you're talking."

"Reckon we'd best go to passenger country first and start checking staterooms."

"No," Fleming said decisively. "This Greenie is smart. We should go all the way down to the Converter Room and work up through the holds to the passenger deck."

"Sounds like a whole lot of work," Exton demurred.

"Listen, dammit, this Greenie snatched Nandi somewhere between B-Deck and here. It's obviously mobile and clever. The only way to nail it is to start at the bottom and work upwards until we flush him out. If we let him get behind us we're finished." There was a peculiar look on Exton's face, but Fleming was too bemused by the drawing feeling in his groin to notice.

"All right," the Exec said reluctantly, "we search below." He rose, loosing his blaster in its holster. The sight of it reassured Fleming considerably.

"Whatever you do," he said as they left the Control Room, "look natural. We mustn't make the Greenie suspicious if we can help it."

"K," said the Exec agreeably, and began to sing a duet with himself.

Seeing Fleming's astonishment, he broke off. "Forgot; you don't know. I was born on Harmony, a pleasant little place where we feel that music is the bedrock of true culture. Most of us had biomod work done on our larynxes, sort of improved on nature. I've got a five-octave range myself, and I can handle up to three voices at once. Handy—gets the women. And I guess it's how come I'm so partial to Triple Ripple, now I think about it."

Fleming puzzled over this as they made their way below. He had heard of biomodification even on the rather provincial planet of his birth, but he had always considered it a rather blasphemous attempt to distort the Creator's intentions. Now, however, he admitted to himself that there were advantages to more versatile vocal chords. Exton was pretty good a cappella.

When they reached the Converter Room, the Chief Engineer was nowhere to be found. "Probably sound asleep somewhere, if I know Reilly," chuckled the Exec, but Fleming was filled with dark suspicion. They searched the power room thoroughly and found nothing.

"Well," said Fleming at last, "I guess that makes it fifty percent of the crew gone."

"Oh, listen here young fellow, Reilly's around somewhere. He's got a lonely job, probably off brewing himself some rocket juice someplace or other." They started up the ladder.

"Listen Exton," Fleming insisted as they reached the cargo level, "I don't think you're taking this whole thing seriously enough. There's a *killer* on board."

"That remains to be proved, son."

"But by the nature of the problem it may be almost impossible to prove before we're dead. *Won't* you call the Patrol?"

"With no evidence to show the Captain? Hah! I'll take my chances with this killer of yours."

"Well, keep your gun handy," grumbled Fleming, disgusted with the Exec's refusal to behave by adventure-story standards. Exton snorted, but drew his blaster. Together they began to search the cargo hold, a huge steel cavern piled high with stacked crates and tarpaulin-covered machinery of all sizes and shapes. The lighting was dim, and Fleming had imagined crazed Greenies in every pool of shadow, but none materialized. Neither did Reilly. Finally every cranny had been poked into unsuccessfully, and Exton started to return to the stairshaft.

"Wait," said Fleming suddenly. "I've got an idea. It seems to me that if I wanted to hide on a ship like this, I'd stay right here in the hold."

"But we've looked . . . " Exton said wearily.

"Not in the cargo itself," Fleming broke in. "I can see five crates from here that are large enough to fit the two of us in."

"Well, I'm sure," snapped Fleming. Turning to the nearest crate of sufficient size, he slapped its pressure seals. Exton yelped in protest, but it was too late—the top of the crate slid open.

Fleming levered himself up on his elbows, peered down into the crate. "No luck with this one. Full of some kind of white powder.

"No, wait!" gasped Fleming, excitement in his voice. "This is not sugar, Exton—it's thionite! Kilos of it!"

"No shit!" the Exec said weakly.

"Sure. That lemony odor is unmistakable. Well I'll be damned. There's more here than meets the eye. *Now* will you call the Patrol?"

"I reckon I'll have to do *something*," said Exton, looking grim.

Very suddenly a dark form detached itself from the shadows, landed on Exton's shoulders and knocked him sprawling to the deck. A gun butt rose and fell, and Exton gave three cries simultaneously and lay still.

As Fleming dropped to his feet, numb with terror, the attacker rose and covered him with a vicious-looking little handgun. It tempered the relief with which Fleming noted that his assailant was human. "Who . . . who're you?" he stammered.

"Chief Engineer," snarled the other, "as if you didn't know."

"Listen, Reilly, give it up. You'll never get away with this."

"Shaddap and come here. You're going to carry this sleeping beauty right up topside to Lifeboat Number One, and then the two of you are going for a nice little ride. Without an astrogational computer."

Fleming went cold. This sort of thing happened all the time in the adventure stories, but the hero was always prepared for something: a special plan, an unsuspected ally, a concealed weapon. Fleming had none of these; it had never occurred to him that the Greenie might have human confederates. The fact disgusted him.

Under the unarguable direction of Reilly's gun barrel, Fleming heaved Exton awkwardly over one shoulder and began climbing. When they reached C-Deck he set the Exec down as gently as he could and began dragging him past the passengers' cabins to the lifeboat locks. "Out of shape," he gasped, and Reilly sneered.

When he had dumped Exton's limp, and now dusty, form inside the first lifeboat in line, he turned to face Reilly, who stood just outside the airlock with his gun leveled at Fleming's mid-section.

"Can't we talk this over?" he asked. Reilly smiled, tightened his finger on the firing stud.

Suddenly voices came from behind him, and the Chief Engineer froze. "Hold it right there." "Patrol, put 'em up." "Drop it, Reilly."

At the last voice, Reilly suddenly unfroze again, and his grin returned. "Nice try, Exton, but it won't work. That fancy throat of yours makes you a better ventriloquist than a Denebian Where-Is-It, but you can't fool me. If the Patrol really was behind me, they'd be calling me by my real name—which is *not* Reilly."

Exton sat up, shrugged. "Can't blame a fellow for trying."

"Maybe not," said Reilly, "but I can kill you for it." He broke off as the sound of shod feet on deckplates came from behind him. "Say, that's pretty good. I didn't know you could imitate sounds too."

"He can't," said Nandi as she brought an oxy-bottle down hard across Reilly's skull.

The Greenie, Nandi explained, had spotted her on her way up to the Control Room and taken a shot at her that barely missed. Fortunately, she was able to elude the monster and hide in Number Two Lifeboat, where she had remained in terror until the noise of Fleming dragging Exton into the neighboring boat had drawn her out.

"You've been very brave, Nandi," Fleming said approvingly as he checked the clip on Reilly's gun. "Well, Exton, now do you believe me?"

"Guess I sort of have to," the Exec drawled. "Wasn't for the young lady here, we'd be trying to astrogate through deep space by eye about now."

"What I don't understand," Fleming mused, "is why the Greenie took Reilly into cahoots with it. There's something going on here I don't understand. Well, anyway, it's past time we notified the Patrol."

"Suppose you're right," Exton agreed.

"Where do we find the Captain?" Nandi asked. "He should send the message."

"He usually hangs out on A-Deck," Exton decided. "We'll probably find him in the crew's lounge there, playing whist with the computer."

"Okay," said Fleming decisively, tightening his grip on the gun. "Let's go."

The three ascended together cautiously, Fleming in the lead, Exton covering their rear. As they climbed, they conversed in whispers.

"How do you suppose all that thionite you boys found ties in with Carmody's murder?"

"I don't know, Nandi. There are more questions than answers in this case." Fleming was a little short-tempered; the peculiar not-quite-pain in his groin was still troubling him.

"Maybe Reilly, Carmody and the Greenie were in partnership on the thionite," suggested Exton from beneath them.

"Could be," Fleming agreed, pausing to peer cautiously over the hatch coaming before exposing himself. "Then Carmody tried to double-cross them somehow—the Greenie said something about him trying to keep all that money to himself." He climbed through the hatch and reached down to help Nandi up, looking around for the Greenie.

"But where're all the bodies?" Nandi asked. "You found nothing in the Converter Room or the hold, and it would make no sense to hide them where there are more people around."

"I dunno, maybe the Greenie spaced them all. What do you think, Exton?"

No answer.

"Exton!" Fleming stuck his head down through the hatch and looked around. The Exec was nowhere in sight.

Nandi gasped, began to tremble. Fleming set his jaw grimly and closed the hatch, dogging it as tightly as he could. "Let's go," he rapped, and began climbing again, pulling Nandi after him.

They found the Captain just where Exton had guessed they might, in a lounge on the uppermost of the two crew's levels, engrossed in a card game with a relatively simple-minded recreational computer. He was a patriarchal figure, massive and heavily-bearded, authority obvious in both the set of his broad shoulders and the disrupter that hung at his hip. He rose as the two entered, bowed to Nandi, and raised a shaggy eyebrow at Fleming. "Yes? What can I do for you?"

"You can call the Galactic Patrol," said Fleming, and without preamble launched into his third retelling of the past day's events. The sincerity in his voice was unmistakable, and when he finished the Captain had a dark look on his craggy face.

"Your story is easily checked, young man," he rumbled. He closed a switch on the wall beside him and said, "Exton. Reilly. Report on the double to A-Deck rec lounge. Hop." His voice seemed to echo in the distance, and Fleming realized he had cut in the command intercom.

They waited for a minute or two with no result. Then the Captain rose to his feet and put his right hand on the butt of his blaster. His mouth was a tight line and there was thunder in his eye. With his other hand he removed a remote control unit from his tunic, dialed a frequency and said clearly, "Computer: broadcast, this frequency. 'Emergency. Emergency. Interstellar Vessel *This Train*, Captain Cavendish speaking. Request Patrol lock onto this carrier and rendezvous at once, report at once, prepared for armed resistance. Cavendish out.' Repeat and maintain carrier."

Fleming breathed a sigh of relief. Whatever happened now, the Patrol would be here soon. He began to relax—then stiffened as he realized that the intercom was still live. The Greenie must have heard every word! He waved frantically to get Captain Cavendish's attention and pointed to the wall switch. Cavendish paled, put down the computer-relay link and slapped the switch open, but the damage was done.

"Look," rapped the Captain, "I've got to get down to the lifeboats and make sure that damned creature doesn't escape before the Patrol arrives. You stay here, barricade the door and don't stick your head out until I knock shave-and-a-haircut. You've got to keep this young lady safe," he put in as Fleming began to object. "I'll be all right— I've had some experience with hijackers before."

Fleming reluctantly agreed. He hated to lose out on potential heroics, but protecting the fair maiden was definitely a duty no hero could dodge. Besides, it was safer.

As soon as the Captain had left, Nandi came into his arms and captured his lips in an urgent, demanding kiss. "Hold me, Fleming," she breathed, "I'm so afraid."

"Don't worry, Nandi," Fleming reassured her with all the bravado he had left. "I'll keep you safe." His arms tightened protectively around her.

"Of course you will, my hero," Nandi said, "Just as you are keeping my jewels safe. Where did you put them, by the way? I've been meaning to ask you since that Reilly almost . . . I mean . . . "

"I understand," he said quickly. "I should have thought of that. They're in my stateroom, under my pillow. Who'd ever." He trailed off. Nandi's hands had begun to wander, and while that confoundingly indefinable sensation had not left his groin, Fleming discovered that whatever it was did not interfere with performance. *What the hell*, he was telling himself, when suddenly something caught his eye and made him go rigid from the waist up as well. "My God," he breathed.

"What is it?" asked Nandi, sensing that he was no longer responding.

"That communications relay the Captain used. It's not set for emergency band at all—way off, as far as I can tell. Cavendish must have accidentally dialed the wrong frequency. Good lord, if I hadn't noticed . . . " He let go of Nandi, picked up the device and reset it, then repeated the Captain's message as best he could remember. "That was too damned close. We would have waited for the Patrol till we were old and gray." He frowned. "I'd better let the Captain know what happened, so he doesn't do something foolish if the Patrol is late in showing up."

He activated the intercom. "Captain Cavendish?" No reply. "Captain, this is Fleming. Come in, please, it's urgent." There was no response at all for a long minute, and then the speaker came alive.

"Mr. Ayniss," came the unmistakable booming voice of the Greenie, "I would advise you not to meddle in criminal matters. They do not concern you."

Fleming jumped a foot in the air, his pulse rate tripling instantly. Somehow the giant killer had gotten the drop on Cavendish, turned the tables again. The youth made a quick decision, a decision based on pure heroism.

"Wait here," he barked, killing the intercom again, "and don't let *anyone* in. I'm going to do what the Captain failed to do—keep that damned creature here until the authorities arrive. We can't let it get away."

Nandi began to protest, but Fleming ignored her and stepped out into the corridor, gun in hand. He was genuinely terrified, but a cold anger sustained him and steadied his weapon in his inexperienced grasp. He felt partially responsible for the carnage that had resulted from his discovery of the original murder, and he meant to avenge the crew and passengers of *This Train*. The Colonel, the steward, the Exec, the Captain, Nandi, all had been innocent victims, ordinary decent folks attacked without knowing why, given no chance to defend themselves. The murdering alien would pay for its crimes—Fleming intended to see to it. He made his way to the lifeboat locks, his peripheral vision straining to meet itself behind his head.

Unfortunately, it failed in this endeavor. As he approached the lifeboat locks, agony exploded in the back of his skull and extinguished the lights one by one. He never felt the deck smack him in the face.

The blow had been startling, but he was considerably more surprised to regain consciousness, alive and unharmed, his gun still nearby where he had dropped it. He reclaimed it, rose shakily to his feet and staggered to the locks.

All six lifeboats were gone.

Got away, dammit, thought Fleming. *Probably fired off all the other boats to make itself harder to track*. He was furious, with himself as much as with the Greenie. His only consolation was that the murderer had been careless enough to fail to finish him off. He decided to make sure Nandi was all right, and headed back up to the lounge.

Nandi was not all right. At least, she was

missing from the lounge. Fleming knew one timeless moment of pure fury, the frustrated rage of undeniable failure. The Greenie had obviously taken her along as a hostage in case the Patrol caught up with it.

The youth sank down into a chair and buried his head in his hands. He was bitterly sorry that he had ever heard the word "adventure," and he cursed the nosy curiosity that had precipitated this slaughter.

After a long, black time he began to think again. Humbly, he decided to go below and check whether the Greenie had removed the thionite from the hold. Perhaps it had been in too much of a hurry.

But when he reached the hold, he heard noises from close at hand and melted quietly into the shadows, his gun growing out of his fist.

It was the Greenie, it had to be! How, Fleming couldn't imagine and didn't care; the song of blood rushing in his temple had a one-word libretto: vengeance. He smiled grimly to himself and clenched his gun tightly, peering with infinite caution around the fender of a half-track farming vehicle.

The Greenie was just resetting the seals on the opened crate of thionite, an ominous expression on its face. Fleming took careful aim at the massive head, but before he could fire, the alien strode rapidly to the stairshaft and climbed above. Fleming slipped from concealment and followed it, reaching the shaft in time to see the Greenie step off two levels above, on C-Deck.

Narrowing his eyes, Fleming ascended noiselessly to C-Deck, just quickly enough to spot the Greenie entering Carmody's stateroom, the scene of the original murder. He waited, hidden by the hatch cover, until the creature had exited and turned a corner. Fleming padded silently after it. As he passed Carmody's room, he glanced in, and was not even mildly surprised to discover that the corpse was missing. It figured. The Greenie was housecleaning.

Fleming intended to do a little housecleaning of his own.

He eased around the corner with care, but the corridor was deserted. The nameplate on the third door he came to read, RAX CH'LOOM, SIRIUS II. Jackpot!

Fleming took hold of the door-latch, paused for a long moment to bid goodbye to his adolescence, then yanked open the door. The first thing he saw was the Greenie, surprised in the act of changing clothes, literally caught with its pants down. The second thing he saw was Carmody's body on the bed, neatly trussed up with nylon cord. A part of him wondered why the Greenie would tie up a corpse, but the majority of him simply didn't give a damn.

"This is for Nandi, you bastard," he said clearly, and aimed for the trifurcate nose.

And then something struck him between the shoulder blades, smashing him to the deck. His chin hit hard enough to drive a wedge of black ice up into his brain, where it melted, turning everything to inky dark.

❊❊ ❊❊ ❊❊

"Shit," Fleming said as consciousness returned.

"You bet, old son," said a pleasant baritone. "Several fans-full of the stuff, in fact."

Fleming looked up, startled. A smiling lieutenant of the Galactic Patrol knelt over him, smelling salts in one hand and a vortex disrupter in the other.

"Did you get him?" Fleming cried. "Did you get the Greenie?"

"Ch'loom? Hell no, Mr. Ayniss, but we got damned near everybody else. God-damnedest thing I ever saw—a freighter along practically empty, and six lifeboats full of crooks heading away from it in different directions like the Big Bang all over again. We picked 'em all up okay, but what I'd like to know is what put the wind up all of them? Their stories didn't make much sense when you put them all together."

Fleming shook his head confusedly, allowed the patrolman to help him to his feet. "I don't understand," he said weakly. "Lifeboats full of crooks?"

"Sure," said the patrolman, holstering his sidearm. "First one in line was a Colonel Underwear-Waist or some such, claimed you were the first sucker in ten Standard years to catch him stacking the cards."

"Huh?" gasped Fleming, thunderstruck.

"Yep. Old time cardsharp, according to our computer records. Been working the tramps for years, ever since the regular lines got on to him. How'd you tumble to him, Ayniss?"

"Uh," Fleming explained. He tried to recall

the exact wording of the message he had slipped into *Captain Galaxy Meets His Match* a hundred years ago. "Who was next?"

"Next was the ship's steward, chap named Blog. Says you found out he was rifling staterooms and threatened to tip off the Captain, so he lit out as soon as he could. We found a lot of bootle with him—guess you've got a reward or two coming. Then there was an engineer who claimed his name was Reilly, but he turned out to be a guy named Foster, wanted for murder over on Armageddon. Had his fingerprints changed, of course, but he couldn't afford biomod work on his retinas. According to him, he heard you and the Executive Officer talking, realized you were on to him and stuck the two of you up. Then, he claims, somebody else sapped him, and he woke up alone in Number One Lifeboat, which he did not hesitate to use.

"But the next customer was the Exec himself, Exxon is it? And under questioning he broke down and admitted smuggling thionite on board to sell at Forced Landing. We found the thionite just where he said it would be. Say, did you know he's got a modified voicebox? Cursed you out in three-part harmony.

"But the strangest of the bunch was Captain Cavendish himself. He was really surprised to see us—kept insisting that he'd called us himself and he was *sure* he'd used the wrong frequency, which doesn't seem to make much sense. But he was so flabbergasted he slipped up and mentioned what frequency he *had* used. Just for fun we broadcast, 'All clear, come ahead,' on that frequency, and a whole gang of pirates walks into the surprise of their life. Apparently Cavendish was in cahoots with them on some kind of insurance fraud scheme, figured to let them rob the ship without a fight. We've got 'em all, and we didn't lose a man."

"What about Nandi?" Fleming asked groggily. "She has to be honest—she gave me a fortune in jewels for safekeeping."

"Nandi *Tyson*—honest? Say, we've been looking for her for years, ever since she started passing out counterfeit Carezza Fire-Diamonds in the outworlds. She was the last one we picked up—she had those diamonds with her, by the way—and boy was she ever mad at you."

Fleming's head spun. "Does this mean that the diamonds are worthless?" he asked.

The Patrol lieutenant had studied classical humor in college, but even as the phrase "Ayniss and Nandi" exploded hilariously into his brain, he felt a flash of compassion for the crestfallen youth and kept a straight face.

"Put it this way, Ayniss," he said gravely. "Yes."

"But—but what about the Greenie? Didn't you get him too? He's the one that started all this madness."

"No, my friend," came a booming voice from the doorway, "I am afraid you did that all by yourself."

Fleming whirled. The Greenie stood there smiling, a gun at its hip, a Patrol officer at its side. "Get it," Fleming screamed at the lieutenant, "It's a murderer."

"Ch'loom a murderer?" the officer said dubiously. "That's a little hard to believe."

"I tell you I saw it," gibbered Fleming. "That damned thing killed a man named Carmody."

The Greenie's smile deepened, exposing more fang. It stepped aside, to reveal Carmody standing behind it, demonstrably alive. Their wrists were handcuffed together. Fleming's mouth opened, and stayed that way.

"Allow me to introduce Rax Ch'loom, Official Equalizer of Carson's World," said the lieutenant. "My name's Hornsby, by the way, pleased to meet you."

"Equalizer?" mumbled Fleming dazedly.

"Sure," Hornsby replied cheerfully. "Rax showed up on Carson's World about thirty years back and commenced stealing from the rich and giving to the poor. The idea caught on so well that they institutionalized him—gave him legal immunity from prosecution, quasigovernmental status, subsidies, the works."

"What did the rich do?" exploded Fleming.

"Squawked like hell," Rax grinned. Wasn't much else they could do."

"But don't the rich hold the political power?" asked Fleming, stunned.

"Hey," Rax replied, "we got democracy. *Lots* more poor people than rich people on Carson's World."

"Sounds like a crazy place to me," Fleming snapped, his confusion turning to unreasonable irritation.

"Oh, I dunno," Hornsby intervened. "You get hungry, you go see Rax. You start hogging,

Rax rips you off. Sounds pretty comfortable to me."

"Suppose you rob a rich man, and for want of capital he's utterly ruined the next day?"

"You get hungry, you go see Rax."

"But there's more to life than food."

"Hey listen, Rax don't steal no women . . . "

"Other things."

"Like what?"

"Er . . . "

"Carmody here thought he could take thirty thousand credits out of circulation," Rax boomed contentedly. "Not a chance." Carmody snarled impotently.

"But I felt his wrist," Fleming objected feebly. "It was cold."

" . . . as a corpse's wouldn't have been for at least an hour," Rax pointed out. "I put him in a cryonic stasis for my own convenience, and spent the whole rest of the voyage trying to figure out what in the name of the seven bloody devils of Old Terra you were doing."

Fleming gave up, began shaking his head. "Then it's all over?" he asked resignedly.

"Er . . . not quite, Ayniss," Hornsby said with curious reluctance. "There's one more little matter. Did you and the Tyson woman . . . ? I mean, did she . . . ? Did you . . . ?"

"Well, yes," Fleming admitted, remembering that he did have at least one thing to be proud of. "She's from Do It, you know."

"You knew that and still let her?" gasped Hornsby, his jaw dropping.

"Hell, yes. She said Do It was based on total

sexual freedom, so as to eliminate tension and frustration. It sounded like a good idea to me."

"It sounds like a good idea to me too, but that's not what Do It is like. It's a world full of fanatical feminists, not hedonists. All the women have had the same biomod work performed on them."

"What kind?" Fleming asked, feeling that strange and undesirable feeling in his crotch again.

"Uh . . . well, you may as well know. It has to do with modifying the ovum, giving it the mobility and the seeking instinct of a sperm cell. Only a psychotic female supremacist could have conceived of it." He broke off, embarrassed.

"Well?" said Fleming. "*Tell* me, dammit."

"I'm afraid, Mr. Ayniss," said the Greenie with genuine compassion, "that you are pregnant."

TOO SOON WE GROW OLD

The first awakening was awful, and she enjoyed it.

She was naked and terribly cold. She was in a plastic coffin, from whose walls grew wrinkled plastic arms, with gnarled plastic hands that did things to her. Most of the things hurt dreadfully—but they were all physical hurts. Her soul was conscious only of an almost terrifying sense of relief. Until you have had your neck and shoulders rubbed for the first time, you can have no conception of how tightly bunched they were. Tension can only be fully appreciated in its release. To her mind came a vivid association from long decades past: her first orgasm. A shudder passed over her body.

A voice spoke in a language unknown to her. Even allowing for the sound-deadening coffin walls, it sounded distant.

Eyes appeared over hers, through a transparent panel she had failed to see since it had showed only a ceiling the same color as the coffin's interior. She refocused. The face was masked and capped in white, the eyes pouched in wrinkles. He said something incomprehensible, apparently in reply to the first voice.

"Hi, Doc," she shouted, finding her voice oddly squeaky in the high-helium atmosphere of the cryogenic capsule. *"I made it!"* She found that she was grinning.

He started, and moved from view. One of the plastic hands did something to her left bicep, and she felt her hurts slipping away—but not her joy. *I knew I could beat it*, she thought just before consciousness faded, and then she dreamed of the day her victory had begun.

She was not at all sure just why she had consented to the interview. She had rejected them for over twenty years, on an impulse so consistent that it had never seemed to call for examination. To understand why she had granted this one would, it seemed to her, call for twenty years' worth of spadework—it was simpler to posit that impulse had merely changed its sign, from negative to positive.

Yet, although she relied implicitly on the automatic pilot which had made the decision for her, she found apprehension mounting within her as the appointed day led her inexorably to the appointed time. An hour before the Interviewer was due, she found herself *examining* a capsule of an obscure and quite illegal tranquilizer, one which had not even filtered down to street level yet. It was called Alpha, according to her source and he claimed it was preternaturally effective But she hesitated—he had said something about it tending to suppress *all* the censors, something about it being a kind of mild truth drug. She turned the capsule end on end in her palm, three times.

The hell with it, she decided. *This is the true measure of my wealth; I can even afford to be honest with an interviewer*. The realization elated her. *Besides*, she afterthought, *I can always buy the network if I have to*.

She washed the capsule down with twice-distilled water.

The lights were not as blinding as she had expected. In fact, none of the external irritations she had anticipated materialized—not even the obtrusive presence of a cameraman. The holocamera was *not* entirely automatic, for newstaping is an art (with a powerful union)—but its operator was nearly a hundred miles away in the network's headquarters, present only by inference. She was simply sitting in her own familiar living room, conversing with a perfect stranger whose profession it was to seem an old and understanding friend. Although she had never seen his show—she never watched 3V—she decided he was one of the best in his field. Or was that the drug? In any case, they went from Ms. Hammond and Mr. Hold to Diana and Owen in what was, for her, a remarkably short time. As she realized this, alarm made one last attempt to take over her controls, but failed miserably.

" . . . clearly done a number of remarkable things with your half-century, Diana," Hold was saying with obvious sincerity. "Today it is no longer inconceivable for a woman to become wealthy by her own efforts in the economic marketplace—but you began your fantastic career in an age when as a roe, only men had such opportunities. In fact, you've done as much as, perhaps more than, anyone else to bring our society out of that restrictive phase."

The words warmed her. "Oh," she said lightly, "it's not a difficult trick to become terribly rich. All it takes is a lifetime of devotion."

"I'm familiar with the quote," Hold agreed. "All the same, it must have been an incredibly difficult, demanding task to carve yourself a navigable path where none existed. And so perhaps the foremost question in my mind is, 'why?'"

"I beg your pardon?"

"Why did you choose the life you have led? What was your motivation for this lifetime of devotion?"

"Because," she said almost automatically, "given the nature of the world I found myself in, it seemed the most sensible . . . the most mature . . . the most *grown-up* thing to do."

"I'm not sure I understand," Hold said, and he *was* the best in his field, because he had the rare gift of listening totally, of conveying by his utter attention to her every gesture and nuance his eagerness to *understand*. Since everyone knows that to understand is to forgive all, no one who genuinely wishes to understand can be an enemy—can they?—and so she found herself explaining to another the agony that had been her childhood.

" . . . and so with Father dead and five girls to raise, Mother entered the business world. She had to—Father's insurance company flatly refused to pay. They claimed it was clearly a suicide, and three judges agreed. There was still a sizable estate, of course, but after the deduction of lawyers' fees and nonrefundable losing bids on three judges, it wasn't enough to provide for all six of us for very long. So Mother converted it all to capital and tried to become a businesswoman, about the time I was twelve. In today's world she might have succeeded—but she was terribly ignorant and naive. Father's inherited wealth had sheltered her as effectively as it had him. The only people who paid her any attention, let alone respect, were the sharks, and they had picked her clean by the time I was twenty. That was . . . let me see . . . 1965 or 66.

"And so it was up to me, the oldest. Mama had gotten clever in the final extremity: no one ever called her death anything but accidental. But even so, the inheritance I received was almost nominal.

"But it was enough, for me and for my sisters."

"Clearly," Hold agreed. "Then you would say your initial motivation was to provide for yourself and your sisters."

"More for them than for myself," she said, and was gratified to hear herself say so. "Mother had passed on to me her own overwhelming sense of responsibility. As a matter of fact, my own strongest interest was in music. But I knew I could never provide for five siblings on a musician's wage, and so I put all that away and buckled down."

"You must be deeply happy, then," he said, "to have so thoroughly realized your life's ambition."

And she surprised herself. "No. No, I can't say that I am."

His face, his posture, his body language all expressed his puzzlement.

"Perhaps," she said slowly, hearing the words only as they came from her mouth, "perhaps one's life ambition oughtn't to be something that can be achieved. Because what do you do *then*? Perhaps one's life ambition should be something that will always need to be worked at."

"But surely you're a long way from retirement!"

"Medically, yes," she agreed. "My doctors tell me I can look forward to at least twenty more years of excellent health. Surely I can contrive to push mountains of money back and forth for that long. But *why*? I have already achieved total security. If I were to seal myself up in my bathroom, my fortune would continue to grow—it has passed the critical point for self-sustaining reaction. And all my sisters are now independent, one way or another.

"I have been . . . uneasy, for months now, discontent in a way I could not explain to myself. But I see it now; I've achieved all I set out to do. No wonder I've been so . . . " She broke off and lapsed into deep thought, utterly unaware of the holocamera.

"But surely," Hold began again, "there are other goals you can turn your attention to now."

"What goals?" she asked, honestly curious.

"Er . . . well, the classic ones, of course," he said. "That is . . . well, to make the world a better place . . . "

"Owen," she said, "I confess that after nearly half a century of living, I haven't the faintest notion of how to make the world a better place. I wouldn't know where to begin."

"Well then, leave something behind for . . . "

"For posterity!" she finished. "Look at me. I'm fifty-four years old."

Hold was silent.

"In fact, that may be the single craziest thing about this society," she said, her voice rising. "We're best prepared to bear children, biologically, in our teens—and we're best able to raise them, socially and economically, in our middle and later years. For the first time in my life, my responsibilities have eased to the point where I can consider children of my own—and now I'm too old to *have* them." The camera unobtrusively tracked her as she rose and paced around the spacious living room. "I've been a surrogate mother for years, and now I'll never be a *real* one."

"But Diana," Hold cut her off, "surely parenthood is not the only form of immortality available to someone of your . . . "

"You don't understand," she cried. "I don't want immortality, even by proxy. I want *children*.

Babies, of my own, to cherish and teach and raise. All my life I've sublimated my maternal drive, to feed and clothe and house my sisters. Now that's ended—and it was never really enough to begin with. Oh why didn't . . . " She flung out an arm, and the very theatricality of the gesture reminded her all at once that she was being recorded. She dropped the arm and turned away from the camera in confusion. "Owen . . . Mr. Hold, I must ask you to leave now. I'm sorry, but this interview was a mistake."

With a total absence of dismay, Hold rose fluidly from the powered armchair and faced her squarely. Perhaps it was coincidental that this presented his best profile to the camera. "You know yourself better now, Diana." he said. "That may sting, but I hardly think it can be a mistake."

"If you're trapped in a canyon, aren't you better off not knowing?" she asked bitterly.

"Subconsciously you knew all along," he countered. "At least now you're facing the knowledge. What you *know* can't be cured, you know you can endure."

She examined her fingertips. "Perhaps you're right," she said at last. "Good day, Mr. Hold."

"Goodbye, Diana."

He collapsed the camera and left, looking rather smug.

A long time later, seated on a couch which had cost the equivalent of her father's total worth at the time of his death, she said to the empty air, " . . . but I never have been a quitter."

And after the sun had come up, she called her

local Cold Sleep center, made an appointment to speak with its director, and then called her attorney.

The second awakening was much better, and she did not enjoy it nearly as much.

Objectively, she should have. She no longer hurt anywhere that she could detect, and the bed—she corrected herself—the artifact on which she was half-sitting was the next best thing to an upholstered womb for comfort. She was alone in an apparently soundproof hospital room, in which the lighting was soft and indirect. She was neither hungry nor unhungry, neither weary nor restless.

But she was uneasy, as though in the back halls of her mind there faintly yammered an alarm bell she could not locate, an alarm clock she could not shut off. It was an unreasoned conviction that *something is wrong*. Unreasoned—was it therefore unreasonable?

That called for a second opinion.

Before she had given herself up to cryogenic sleep, she had firmly instructed herself not to be childishly startled by unfamiliar gadgetry when she woke. All the same, she was startled to learn that her nurse-call buzzer was a) cordless, b) conveniently accessible, and c) non-spring loaded, so that it could be thumbed without effort. It was not the technology that was startling—she realized that such technology was available in her own time—it was the thoughtful compassion which had opted to *use* technology for patient comfort. *Maybe they've repealed Murphy's Law,* she thought wildly, and giggled. *Now there's a dangerous vision for you.*

She was even more profoundly startled to learn that the *other* end of the process had been equally improved; her summons was answered at once. A tall, quite aged man with a mane of white hair swept aside the curtain at the far corner (The room couldn't be soundproof, then. Could it?) and stepped into the room. His clothing startled her again. She was somewhat used to the notion of purely ornamental, rather than functional, clothing—but to her mind, "ornament" involved not-quite concealing the genitals. Embarrassed, and therefore furious with herself, she transferred her gaze to his face, and felt her emotional turmoil fade, leaving only that original undefined unease like a single rotting stump protruding from a vast tranquil lake.

His mouth was couched in strong wrinkles that spoke of frequent laughter and tears, and his eyes were a clear warm blue beneath magnificent white eyebrows. She was . . . not captured . . . held by those eyes; to meet them was to be stroked by strong, healing hands, hands that gently probed and learned and comforted. They made her smile involuntarily, and his answering smile was a kind of benediction, a closing of a circuit between them.

And then those eyes seemed to see the rotting stump; the great white brow frowned mightily. "What's the matter, Diana?"

She could not frame the words, they simply spilled out. *"How much time has passed?"*

Comprehension seemed to dawn, yet the

frown deepened. "Even more than you stipulated," he said carefully.

She knew, somehow, that he would not lie, and
tried to relax. It did not entirely work. *I've
achieved what I set out to do*, she thought, *but
there's a catch of some kind somewhere. Now
how do I know that?* Then she thought, *More
important, how did he know that?*

"Who are you?" she asked.

He was perceptive enough to guess which
question she had asked with those words. "I am
Caleb," he said. "You've evidently guessed that
I'm to be your Orientator."

"I'm fairly good at anticipating the obvious,"
she said proudly. "It was inevitable that someone would have to fill me in on current conven-
tions, show me how to recognize the ladies' room
and so forth."

He laughed aloud. "I'm afraid that by 'anticipating the obvious,' you mean straight-line extrapolation of what you were already accustomed
to. That's going to cause you problems."

"Explain," she said, wondering if she should
take offense at his laughter.

"Well, for a start, I can't show you how to find
a ladies' room."

"Eh?"

"I can show you how to find a public toilet."

She registered confusion.

He smiled tolerantly. "Come, now—you're
obviously quite intelligent. What does your term
imply that mine does not?"

She thought a moment. "Oh." She reddened.
"Oh." She went on thinking, as he waited

patiently. "I suppose that makes sense. Earth must be too crowded by now to duplicate facilities without good reason."

He laughed aloud again, and this time she tried to take offense. Since Caleb was not offering any, she failed. "There you go again. You'll simply have to stop assuming that this is your world with tailfins on it. It isn't, you know."

"Will you explain my error?" she asked, battling her own irritation.

"It's not that we needed to stop excreting in secret—it's that we *stopped* needing to *do* so."

She thought that over very carefully indeed, and again Caleb waited with infinite patience, the warmth of his eyes offered but not proffered. He clearly understood that she wanted to work out as much of it as possible for herself—in order to deny that this strange new world was quite terrifying.

"Another question," she said finally. "When was the last war?"

His smile was more than approving—it was congratulatory, quite personally pleased. "Well," he said, "last night a few thousand of us had one hell of an argument over next year's crop program. Some of the younger folk got quite exasperated. But if you mean physical violence, deliberate damage . . . well, I'm an historian, so I could give you the precise date. But if you were to step out into the hall and ask someone, you'd probably get a blank stare. Does that answer your question?"

"Yes," she said slowly. "You're telling me that we've . . . that the race has actually . . . "

She paused, found the word. "Actually grown up."

"We like to think that we're adjusting well to adolescence," he said. "Of course, that implies the same sort of extrapolation you've been trying to use—but that's the best *we* can do, too."

"You are wondrously tactful, Caleb." she said. "But dammit, my whole life to now has been based on extrapolation."

"Oh, on a short time scale it works just fine." Caleb agreed. "But over long range, it only works as hindsight. It's a matter of locating the really significant data from which to extrapolate. An extrapolator in the early 1900s might have been aware that a man named Ford invented a mechanical horse—but how could that observer have guessed how *much* significance that should have in his projections? All the seeds of today were present in your world, and you were almost certainly aware of them. But if I hand you a thousand seeds, most of which are strange new hybrids, how are you to know which will be weeds and which mighty trees?"

"I understand," she said, "but I must admit I find the idea disturbing."

"Of course," he said gently. "We all like to think ourselves such imaginative navigators that no new twist in the river can startle us. The one thing that every Awakened Sleeper finds *most* surprising is the depth of his own surprise. The fun in all stories is trying to guess what happens next, and we like to feel that if we fail, it's either because we didn't try hard enough or because the author cheated. God is a much more talented author than that—thank God."

"I suppose you're right," she agreed. "All right, what were the seeds—the data I overlooked?"

"The biggest part was, as far as I can tell, right under your nose. The spiritual renaissance in North America was already well under weigh in your time."

Her jaw dropped in honest astonishment. "Do you mean to tell me that all that divine mumbo-jumbo, all those crackpot holy men, actually produced something?"

"The very success of such transparent charlatans proved that they were filling a deep and urgent need. When the so-called 'science' of psychology collapsed under the weight of its own flawed postulates, its more sincere followers perforce turned their attention toward spirituality. Over the ensuing decades, this culminated in the creation of the first self-consistent code of ethics—one that didn't depend on a white-bearded know-it-all with thunderbolts up his sleeve to enforce it. It didn't have to be enforced. When completed, it was as self-evidently superior to anything that had gone before as the assembly line was in its time. It sold itself. Behaviorally-determined helplessness may be a dandy rationalization—but it isn't any *fun*.

"At more or less the same time, there was a widespread boom in the use of a new drug called Alpha . . . why are you frowning?"

"I'm familiar with Alpha," she said sourly. "Salvation by drug addiction—that sounds just great."

"You misunderstand," he said gently. "It's not that the drug is addictive. Happens it's not. It's Truth that's addictive."

"Go on," she said, plainly not convinced.

"An interest in spirituality, combined with volitional control of rationalization, led inevitably to the first clear distinguishing between pleasure and joy. Then came the first rigorous definition of sharing, and the rest followed logically. Shared joy is increased; shared pain lessened. Axiomatic."

"But I knew that," she cried, and caught herself.

"If so," he said with gentle sadness, "then—as I have just said—you did not know how much significance to assign this awareness. What clearer proof is there than your presence here—than the inescapable fact that you used a much greater portion of the world's resources than you deserved, specifically to remove yourself from all possibility of sharing with anyone you know?"

"Wait a damn minute," she snapped. "I *earned* my fortune, and furthermore . . . "

"It is impossible," he interrupted, "to *earn* more than you can use—you can only acquire it."

" . . . and *further*more," she insisted, "I risked my life and health on the wild gamble that your age would Awaken me, specifically so that I *could* share—share my life and my experience with children."

"Whose children?" he asked softly.

She blew up. "You garrulous old fool. What in the HELL was the point in considering that until it was a physical possibility? How do I know whose children? Perhaps I'll have myself artificially inseminated, perhaps I'll have me a virgin birth, what business of yours whose children?"

"Am I not my sister's keeper?" he asked, unmoved by the violence of her rage. "Admit it, Diana; you *have* considered the matter, even if only subconsciously and those flip, off-the-top-of-your-head suggestions are all you've come up with. Sharing the job of parenthood might just be one of the most exciting challenges of your life—but what you really want is to recreate a game you already know how to win; raising images of yourself by yourself."

Implied insult could enrage her, but when she felt directly attacked she invariably became calm and cold. The anger left her features, and her voice was "only" impersonal. "You make it sound easy. Being father and mother both."

"Easy!" he said softly. "It cannot be done— save poorly, when there is no alternative. 'Poorly,' of course, is a relative term. Fate gave you that very burden to shoulder, and you did magnificently—from the records I have. It appears that none of your sisters turned out significantly more neurotic than you."

"Except Mary," she said bitterly.

"There is no reason to believe that you could have prevented her tragedy," he said. "I repeat: Given what you had to work with, you did splendidly. But if you persist in trying to repeat the task with no more than you had to work with then, you will end in sorrow."

"It would be challenging." she said.

"If it's challenge you want," he said in exasperation, "then why don't you try the one that occupies our attention these days?"

"And that is?"

"Raising the sanest children that it is within our power to raise. It's the major thrust of social concern, and the only ethical approach to procreation. How else are we to grow up than by growing ourselves up?"

"And how do you do that?" she asked, intrigued in spite of herself.

He tugged at the ends of his snow-white hair. "Well, some of it I can't explain to you until you've learned to talk—in our speech, I mean. I like this old tongue, but it's next to impossible to *think* coherently in it. But one of the basic concepts you already know.

"I reviewed a copy of that final interview you gave, to that man with the unbearably cute name. Owen B. Hold, that was it, of *Lo and Behold*. It's a rather famous tape, you know: you made a big splash in the media when you opted for Cold Sleep. Richard Corey has always been a popular image.

"And in that interview you raised one of the central problems of your age: the biological incongruity by which humans lost the capacity for reproduction at just about the time they were acquiring the experimental wisdom to raise children properly. People were forced to raise children, if at all, during the most agonizingly confused time in their lives, and by the time they *had* achieved any stability or 'common' sense, they tended to drop dead.

"Technology gave us the first phase of the solution; rejuvenation treatments were developed which restored fertility and vigor to the aged. The second phase came when the race abandoned technology—that is, clumsy and dangerous technical means of birth control—and learned how to make conception an act of the will. The ability was always there, locked in that eighty-five percent of the human brain for which your era could find no use. Its development was a function of increased self-knowledge.

"The two breakthroughs, combined, solved the problem, by encouraging humans not to reproduce until they were truly prepared to. The effects of this change were profound."

He broke off, then, for she was clearly no longer listening. *That's it,* she thought dizzily, *that's the final confirmation, he's just told me I can do it, so why am I still* sure *there's a catch to it somewhere? There's too much happening at once, I can't think straight, but* something's wrong *and I don't know what it is.* "Have you supermen figured out what a hunch is?" she said aloud.

Apparently Caleb had the rare gift of moving without attracting attention, for he was now in a far corner of the room. He seemed to have caused the wall to extrude something like a small radar screen; his eye movements told her he was studying some display on the face she could not see. When he spoke, his voice was grim. "That was known in your time. A hunch is a projection based on data you didn't know you possessed. Like the one that's been bothering you since I came into this room—the one that's been mystifying me for the same period."

She shook her head. "I've had this hunch since before I could possibly have had *any* data—from the moment I regained consciousness in this room."

"Except while actually in cryogenic stasis," he said, "no one is *ever* unconscious."

She started to argue, and then remembered the time she had been involved in a traffic accident on her way through South Carolina. She had spent a week in a coma, and awakened to find that she was speaking in a pronounced Southern drawl which mirrored that of her nurses. "Perhaps you're right," she conceded. "But what data could I have?"

He gestured to the screen. "This device monitors the room, so that if you should be found in the midst of some medical crisis, the Healers can study its beginnings. I've run it back, and I've found the problem."

A sudden increase of anxiety told her that Caleb was right. "Well?"

"A man with a habit of talking to himself did so as he was wheeling you in here from surgery and tuning your bed to you. This might not have mattered—save that he too is a recently awakened Sleeper, who still thinks and speaks in his old tongue. Since that tongue is Old Anglish, his mutterings upset your subconscious—and forced my hand. I hadn't wanted to go into this on your first post-Awakening conversation, Diana—but now I have no choice."

She tried to tense her shoulders, but the bed would not permit it. She settled for clamping her teeth together. "Let's get on with it."

"I'm afraid you *can't* have children—yet. Possibly never."

"But you said . . . "

"That even more time had passed than you stipulated, yes. Your instructions were to Awaken you as soon as it became medically possible for a woman of your age to bear optimally healthy children in safety. That condition obtains, and has for some time."

"And you're telling me *I can't*, even though it's medically possible." Her lip curled in a sneer. "I thought this Brave New World was too good to be true. Go on, Caleb—tell me more about your little Utopian tyranny."

"You misunderstand."

"I'll bet. So procreation is an 'act of the will,' eh? Just not mine."

"Diana, Diana! Yes, procreation is everyone's personal responsibility. But it requires *two* acts of the will."

"What?"

"I am not saying that you are forbidden to procreate. I'm saying that you won't find a male—or a clinic—willing to cooperate with you at this time."

"*Why not?*"

"Because," he said with genuine compassion, "you're not old enough."

Before shock gave way to true sleep, she became aware of Caleb again, realized that he had never left her side. He was holding her hand, stroking it as gently as a man removing ashes from a third-degree burn.

It was an enormous effort to speak, but she managed. "Will . . . will I . . . "

Caleb bent closer.

"Will I ever be old enough?" she whispered.

A faint smile came to his thin, old lips. "Perhaps." he said softly. "Barring accident, you will live at least another seventy years, years of youthful vigor. But I must warn you that, by our standards, you are a backward child."

"Hell with . . . hell with that. Only thing you've . . . got I haven't . . . s'healthier background."

"That is true."

"Jus' . . . watch me. Never was a quitter."

"I know." he said, his voice widening. "Your file told me that. That's why I overruled my colleagues, and Awoke you. I think that you will find joy, Diana. It's right in front of you. It always was."

"Think I'll . . . study music now."

He radiated approval. "An excellent idea. A life's ambition ought to be something that will always need to be worked at."

Peace washed over her, in something too gentle to be called a wave. She felt sleep reaching for her. But as her vision faded, curiosity birthed one last question.

"How many . . . how many thousands of years . . . has it been?"

His grin was something that could be heard and felt.

"Less than a century."

PLUS ÇA CHANGE...

Isaac Asimov used to say that when his father was born, man had not yet left the surface of the Earth in powered flight; when he died there were footprints on the Moon and color video cameras halfway to Saturn. Progress has certainly been progressing, and perhaps you agree with the cat who, after making love to a skunk, said, "I reckon I've enjoyed about as much of this as I can stand."

For some time now, it has been getting harder to dream a dream that isn't apt to up and come true on you, forcing you to live with all its new complications and implications, which once could have been safely left for your grandchildren to worry about.

If you worry that accelerating future shock may make you a Stranger in a Strange Land, allow me to reassure you. Let me tell you about the familiar, bedrock universals that will carry over into any world of tomorrow, reminding you of the world you know now. Every so-called "law of nature" is vulnerable to new and better observations, save one.

I'll bet cash on it: Murphy's Law will outlive thee and me.

• If tickets become available in your lifetime for regular passenger service to Luna, or Neptune, or even Alpha Centauri, you can reliably expect that the seats will be too cramped for an Ewok, the in-trajectory movie will be one you have already seen and hated, the food will be tasteless and toxic, and the coffee will qualify as an industrial solvent. The flight you wanted will be overbooked, and you'll never see your luggage again.

• Similarly, if vacation paradises are built in orbit during your lifetime, you will find them full of the wrong kind of people, infested with *tourists* rather than thoughtful travelers like yourself. Everything will be mercilessly overpriced, including air. If your hotel is in "luxurious free fall," you will need bellhops not only to handle your luggage, but to handle *you*; they and all resort employees will customarily be found floating a few feet distant, one hand drifting your way, palm upward—relative to you. (Be *certain* to tip the air steward adequately.) The plumbing will be indescribably barbaric, and give you at least one disease unknown to your doctor at home. The promised "romantic spacewalk" will consist of fifteen minutes in something very like a coffin with arms, with plumbing that makes the stuff inboard look good. Half the photos you snap will be spoiled when you forget to keep the Sun out of frame; the rest will be ruined by cosmic rays. The entertainment *will* probably be truly spectacular, but the drinks will cost two weeks' pay apiece, and their essential recipe will be two parts hydrogen to one part oxygen. Upon reentry, you will sprain something, and when you land a horde of sadistic customs inspectors will gleefully insult you, confiscate your souvenirs, subject you to something like a full-body CAT scan with unshielded equipment, stick a hundred needles into you, and fog any surviving film. Then you'll get home to find out that (as Tom Waits said) everything in your refrigerator has turned into a science project, the water was left running in the bathroom, and your next-door neighbors had a *much* better time at the Luna City Hilton for half the money.

• When it becomes possible for you to buy an antigravity flight belt, you will find that fresh out of the showroom it requires expensive repair; that the warranty is worthless, that the resale value plummets with every passing second; that the device wastes immense amounts of precious resources, has inadequate safety features and requires expensive licensing, registration, insurance and inspection rituals every year; that parts are unobtainable; that the roofs are full and there's no place to park; and that Japan makes a better one cheaper.

And presently you'll notice that the sky is full of idiots. The wise will tend to stay indoors . . .

• When fusion power finally starts to come

on-line, its implementation will be delayed by a vocal environmental lobby demanding a return to something safe, clean and natural, like fission.

• When you can afford a TV linkup that offers you 245 channels in 3-D with digital stereo sound, there won't be a damn thing worth watching on any of them.

• About the time they complete a Unified Field Theory, someone will identify a fifth, incompossible force. You'll never be able to understand it. Your teenager will grasp it at once.

• Then they perfect a method for keeping people sexually vigorous into their nineties, they will simultaneously extend the lifespan to a hundred and fifty. (And you won't be allowed to retire much before a hundred.)

• If intelligence-enhancing drugs are ever perfected, they will for some reason fail to work within the city limits of Ottawa, Ontario, Washington, D.C., or Moscow, Russia. (Note: the same may not be true in Tokyo . . . or Beijing . . . or . . .)

• When the whole world is linked together by computer network, and you have a billion terabytes of information available to you, you will not be able to find the little piece of matchbook cover on which you jotted down that essential access code.

• Finally—perhaps most ominously—as computers become smarter, as they reach the threshold of human intelligence, it will become possible . . . and soon after that, *necessary*—to *bribe* them.

❄ ❌ ❄

Myself, I take comfort from one final rock-certainty: No matter what marvels tomorrow rains on us, science fiction writers like me will always manage to dream up something absolutely far-fetched and preposterous for the day *after* tomorrow.

THE GIFTS OF THE MAGISTRATE

"Merry Christmas, Mr. Chief Justice," the Captain of the Guard said; but his subsequent behavior scarcely reflected the holiday spirit.

Wolfgang Jannike submitted philosophically to the fingerprinting, retina scan and close body search which were his Christmas presents from his subordinate. Jannike could hardly protest an order he had written himself. Nor would any conceivable protest have made the slightest difference; all the human guards at this stronghold were—again, by his own direction—Gurkhas, the deadliest humans alive.

Scanners had shown him unarmed, and the ID signal broadcast by the chip in his skull had been confirmed as legitimate and valid, else he would not have lived to reach Captain Lal. But even after Jannike had been positively identified as the person described by that ID chip, and therefore as the Chief Justice of the Solar High Court—nominal master of this prison—Captain Lal remained vigilant.

That was understandable. Of the four assassins who had come here to date, two had gotten this far; one of them so recently that Jannike could still see the stains on the wall. That one, he knew, had been a friend of the Captain's.

"How may I help Your Honor?" Lal asked when the ritual was done.

"I will speak with the prisoner alone for a time," Jannike replied firmly. He was committed now; at least three microphones had recorded those words.

There was a long pause, during which Captain Lal's eyes made all the responses his lips dared not—even a Gurkha must sometimes tread cautiously—and at last his lips made the only reply they could. "Yes, sir."

"Have you ever read the works of Clement Samuels, Captain?" the Chief Justice was moved to ask then.

"No, sir," Lal replied, doubtless baffled but showing nothing. He spun smartly in place and headed for the door, motioning to two of his men. They fell in behind Jannike in antiterrorist mode, one facing forward and one facing back, weapons out and ready. Somehow, he noted over his shoulder, they contrived to make it seem merely ceremonial. Then he faced forward and followed the Captain, to the cell which held the Vandal, the worst vandal of all time.

"Cell" it was in a legal and actual sense, but most of the humans alive in the Solar System

in 2061 occupied meaner quarters. The Chief
Justice himself owned slightly more cubic, and
more flexible hedonics therein—but not by
much. It was odd. The whole System was angry
at the Vandal, murderously angry, but it seemed
to be a kind of anger that precluded cruelty. The
execution would be retribution, but not vengeance. Revenge was not possible, and the crime
was so numbingly enormous and senseless that
deterrence could have no meaning. Nonetheless
society would do what it could to redress the
balance.

The Vandal was in an odd and striking position, both legally and morally, and—Jannike saw
as Captain Lal waved him into the cell—physically as well. Virtually all humans in free fall are
uncomfortable if they can not align themselves
with an arbitrary "up" and "down"; since the
earliest days of spaceflight men have built rooms
with an assumed local vertical, and the occupants
have oriented themselves accordingly. This occu-
pant was crouched upside down and tilted
slightly leftward with respect to the Chief Justice, drifting slightly in the eddy of the airflow.

The prisoner was studying the display wall:
the cell had a better computer and much greater
data storage capacity than Jannike's own home.
(On the other hand, Jannike's computer was
plugged into the Net, could send and receive
data; the prisoner's could only manipulate it. And
Jannike's door unlocked from the inside . . .)
Most of the datawindows that were open on the
wall displayed scrolling text or columns of changing figures, which must have been hard to read

upside down. So the Vandal's attention must have been chiefly devoted to the central and largest window, which showed a detailed three-dimensional model of the Solar System as seen from above the plane of the ecliptic.

She rotated slowly to face Jannike. Recognizing him, she starfished her body until it precessed around to his local vertical, a polite gesture that touched him. "Clear sky, Chief Justice," she said.

"And delta vee to you, Citizen," he responded automatically.

Behind him, Captain Lal made a frown Jannike could actually hear, over the muffled pounding in his own ears, and left them alone; there was an audible click just after the door had irised shut.

Vonda McLisle (ironic that her name should look and sound so much like the word Vandal) almost smiled at her judge. "May I offer you refreshment?"

"I'd be pleased to share tobacco with you."

Her eyebrows rose. "You're a user, too?"

Automatically he gave his stock reply. "It gives solace. And costs hours of life, but I don't expect to run short."

"And I won't live long enough to pay the bill," she agreed. He winced. She struck two cigarettes and floated one toward him; a bearing hummed as the room turned up its airflow to compensate. "Have you come to deliver a hangman's apology?"

"No." He picked his cigarette out of the air and took a deep drag. "It is Christmas Eve on Terra. I've brought you three gifts."

"But we don't even know each other."

"On the contrary, we've slept together for weeks."

"I beg your pardon?"

"You and I have both dozed through most of the trial so far, like most of those who've watched it. You're very good, but one of your eyelids flutters when you're deep under."

Again she nearly smiled. "With you it's the nostrils. You're right: as the old joke goes, it's been the equivalent of a formal introduction. But I'm afraid I have nothing to give you in return."

"I think you are wrong."

She pursed her lips quizzically. "Why would you want to give me presents, if deciding whether I live or die isn't enough to keep you awake?"

"Oh, it does keep me awake, Ms. McLisle—at night. But why *not* sleep through the trial itself? It's merely the formal public recitation of facts we both know already, that *everyone* knows already. You nap because my court has nothing to say to you. I nap because you have something to say to me, and will not."

She let smoke drift from her mouth, hiding her face. "The trial told you everything you need to know. The prosecution's case was exhaustive."

"But the defense stood mute. I am so constructed that I cannot condemn a woman to death without knowing the motive for her crime. Even if I cannot understand it, I must know what it is, what she at least conceives it to be."

"I will not tell you my motive."

"You do not have to."

She nodded, taking his statement only at face value, and he let her. "That's right, and I don't want to. So if that's the gift you wanted, I'm afraid—"

"Not at all. The gift I want is a much smaller thing. But before we get to that, here is the first of my gifts." He took an item from a pocket and sent it to her.

Her eyes widened when she recognized the gift.

"A modem! I can find out *what's going on*, get the latest figures, find out how bad I—" Her voice trailed off as she turned it over in her hands, tracing its design with sure slender fingers. She looked up at him, and the raw gratitude in her eyes seared his heart. "Have you ever been cut off from the Net? Thank you, *Herr* Jannike."

"You are welcome, Ms. McLisle."

"Vonda."

"Wolf. My second gift, Vonda, may seem disappointing; I ask that you wait until it is completely unwrapped before judging. It is a short speech, entitled, 'How I Spent My Christmas Vacation.'"

She must have been desperately eager to interface her first gift with her computer, but she made herself display polite interest. It faded fast.

"The holiday season was a perfect excuse for a short recess, and I needed one. What you did was perfectly clear and indisputable. You misappropriated the *Tom Swift*, the electrical drive unit your firm owns. Abrogating your contract with Systel S.A., you abandoned their o'neill in mid-deceleration, leaving several thousand colonists in an orbit that caused them to overshoot the Asteroid Belt by a wide margin. You used the *Tom Swift*'s enormous delta vee to intercept Halley's Comet, beyond the orbit of Mars. And then you stole the comet, and threw it away.

"Clear, indisputable—and inexplicable. The experts say you're sane. Your record is admirable. Yet you endangered thousands of innocents, and committed the greatest act of vandalism ever. The comet that led William to Hastings in 1066 and appears in the Bayeux Tapestry, that inspired Newton to write the *Principia*, the greatest scientific book ever, that inspired the first cooperative international space expedition in human history—kicked out of the ecliptic for good, never again to be seen in the sky of Terra after two millenia of faithful punctuality.

"I *had* to know why. I had to understand you, to imagine why you might do the inexplicable. So I went to your apartment."

The modem floated unheeded a meter from her hand. There was no other indication that she was still listening to him; her gaze had drifted away and her body was starting to do the same.

"A thousand reporters must have swarmed over that place, but none did what I did. I sat in it, for two entire days. I was trying to become you.

"I noticed the books at once; I share your fetish. Actual books, bound hard copy on acid-free paper. Naturally I was not surprised to find the complete works of Clement Samuels. He is surely the greatest writer still using that old-fashioned medium, and has millions of subscribers, myself among them. I *was* surprised to find the complete works of Mark Twain. Even though Samuels makes no secret of his debt to his palindromic namesake, few of his readers bother to go back to the source any more."

"Of all the arts," she said softly, "humor travels worst through time."

"I sat there for hours," he went on, "thinking of odd things. The comet, of course. Tom Sawyer. The food riots in New York. Clement Samuels, inexplicably wasting away in his seventies, when most citizens expect to see their hundredth birthday. The way the chief prosecutor sprays spittle when he's especially angry. The color of . . . no matter.

"I felt awful, inexpressibly sad. Samuels' work has always consoled me—but I've memorized everything he wrote, and I couldn't think of one I wanted to reread. So I took a Twain at random from your shelves.

"The first thing I noticed was the letter that acted as a bookmark. I read it without hesitation when I saw the return address. I never knew you and Samuels were lovers; I don't know how the media missed it."

"It was very brief," she whispered, "and a long time ago. His marriage was too good to risk, and I had a career in space, where he cannot live."

"So I gathered. When I had digested the letter, I finally noticed the passage it marked—and everything fell into place at once."

She was looking at him again now, eyes tracking

him as she drifted. "The last eighty years have brought more technological change than the previous two hundred," she said. "That implies an immense amount of pain, Mr. Chief Justice, as you know better than most. One of the things that got us through it, as a society, as a species, was the humor of Clem Samuels. It was gentle humor, humor with no cruelty in it, humor that didn't make you want to curl up and die with the hilarity of it all. Humor that helped you to go on, to endure, to enjoy. Maybe he didn't save us single handed, but we might not have made it without him. I know I wouldn't have; I wouldn't have kept on wanting to. A few hours of stolen passion fifty years ago had nothing to do with it."

"I know," the Chief Justice murmured.

"But he had to identify so damned strongly with Mark Twain. He rarely talked about it, but it tickled him to death that he'd been born at the beginning of 1986, with Halley's Comet at perihelion, just like Twain."

"'Now the Almighty must have said, "Here are these two unaccountable freaks,"'" Jannike quoted from memory. "'"They came in together, and so they must go out together."'" And Twain died on schedule."

"So of course Samuels insisted that he'd go the same way. It was funny—when he was twenty-six."

"And a little pretentious," Jannike said, "so he never mentioned it in interviews. It's not in his authorized biography."

"And then it was 2061 and he was *dying* and nobody knew why," she burst out. "*I knew why!*"

"So you took the most powerful tug in space and hijacked Halley's Comet, flung it out of human space. And now Clement Samuels is said to be recovering. And every astronomer in the System wants a recording of your death agonies, and the rest of the Federation just wants you gone."

She had been ready to die calmly; now she was white with fear. "You mustn't tell anyone, Wolf! *He mustn't know!*"

"That was my first question to myself: why would you conceal your motive? I concluded that you did not want to damage Samuels's marriage by announcing what must have been his first and only infidelity.

"So then I wondered why you had come back, why you did not simply stay with the comet when you knew your life was finished. I decided it was to return the *Tom Swift,* so that the colonists of Systel 2 could be rescued and towed to their proper orbit."

She was calming down as she persuaded herself that he meant to keep her secret. "That's only part of it. I . . . things went out of control out there. I landed on the nucleus, put down the hoses, filled her tanks, lit the fusion torch—and all hell broke loose. The hydrogen I got from the nucleus was even dirtier than I expected, so the drive burned wrong, and the second ion tail I made interacted weirdly with the comet's own and gave me more thrust than I wanted, in an uncontrollable direction. I meant to see that the comet never appeared in Terra's sky again, but I didn't mean to kick it out of the System completely. I had to cut loose, come back and get access to better computer power, and see if there wasn't any way to partially undo the damage. And you let me have this computer—but without the Net, without the precise up-to-the-minute observations of the entire System network, I didn't have the numbers to crunch."

"And because the rest of the System doesn't have your special empirical knowledge of what happens when you set a comet on fire, and is too angry to ask for it, any answers they get will be wrong," Jannike said. "That's why I brought you the modem. Please use it now."

She leaped to obey. It took her almost fifteen minutes to interface, access, download, integrate and get a trial answer.

"There's a chance," she announced. "If I've understood and correctly described all the anomalies I witnessed—if there are no new anomalies waiting to be discovered—there's a chance to keep Halley in the system. But the window closes in a matter of days, and I wouldn't sell insurance to whoever goes. Oh, Wolf, see that they examine this data—make them send someone! She's so . . . she's so *beautiful* I nearly changed my mind. It made me crazy when I saw how badly I'd miscalculated. I hate to think of her alone out there in the cold dark. Make them send someone!"

"I will," he promised. "Vonda, I said I had three presents for you. May I give you the third now? It's a letter from a friend."

"Oh. Okay, tell me the code and I'll access it."

He shook his head. "No. The friend wanted you to have hard copy, for some reason." He passed it across, an old-fashioned letter in an actual envelope, and politely rotated himself to let her read it in privacy.

It read:

24 December, 2061

My dear Vonda,

The bearer of this letter is more arrogant than you are, more arrogant even than myself, and that much arrogance takes my breath away. You were arrogant enough to maim the Solar System to suit yourself. I was arrogant enough to liken myself to Mark Twain, to think that the stars were placed in their courses to enhance the ego of Clement Samuels. Between us we cost mankind one of its favorite comets. But Wolf Jannike makes us look silly. He was arrogant enough to risk the destruction of two human beings and their marriage—and unlike us, he got away with it.

Did you really think you could anger or hurt my wife, by acting to extend my life with her? Yes, I am recovering, slowly but unmistakably, as you knew I would. Dorothy says she remembers you, always liked you, and wishes you to know that you are always welcome in our home.

Perhaps the purpose for your silence was to spare me the humiliation and guilt of knowing what destruction my folly inspired. I don't think I was meant to be spared that humiliation and guilt, Vonda; I think I needed it badly. I've been too successful for too long.

Now that—thanks to you!—I am no longer voodooing myself to death, I intend, in the words of the philosopher Callahan, to live forever or die in the attempt. I don't know if I will survive long enough to assuage my guilt, and I know I'll never live long enough to thank you for what you did, but I promise you I will live long enough to write a book about what you did, a book so funny and so sad that people will stop hating you and start laughing at me.

You took a comet the size of a city, and made it a City of Two Tails. That is a far, far better thing than I for one have ever done, and I'm damned if I'll see you lose your head over it.

Meanwhile, my wife and I thank you with all our hearts. There was never any danger of me forgetting you, Vonda my dear, and now I owe you my life. I'll try not to waste the balance of it.

Very truly yours,
Clement Samuels

Jannike knew when she was done digesting it, because she stopped crying and started trying to thank him. He interrupted her.

"I told you that I brought three gifts, Vonda McLisle," he said formally. "I've also brought you something else, which it would be inappropriate to call a gift. As your magistrate, I bring you your sentence. Are you ready to hear it?"

She shook the tears from her head like a horse tossing off flies, and nodded gravely. "Yes, Chief Justice."

"When Mr. Samuels's book is released and understood, I believe you will be considerably less unpopular than you are now. But that will take time. For now, there is only one sentence other than death which I feel the public might accept without rioting. Therefore I condemn you—"

—so this was what Scrooge felt like on Christmas morning!—

"—to fuel and refit the *Tom Swift* at once, and repair your vandalism as completely and as soon as possible. Charge the fuel to my personal account; I have reason to believe the System Federation will one day reimburse me. And may God have affection for your soul, Vonda my friend."

And he got the gift he had wanted in return: the first smile he had seen upon her face.

DISTRACTION

"Why *that* dump, Angel?"

"Jesus, kid," the smaller man hissed. "What did I tell you about names?"

Thomas Two Bears stopped walking. "Shit, man—"

Angel did not stop. "What did I tell you?" he repeated in a prison-yard murmur, without turning his head or moving his lips. "Say it back to me."

His large companion hurried to catch up, so he could reply without raising his own voice above a whisper. "From the moment you go out on a job, you don't use nobody's name, ever," he recited.

"And why not?"

A sentence was Thomas's limit of memorization; he took refuge in paraphrase. "Then you get into the habit, like, and you don't go blabbin' somebody's name when something goes wrong, and you don't gotta cool no citizens." He was puffing just a bit: the sidewalk sloped uphill.

Angel winced. "The *only* time you cool a citizen is if he's tryin' to cool you first, and you can't run away, and you can't stop him *without* chillin' him. Listen to me, stupid: the Vancouver cops or the RCMP catch you with an armful of VCRs, a good lawyer, you might do a year. You ice a citizen and it's at least a nickel. Especially an Indian kid icin' a rich white dude."

Thomas brushed aside this digression. "I still want to know why *that* shithole back there."

They had reached the big firehouse on the corner. Church across the street; a good place to pause without drawing notice; not in front of anybody's house. Besides, it was quite dark out, a usefully moonless and cloudy night. Angel stopped and lit an Export A, his round face looking like a jack-o'-lantern in the glow from his Bic lighter. "How is that place different?"

"It's a little dinky piece of shit. Peelin' paint. Dirty windows. The friggin' lawn's got herpes, for shit's sake."

"Right. In West Point Grey. You know about this neighborhood?"

"It's where the money is. What else I gotta know?"

Angel shook his head. "He doesn't know the territory. Kid, you're lucky you ran into me: you ain't got the brains to be a thief."

Thomas Two Bears could have twisted Angel's head off with one hand. He thrust both of them deep into his pockets, and whispered, "*I know that*," so loudly that he flinched himself. "So teach me like you said, okay?"

"Pay attention, then. Three or four years ago, all the houses on this block looked like that, little and short and old, only with better lawns. Big like that one, but kept up. Old retired rich people lived here. Then one morning, for no particular reason, all the real estate guys woke up with a hard-on. They all got together and announced this whole area was worth four times what it was the day before, and the citizens all bought it. Next thing you know, a plague of realty rats came through here buyin' up all the nice old wood-frame houses, and they tore 'em all down and built all these giant ugly Martian boxes out of balsa wood and slapped stucco on 'em and sold 'em to airhead yuppies for a couple of mil apiece."

Thomas looked back down the street. Most of the houses *did* look like the box a real house had come in. "So?"

"So tell me: what kind of guy, you go to him and say, 'I'll give you three times what your house is worth,' and he says, 'Take a hike, I like it where I am'?"

"Oh." Thomas lit a Player's Light King of his own, his last, and tossed away the empty pack. "A *real* rich guy."

"Or a real rich broad, or both. Probably old. And *so* rich they don't give a shit what the new yuppie neighbors think of their scraggy lawn."

"And you're sure they're not in there now? For a second there I could of swore I saw somethin' move at one of the windows."

"Kid, I been casin' this block three nights running. There's no car in front of the place or in the alley behind it. There's newspapers and fliers piled on the porch and mail spillin' out of the mailbox. The only sign of life in the whole place is a light inside that goes on at sundown and goes off at dawn. So what do *you* think?"

Thomas grinned. "I think we're half a block from Fat City. How long do we wait?"

"Let's give it until two—another hour or so. A lot of these yuppie jerks stay up late doin' that on-the-line bullshit with each other on their computers."

Thomas grinned again. "Imagine payin' thousands of bucks to shoot the shit with strangers? All they gotta do is go down to Granville Street, for Christ's sake."

"Not safe enough for a yuppie. Hell, *I* wouldn't talk to a stranger on Granville Street."

"Unless she had a real short skirt on," Thomas said, still grinning.

Angel snorted. "Kid, you not only don't know nothin', you don't even *suspect* nothin'. You mess with a street hooker, you might as well marry Lorena Bobbit and get it over with."

Thomas's grin vanished. "Aw, Angel, I was just—"

"Goddammit, you say my name one more time, I'm gonna tattoo it on your forehead with this cigarette!"

"Not so loud! Jesus. I'm sorry, okay?" Thomas drew on his smoke to cover his embarrassment. "So where are we gonna chill for an hour in this neighborhood, Mr. Mastermind?"

Angel pointed south, to the forests of the University Endowment Land a few blocks distant. "One of those hiking trails."

A boring hour later, the pair emerged from the woods onto 16th Avenue, walked north again, and turned at the firehouse.

"How do we go in?" Thomas Two Bears asked. "Front or back?"

"See them advertising fliers there on the porch, with all the newspapers? You get caught on that porch at 2 A.M., you could always try and make like you just put a flier there. You get caught in the backyard, end of story. Besides, I can see the front-door locks from the street, and they're candy. We'll only be exposed for a matter of seconds. Just stay cool."

"Man, I'm cool," Thomas said.

Angel looked at him. "You're about as cool as Regis Philbin."

"Who?"

"Forget it. Now don't look around, all right? Try and act like you're an invited guest, like I told you."

They left the sidewalk at the target house, climbed three cracked cement stairs, strode boldly up the walkway across the scruffy lawn, and climbed eight more stairs to the porch. The curtains behind the big picture window were translucent, and that light was on somewhere deep inside the house; it was just possible for Thomas to see into the dark living room while Angel worked on the locks. "Far out, man: looks like he's got a real nice sound system." He squinted, and frowned. "Lot of fuckin' books, too: he must be a prof from the university. I like rippin' off teachers; a lot of them ripped me off."

"Forget books—you can't fence a book for shit. Who wants 'em?"

"I was just saying."

Click. "Okay, kid, we're in. Come on."

Once they were inside, Angel almost-but-not-quite closed the door behind them, and then they simply stood there for a moment together. It was always a thrill, being inside some citizen's home. The silence of an empty house was pregnant with promise. It was like Christmas morning, or finding a woman asleep in the woods: the delicious suspense of presents received but as yet unopened, pleasures present but as yet unsampled.

"All right," Angel said at last. "Let's do it."

He spoke at normal conversational volume, for the first time since they'd entered this neighborhood; Thomas flinched slightly, and then smiled. "Yeah," he said, just as loudly. "Let's fucking *do* it."

He crossed the carpeted floor to the entertainment area. In the corner stood a massive floor-to-ceiling shelf affair packed full with CDs, cassette trays, and an enormous number of phonograph records. "Guy must be an old fart," Thomas said, indicating the records. "Look, he's got one of them antique turntable things." The turntable sat on a shelf of its own, with plenty of clearance over it.

"Yeah, well, he's got some good gear, too," Angel said. Beside the shelves was a waist-tall table, on which sat a huge, expensive-looking up-to-the-minute Personal Entertainment Center incorporating a six-disk CD player, a tuner, a double-cassette deck with both kinds of Dolby, and built-in speakers that looked like jet engine nacelles. A second pair of stand-alone speakers shaped like huge elongated pyramids stood against the opposite wall, flanking an enormous bookcase, aimed at the living room couch that sat beside the sound system. "That's at least a couple of grand worth of sound system right there. I can't wait to see the TV and VCR in his bedroom. This is great. Take that overgrown ghetto blaster and put it over by the front door; we'll make a pile and come back for it with wheels."

Thomas nodded. "You got it, man. Jeeze, this is great!"

"Let me see if he's got any music worth copping. I like some of that old shit . . . "

Thomas stepped up to the music monolith. It sat on short little legs, leaving a convenient space to get his hands under it on either side. He did so. To his surprise, it felt wet under there. Slimy wet. "Huh." He tried to take his hands back out and see what he'd gotten on his fingers, and failed. "Huh." He tried again, with no better result. "Hey, Ang . . . I mean, hey, man?"

"What is it now?" Angel, with tilted neck, was studying the CDs by the light of his Bic.

"Uh . . . I'm, like, stuck."

"What are you talkin' about?"

"I'm . . . you know: like, stuck."

"Hey, you can leave any time you want. You losin' your nerve or what?"

"No, man, I mean I can't let go of this fuckin' thing. I'm stuck to it."

"What do you mean, you're stuck to it?"

Thomas shook the heavy thing vigorously, picked it up and set it down twice. "I can't let go of it. My hands are like, stuck to it."

"*What?*" The Bic lighter went out.

"It felt wet when I went to pick it up . . . and now I can't let go."

"Jesus Christ, Tommy—"

"For Christ's sake, Angel, don't use my *name!*"

Angel relit the lighter, held it near and peered at Thomas's hands. "You really can't get loose? You're not shitting me?"

Thomas's big shoulders swelled, and then swelled further. "Not without ripping the skin right off 'em. I mean it, man: I'm *stuck.*"

Even in the feeble light of the lighter, Thomas could see the blood draining from Angel's face. "Holy *shit,*" the older man said softly.

Thomas thought as hard as he ever had in his life, an effort greater than the earlier physical effort of trying to free his hands from this technophile Tar-Baby. The results were disappointing . . . but crystal clear. "I'm screwed, ain't I? Ain't I, Angel? I'm completely screwed. I can't even change my mind and go home empty now, can I?"

"What do you mean, you can't—"

"Angel, think about it. How far is an Indian kid carrying a two thousand dollar sound system through Vancouver at two in the morning gonna get? I can't pay a bus driver, or a cabbie if I could get one to stop. Even if I make it to cover somehow, how long can I hide from the heat with *this* goddam thing on my hands? I'm screwed, right?"

Angel grimaced. "So we do what you said: bite the fuckin' bullet and rip the skin off your fingertips. It'll hurt, but not like a nickel will."

"I know you told me leaving fingerprints don't matter as much as everybody thinks—but Jesus, man, if I leave 'em the goddam *fingertips*, they'll make me for sure."

Angel shut his lighter down again. "Kid," he said finally, "you're right: you're totally fucked." It was irritating that Thomas had thought it through faster than he had. Then again, the kid probably had a lifetime of experience in reaching the conclusion that he was screwed. "Jesus *Christ*, this pisses me off."

It didn't piss Thomas off. He was too miserable, and too confused.

"Son of a *bitch*," Angel said suddenly. "He's *here*. The bastard is here in the house, right now. He's gotta be: the kind of glue that bonds to skin don't stay wet very long. He saw us coming and he put Wonderglue on the damn stereo. He figured out the first thing we'd touch and he boobytrapped it. I'm gonna *kill* the son of a bitch!" He took a gun from his jacket—far too angry to remember his own lecture on when and when not to cool a citizen—and started to leave the living room.

"Angel, wait—maybe he's got a piece!"

"If he had a piece, he wouldn't be screwin' around with glue," Angel said, and left the room.

❦ ❈ ❦

He found himself at once in a small foyer of sorts, presented with three choices. Right oblique, an open doorway that led to a dark kitchen. Left oblique, a door, slightly ajar. Far left, a dark hallway that ran back parallel to the living room he'd just left, doubtless leading to bedroom and bathroom. The light by which he had been seeing since he'd entered the building was coming out from behind the partly closed door. *That* was where the sneaky bastard was, in his goddam den, probably trying to phone the police. Angel reached for the doorknob—and paused. Tricky prick wasn't going to get Angel McKee to put his hand on any doorknob full of glue, no sir. He laughed, butted the door open with his crotch, and entered the new room.

He got a very brief look at his antagonist, barely time to register a tall skinny geek with glasses, long hair and a beard—then was distracted by a visual phenomenon much nearer and too transient to grasp.

His feet exploded.

He glanced down in shocked surprise. An extremely large, heavy book—a dictionary—had fallen from a perch on top of the door, passed before his eyes, and landed, spine downwards, on both his feet.

They *hurt*.

As he was absorbing this news, he looked back up again—and met a large, heavy cut-glass ashtray, traveling in his direction at high speed. It impacted on the bridge of his nose, and would have hurt terribly—but he just had time to register the hideous sensation of cigarette ashes in his eyes before consciousness tactfully left him.

When it returned, his first sensation was utter disorientation—too many things to sort out. His whole face hurt, even more than his feet, the ashes still in his eyes were an intolerable annoyance, his neck ached from being in a bad position for a long time, and for some reason his feet felt unbelievably cold—but these were *not* the first things he noticed.

He was outside, and it was broad daylight. He was sitting on the porch, *barefoot*, head on his knees. Out on the sidewalk, a small boy was regarding him with grave curiosity.

"Oh shit," he croaked, sitting up straighter with considerable pain.

"You got that right," Thomas said mournfully.

He whirled his head around, sending cut glass slivers through his stiff neck muscles. Thomas Two Bears was sitting beside him, his legs spread wide—for the Personal Entertainment Center was still attached to his hands.

Figuring all this out might well prove to be impossible—but short-term tactics, at least, were easy to decide. "Let's book!" he said.

"Go for it," Thomas suggested.

He realized, in failing to get to his feet, that his soles were glued to the porch. "Aw, *shit*."

Thomas's voice had a dreamy, singsong quality. "You're so fucking smart. You figure shit out all the time, with that big brain, and explain it to me like I'm five years old. And now you got us both in this jackpot. Man, you're no smarter than me. You're just a fancier kind of stupid."

Angel might actually have been willing to concede the point—but had more pressing things on his mind just then. "Jesus Christ, kid, what the hell *time* is it? How long we been sitting here like this, sitting fucking ducks?"

"Hours," the Indian chanted. "Hours. Lots of hours. It's almost sundown again."

"*Sundown the next day?* And that bastard didn't call the cops?"

"You're the genius. You figure it out. It's past me."

Now it was Angel's turn to think harder than he ever had in his life. His temples swelled. Finally they relaxed, as his jaw sagged. "Oh, *no*. Man, we're in *trouble*—"

"You don't know the half of it," Tommy told him. "I've had to take a shit for the last five hours."

Oh God, me too, Angel thought, and swept the thought aside. "Oh my God, kid," he moaned. "I think I know where I fucked up. He lives like a bum in a rich neighborhood. He wouldn't move if you gave him a million dollars. He stays up all night long and never goes out. You know what we did? Oh Christ, it would of been safer to tease a wolverine . . . "

"What'd we do, Angel?"

"God help us, Thomas: we disturbed a writer while he was working." He frowned. "Shit, he'll just leave us here until he's made his deadline. We could fucking starve. It could be *weeks*, if he's a novelist. He might not even *remember* us by then." He turned away from his accomplice and faced the street. "Hey—*kid!* Go home and tell your mother to call the cops, would ya? *Please*? We want to surrender . . . "

ORPHANS OF EDEN

Well, what would *you* have done?

Begin at the front part, Spider:
It was just after two in the morning. I was right here in my office (as we call the dining room in this family), about to write a science fiction story called "Orphans of Eden" on this loyal senescent Macintosh, when he appeared in the doorway from the kitchen, right next to my Lava Lamp. I don't mean "came through the doorway and stopped"; I mean he *appeared*, in the doorway. He sort of shimmered into existence, like a Star Trek transportee, or the ballplayers disappearing into the corn in *Field of Dreams* in reverse. He was my height and age, but of normal weight. His clothing was crazier than a basketball bat. I never did get the hang of the fashion assumptions behind it. I'd like to

say the first thing I noticed about it was the ingenious method of fastening, but actually that was the second thing; first I observed that his clothing pointedly avoided covering either genitals or armpits. I kind of liked that. If you lived in a *nice* world, why would you want to hide your smell? He stood with his hands slightly out from his sides, palms displayed, an expectant look on his extraordinarily beautiful face. He didn't look afraid of me, so I wasn't afraid of him. I hit command-S to save my changes (title and a handful of sentences) and forgot that story completely. Forever, now that I think about it.

"When are you from?" I asked him. "Originally, I mean."

I'm not going too fast for you, am I? If a guy materializes in front of you, and you're sober, he *might* be the genius who just invented the transporter beam . . . but if he's dressed funny, he's a time traveler, right? Gotta be. *Thank God the kitchen door was open* had been my very first thought.

He smiled, the kind of pleased but almost rueful smile you make when a friend comes through a practical joke better than you thought he would. "Very good," he told me.

"It was okay, but that's not a responsive answer."

"I'm sorry," he said. "But I can't say I think a lot of the question itself. Still, if it really matters to you, I was born in the year 2146 . . . though we didn't call it that at the time, naturally. Feel better, now?"

He was right: it hadn't been much of a

question. Just the only one I could come up with on the spur of the moment. But I thought it small of him to point it out. I mean, what a spur—what a moment! And the information was mildly interesting, if useless. "You don't go around pulling this on *civilians*, do you?" I asked irritably. "You could give somebody a trauma."

"Good Lord, no," he said. "Why, half the other *science fiction writers* alive now would lose sphincter control if I materialized in their workplace like this."

It was some comfort to think that my work might survive at least another hundred and fifty-five years. Unless, of course, he had run across one of my books in the middle of next week. "That's because they think wonder is just another tool, like sex or violence or a sympathetic protagonist."

"Whereas you know it is a religion, a Grail, the Divine Carrot that is the only thing that makes it possible for human beings to ever *get* anywhere without a stick across their ass, yes, it shows in your work. You understand that only by putting his faith in wonder can a man be a moral being. So you're not afraid of me, or compelled to disbelieve in me, and you probably hadn't even gotten around to trying to figure out a way to exploit me until I just mentioned it: you're too busy wondering."

I thought about it. "Well, I'm sorry to say I've been wasting a good deal of time and energy on trying not to look stupid in retrospect—but yes, most of my attention has been on wonder. Before we get to the question and answer section, though, what's your name?"

"Why?" he asked. "There's only one of me."

"Suppose I want to swear at you."

He gave a smaller version of that faintly annoying smile. "Good point. My name is Daniel."

My wife's ex-husband is named Daniel. Also amazing, also faintly annoying at times. "Would you mind if I went and woke up my wife? She'd be sore if I let her sleep through this." Jeanne enjoys looking at very beautiful men. Obviously. Our teenager, on the other hand, would doubtless find a two-hundred-year-old grownup five times more boring than me—and enough music to wake her (the only thing that will do the trick) would probably also wake the tenants downstairs in the basement suite. "And would you care for some coffee?"

He shuddered slightly—then saw my expression. "Sorry. That was for the coffee, not your wife. Imagine I brought you back to a Cro-Magnon's cave, and he offered you refreshments."

My turn to apologize. "Sorry, I wasn't thinking."

"As to Jeanne . . . please don't misunderstand. I would be honored to meet her under other circumstances, another time. Your collaborations with her are even better than your solo work." I nodded strong agreement. "But if I correctly decipher her input therein, she is a Soto Zen Buddhist and a sentimentalist."

"What's wrong with that?" I demanded.

"Nothing at all. But I seek advice on a practical matter of morality . . . and *you* understand how omelettes are made."

I frowned. "Do you mind if the Cro-Magnon has a little cup of jaguar blood to help him think?"

"This is your house," he said simply.

Well, actually it isn't—I'm a writer; I rent— but I knew what he meant, and agreed with it. I thought about that while I turned another cup of water into dark Tanzanian magic and spooned in sugar and whipped cream. By the time I tipped the Old Bushmill's into the coffee my Irish was up. "Before we start," I said.

"Yes?" He was watching my preparations with the same gravity I'd like to think I could bring to watching an autopsy.

"You have managed to be sufficiently inter- esting that I will forgive you this once," I said. "But if you *ever again* drop in without phoning ahead first like that, I'll set the cat on you."

He did not quite look wildly around. "Do you have a cat?"

I winced. Smokey was killed a month ago, by some asshole motorist in a hurry. One of the best masters I ever served. "I'll get one if necessary. And I don't want to hear any guff when you reach my answering machine, either. It's always on. People should be grateful I let 'em leave messages."

"Understood and agreed," he said. "And I apologize. But in my defense: what would you have done if I had left a phone message?"

I nodded. "That's why I forgive you this once." I made one last try at hospitality. "I can offer you charcoal-filtered water."

"Thank you, no."

I pointed to a kitchen chair, and took the one across the table from it for myself. He sat beautifully, like a dancer, or one of Jeanne's Alexander Technique students.

I took a long appreciative sip of my Irish coffee. "I'm listening, Daniel," I said.

"Before we start."

"Yeah?"

"When will you begin to get excited?"

"About a minute after you leave, I hope. By then I can afford to."

He nodded. We both knew I was lying; the cup was trembling. He really was trying to be polite.

Why was he trying so hard to be polite?

"You spoke of wanting my advice on a practical matter of morality," I went on. "Is this an ends-justifying-means kind of deal?"

I had succeeded in impressing him. "You have succeeded in impressing me," he said. "Yes."

I sighed. "You've read *Mindkiller*."

He nodded.

It's one of my scarier books. One or two critics, after having had someone literate summarize it for them, have declared that it says the end justifies the means. Beginning for the first time to be a little scared myself, I said, "And have *you* got the secrets of mindwipe and mindwrite?"

"Oh, no," he said convincingly enough to make me relax again.

"What's holding things up?" I asked. "I expected that stuff to come along well before 2040."

"You vastly underestimate the complexity of modeling the brain."

I nodded philosophically. "It's going around these days. Well, I'm relieved, I guess. I had to force that happy ending. That happens to me a lot in the serious books."

He nodded again. "But you keep doing it. Splendid."

"Thank you." The better the flattery, the warier I become. Back to business. "Then I am to assume that you have another moral dilemma, as sharp as the one faced by Jacques in *Mindkiller*?"

"It is to me. I want you to tell me if I am a monster . . . or simply a victim of my inability not to ask the next question."

"Or both," I pointed out.

"Or both," he agreed.

I took another long gulp of Irish coffee. I've long since worked out to my own satisfaction the one about a writer's responsibility . . . but I'd always known that book would come back to haunt me one day. "Let me get this straight. You have already done . . . whatever this thing is. Some would call it monstrous. And now you want my opinion on whether or not you were right to do it. Why? Since it's too late."

"I need to know if I dare go public—in my own ficton, my own space/time. If I can't persuade you, I can't persuade anybody."

I always had the sneaking idea I'd make a good judge, if only there weren't so damned many laws. Time to find out if I was right. "First tell me your ends. Then your means. If you can do it that way."

"I can approach it that way," he said, "but the ends imply the means. I can put it in a nutshell. I wanted to do meaningful sociological experiments."

I understood him at once, because he was speaking to the heart of the science fiction story I'd intended to write. But in case I only *thought* I understood him, I dragged the exposition out of him like a good character should. "What do you mean?"

"I think you suspect," he said. "Most of the really important questions about human societies are unanswerable because you can't contain the size of the question. You can't understand the ancient Romans if you don't know about all their neighbors and trading partners and subject peoples, and you can't really grasp any of *them* any better because they all influence each other helter skelter— and you can't even get a start on any one of them until you know *their* whole history back to their year one. It's the history that's even worse than the local complexity: so much of any society is vestigial, the original reasons for its fundamental assumptions forgotten.

"And it's the *history* that always gets in the way of trying to make things better. Look at your own contemporary ficton. Can you imagine any solution to the Irish problem or the Serbo-Croatian problem or the Palestinian-Jewish problem or any one of a hundred others like them that does not involve giving everyone involved mass amnesia and erasing all the history books?"

"Well, yes," I said. "But it won't come soon.

Now that you tell me telepathy isn't even going to be as easy as time travel."

"For all I know telepathy could come along before 2300," he said. "I left in 2292 . . . " (I calculated without much surprise that he was at least a hundred and forty-four subjective years old) " . . . and one of the limitations of time travel—a blessed one in my opinion—is that you cannot go further *forward* in time than you have already been. The only way to see the future is to live it. But I'm not expecting telepathy soon—then/soon—either."

I finished my coffee. "I'm sorry to hear that. Still, there's no real hurry. Once we have telepathy *and* time travel, we can build Heaven or a reasonable facsimile retroactively."

"As in your book *Time Pressure*," he agreed. "But since I don't expect that soon and can't depend on it ever, I'm trying to save the human race in a different way. There is some urgency about the matter. When I come from, we have come very close to destroying ourselves in catastrophic warfare."

"Nanotechnological?"

"Worse. I strongly advise you to leave it at that."

I could not suppress the shudder . . . or the squirm that followed it. I had been wondering if he was too evolved to have immunities for primitive local germs—just wondering, not worrying, as I believe a man's health is his business. Now I was reminded that there are circumstances under which a man's health is your business. Was Daniel carrying anything?

Too late to worry now. "What kind of a ficton is it?"

He hesitated. "It's hard to give you a meaningful answer. Imagine I'm a Cro-Magnon. Tell me: what's your world like?"

"Giddy, with fear and pride and guilt and shame, but trying to be as decent as it can."

He nodded thoughtfully. "Okay. In those terms, the 2290s are sullen, scared and preoccupied with the present. In the immediate past is horror, and just beyond that are the things that inexorably brought it on us, and still we prefer not to think overmuch of the future. We see what went wrong, and don't know how to fix it. As near as we can see, all the future holds is another slow painful climb to the pinnacle which blasts all who stand on it, and those of us who think about that wonder what's the point. So not many of us think about it."

I was more grateful than ever to have lived my life in the twentieth century. But I was also puzzled. "It's hard to square that with your clothes. That kind of outfit in that kind of world doesn't ring true. People like that would cover up."

He smiled sadly. "These clothes were designed elsewhen."

Skip irrelevancies. The night was old. "Okay. So what do you figure to do about your situation?"

He clasped his fingers together before him on the table. With his spine so straight, it made him look as if he were praying. "It's all the history, you see. The weight of all that history, all those mistakes we can't ever undo or forget."

"I can understand that."

"Probably you can; the problem is just now beginning to become apparent. Time was when the maximum length of history was the number of stories an old man could tell before he died. Then we got too damned good at recording and preserving the stories. At about the same time there began to be too many stories, and they all interacted. And then came the Information Explosion. Human beings are only built to tolerate the knowledge of so much failure and tragedy. All the things we've ever done to warp the human spirit, from making wars to making gods, are there in us, at the root of anything we plant, at the base of anything we build. When you try to start all over again from scratch, you find out you can't. Your definition of 'scratch' merely defines the direction history has warped you in, and condemns you to tug in the other direction. But the weave is too complex to straighten.

"It's too late for us to start over. It's too late to try and create a society without taboos: the people who would try it are warped by the knowledge of what a taboo is. It's too late to try and create a society without sexual repression: the parents inevitably pass along to their children at least warped shadows of the repressions they inherited themselves. It's too late to make a society without racism . . . and so on. Every attempt at an experimental Utopian community has failed, no matter how hard they tried to keep themselves isolated from the surrounding world. Sealing yourself up in a self-sustaining space colony and smashing all your comm gear doesn't help. It's just too late to experiment with a society that has no possessions, or conformity, or tribalism, or irrational religions—all possible experimental subjects are compromised by their knowledge of human history. What's needed is some way to put an 'Undo' key on history."

"I think I see where you're going," I said. "I was just about to write a story about—"

"I know," he interrupted. "And you were going to screw it up."

We'll never know, will we? "Go on."

"Well, I think you know the only possible solution. Let's do a thought experiment—I *know* you won't mind the pun. Hypothetically: put a bunch of preverbal children—infants, for preference—in a congenial artificial environment. Plenty of room, plenty of food for the taking, mild climate, no predators, an adequate supply of useful materials and appropriate technology for later. Immunize them against all disease, and give them doctor-robots that will see them into adulthood and then fall apart. Provide AI packages to teach language skills and basic hygiene—both carefully vetted to be as semantically value-free as possible—"

"Have the AI design the language," I suggested.

"Yes. Open-ended, but with just enough given vocabulary to sustain a complicated thought: let 'em invent their own. A clean foundation. When they're ready to handle it, have the machines teach them the basic principles of mathematics and science, using numbers rather than words wherever possible, and just enough philosophy to keep them from brewing up organized religion. And *not a damned word of history.* Then you go away, and come back in a thousand years."

"To find them knifing each other over which one has the right to sacrifice a peasant to the teaching machines," I said.

"You are not really that cynical."

"Of course I am. Why do you think I have to keep writing those happy endings? You know, another writer wrote a story years ago with the same basic theme as your thought experiment—"

"Yes," he said, "and what was the first thing his protagonist did? Saddled the poor little bastards with the author's own religion! Gifted them with shame and sin and an angry but bribeable paternalistic God and a lot of other 'moral' mumbo jumbo. Phooey. He had greatness in his hands and he blew it. That time."

I didn't quite agree, but the differences were quibbles. And I had something else to think about. This wasn't a science fiction story Daniel was describing, or any cockamamie "thought experiment" . . .

I once heard a black woman use some memorable language: she described someone as having been "as ugly as Death backin' out of a outhouse, readin' *Mad* magazine; ugly enough to make a freight train take a dirt road."

All at once a thought uglier than that was slithering around under my hair.

"Talk about cynical," I went on, "why don't we get down to the crucial problem with this little thought experiment, as you call it?"

I was looking him in the eye, and he did not look away. But he didn't answer me either. So I did.

"The problem is, where do you get the infants?"

"Yes," he said slowly, "that was the problem."

I poured more Irish coffee, omitting coffee, cream and sugar. When it was gone I said, "So you're the guy that laid the bad rap on all those gypsies." I was trying hard not to hate him. I try not to hate anybody, no matter how much it seems indicated, until I've walked around it a little while. And he hadn't said he was through talking yet. But so far I really hated this . . .

He looked confused for the first time since I'd met him; then he got the reference. "No, no. That wasn't me, any more than it was gypsies. As far as I know, that child-stealing gossip was sheer wishful thinking on the part of parents, combined with a natural hatred of anyone who didn't have to stay in the village they were born in. I've never stolen a baby, anywhere in Time."

"Then where did you get them? Roll your own? In a test tube or a petri dish or whatever? Were the donors informed volunteers?" Even if the answer was yes, I didn't like this one any better. Call up human beings out of nothingness, to be born (or decanted or whatever) and suffer and die, for purely scientific reasons? At least the first generation of them compelled to grow up without parents or role models, forced to reinvent love and law and humor and a trillion

other things I took for granted? If they could?
Grow babies as guinea pigs?

"I've never made a baby either," he said. "Not
even with someone else's genes."

I frowned. "Den ah give up, Mr. Bones—how
did dat time traveler . . . oh." Then I said: "Oh!"
And finally: "*Oh!*"

"A lot of infants have been abandoned on a
lot of windy hillsides or left in dumpsters since
time began," he said sadly. "If Pharaoh's daughter
had happened to miss Moses, she probably could
have picked up another one the next day. It
tends to happen most in places and times where,
even if the child had somehow miraculously been
found and taken in by some contemporary, it
would have had a maximum life expectancy of
about thirty years. So I denied some of them the
comfort of a nice quick death by exposure or
predator, brought them to a safe place and gave
them the means to live in good health for hundreds of years."

"And used them as guinea pigs," I said, but
without any real heat in it. I was beginning to
see his logic.

He didn't duck it. "That's right. Now you tell
me: are my actions forgivable?"

"Give me a minute," I said, and poured more
whiskey and thought.

Thou shalt not use human beings as guinea
pigs.

Don't be silly, Spider. Accept that and you've
just tossed out most of medicine. Certainly all the
vaccines. *First* you use guinea pigs, sure . . . but
sooner or later you have to try it on a human or

you're just a veterinarian. And meanwhile people are *dying*, in pain . . .

Thou shalt not experiment on human beings without their informed consent.

Many valuable psych experiments collapse with informed consent. You can't experiment with the brain chemistry of a schizophrenic without endangering his life. You can't find out whether slapping a hysteric will calm him down by asking him: you have to try it and see what happens. Daniel's too is an experiment which by definition may not have informed consent: informing the subject destroys the experiment. Is there, Written anywhere, some fundamental law forbidding a man to withhold information, even if he believes it to be potentially harmful?

Thou shalt not use infants as guinea pigs.

Hogwash, for the same reasons as number one above. How do you test an infant-mortality preventative, if not on an infant? Should we not have learned how to do fetal heart surgery? Do not the benefits of amniocentesis outweigh the (please God) few who will inevitably be accidentally skewered? Would Daniel's orphans really be better off dead than in Eden?

Thou shalt not play God.

God knows someone has to. Especially if the future is as grim as Daniel says. And She hasn't been answering Her phone lately. When it comes down to the crunch, humans have *always* tried to play God, if they thought they could pull it off . . .

Ah, there was the crux.

"And what kind of results have you gotten?" I asked.

His face split in a broad grin. "Ah, there's the crux, isn't it? If you examine the data that came out of the Nazi death camps, and profit from that terrible knowledge . . . are you any better than Dr. Mengele?"

I winced.

"That is the question I want you to answer," he said. "You are completely insulated from any possible backlash to your answer—the people who will ultimately judge me will never know you were consulted, even after the fact. There is no stick to be applied to you as a result of your answer. And now I will offer the carrot. The same carrot that got me into this."

I was already reaching for the whiskey. *Dammit,* I thought, *this isn't fair. All I ever tried to do was entertain people . . .*

Balls, came the answer from deep inside.

"If you tell me that constructing the experiment was a moral act," he went on inexorably, "I will tell you everything I can about the results."

Well, what would *you* have done?

PANDORA'S LAST GIFT

Can anyone tell me what is the antonym for the word, "cynic"? After reflection I come up with "idealist," "romantic," "Pollyanna," "Pangloss," and "flower child," all of which are currently considered derogatory. Is it really true that the only opposite of "disillusioned" is "illusioned"? Is the opposite of "despair" "naiveté," or is there still room for "hope" in our vocabulary?

It seems to me that the floodtide of cynicism which has swamped North America was barely a trickle during my childhood. Perhaps it always seems so, to each generation; there seems to be a general societal agreement that it is well to shield children from our own cynicism until they are old enough to get drunk. I was a freak reading prodigy as a child, and my mother placed almost no constraints on my reading, so I was a cynic at six—but I recall distinctly that in those days if you used the term "Murphy's Law" in conversation with adults or other children, you usually had to explain it. Most movies and books seemed to end with the assumption that Virtue Would Triumph and Love Would Conquer All, even if they took satirical potshots at society along the way. It was possible to shock your teachers by quoting Ambrose Bierce. Only the very rich entered marriage planning for the divorce. We did not feel a need to train our children that any adult who smiled at them was a potential rapist.

We understood that living in the Twentieth Century posed new and extraordinary ethical dilemmas, challenges to integrity and decency, challenges to ingenuity and will—but there seemed a general consensus that we were up to it, or at least intended to go down swinging.

Then a whole generation was somehow capriciously inoculated with massive conflicting overdoses of cynicism and hope, just as it was entering puberty. The richest and most favored generation in the history of the world looked about at the best of all possible worlds to date, and found it so vile and despicable that it must be made over, *at once*. The recommended tools for changing the world were prayer, sex, new drugs, rock and roll, and public rioting—anything at all except rational thought plus learning followed by reasoned manipulation of the world as it was. There was, it must be noted, an undercurrent of hope in the notion that the world *could* be changed for the better, by any means at all. But that hope could not be sustained without intelligence, and intelligence was somehow made to seem inferior to intuition—a poor problem-solver. The Sixties flowered and died in a single great convulsion. The Beatles as a phenomenon lasted less than ten years, broken up by apathy and spiritual confusion and ego and greed. We all got the message that protest led you to jail or hospital, new drugs led to the Manson Family or the Funny Farm, sex led to herpes and trichomoniasis and AIDS, prayer led to Jonestown, and rock and roll stopped leading anything and blundered off into disco. And what did it matter, when any moment ICBMs and nuclear winter would fall?

I think the problem may come down to this: that we are the children of the Great Age of The Media, consumers of more news, and more detailed news, than our ancestors would have believed possible—and that bad news outsells good, time and again, reinforcing every panic, complicating every tragedy, cluttering every attempt to cope. I wish I knew why. There have been attempts to start Good-News papers, Good-News radio broadcasts—and they always fold within a few years. For some reason the modern news consumer *insists* on being *either* bummed out *or* distracted with glitter and bullshit, as from ET and Hard Copy and their ilk. No popular news medium in all the world ran with the lead story: Smallpox Eradicated: Mankind's Single Deadliest Enemy Defeated! and so, astonishingly, there has never been anything like the worldwide celebration and victory party that this exhilarating achievement merited. Polio too is dead in this hemisphere, did you know? I found the news on page B-14 of my local paper. It wasn't on the TV news.

But if we are getting more and better Bad News than any generation in history, is it any wonder that we are stunned goofy? Robert Heinlein had his character Jubal Harshaw wonder aloud about the pernicious psychic effects of "wallowing daily in the troubles of six billion strangers"—and sometime later Theodore Sturgeon addressed Harshaw's question, in a bone-chilling story called, "And Now The News . . ." The hero, driven mad by news, quotes John Donne's line about every man's death diminishing him . . . and decides to go out there and diminish mankind right back. The last line is, "He got eight people before they brought him down." Sturgeon wrote this decades before serial killers became a commonplace.

So we all changed . . . in response to relentless, useless alarm signals. Cynical despair suddenly became the very hallmark of intelligence, and if anyone heaped more scorn on the hopeful hippies of the Sixties than the ex-hippies themselves, it was those of their contemporaries and near-contemporaries who had been too timid or nerdy to benefit from the Age of Aquarius. Hair got shorter and became layered, beards were domesticated or exterminated. Bras and pantyhose reappeared, or rather returned. It became impossible to find anyone who would publically admit to having existed in the Sixties, much less participated in its grand experiments. It had been conclusively proven after exhaustive testing—whole weeks of it—that you could not change the system from *outside* the system, and the notion of changing the system from *inside* the system produced such gales of cynical mirth that it could not even be proposed, much less tried. Why, that would be . . . *hard*. Every commentator in the land became determined to remind you that all the hippies have either blown their minds, or sold out in some way or other. A famous *New Yorker* cartoon depicting a 20th Anniversary Reunion at Woodstock—attended exclusively by people in expensive business attire holding martinis—ran *five years* after Woodstock.

When you get afraid enough, you start to get selfish: it's human nature. Cynicism is a clever way of justifying that selfishness, so that you can live with yourself. Just strike the word "cop-out," and substitute the more palatable Post Modern term "burnout." (Be wary, by the way, of any school of thought whose very name is an oxymoron. They're telling you up front that they intend to travel on square wheels.)

As for myself, I was already a cynic when the Sixties began. I'd been reading Fifties and Sixties science fiction. Hope came slowly to me; I didn't actually join a commune until the early Seventies. I married Jeanne there; we birthed our daughter there; an astonishing succession of Good Things have come into my life since then. Hope has been good to me; so I've written cheery, basically optimistic science fiction stories in which responsible individuals solve great problems by applying their attention and intelligence to them.

About ten years ago I found myself backsliding. I was writing about problems whose solutions utterly escaped me, about people plagued by insoluble antinomy. I began to lose faith in mankind's ability to get itself out of the messes it has made. I ran out of optimistic guesses about the future. I became infected with a threshold dosage of the conviction that we are all merely rearranging deck chairs on the Titanic, waiting for the end to come in the form of nuclear apocalypse or worldwide financial catastrophe or new ice age or meteor strike or planetary race war or bubonic plague mutation or any of a thousand dooms. Despair, like heroin, relieves you of all responsibility. If you truly believe the saw that "No good deed goes unpunished," life is simpler. I told myself that I could take despair or leave it alone, that I'd only do it on weekends . . . well, on alternate days . . . okay, only on days ending in "y" . . .

There was a crazed genius around at that time who made it his holy mission to create a computer for normal human beings, a computer that spoke Human, a supertool a child could use. He achieved his dream—but along the way, he made so much money as a side effect that his enterprise grew too huge for him to manage. So he went to a manager, and said, "Do you want to spend the rest of your life selling sugared water, or do you want to change the world?" Note the Sixties word choice. The manager took the plunge . . . and soon took undisputed control of that enterprise; the founder, Steven Jobs, was "promoted to Global Visionary," lost his parking space in the Apple lot. The news depressed me.

And just then, Theodore Sturgeon died on me.

Everyone dies, but somehow I had expected that some sort of exception would be made for Theodore. He was one of the finest writers who ever worked—in any genre—and everything he wrote was about need, one way or another. He may have known more about need than anyone who ever lived, and he shared it all with us for over forty years. He was also a gentle and loving man, who when I was 35 years old taught me how to hug. His death hit me very hard.

And then summer came, and synchronicity (a fine old Sixties word) struck. Chance brought Jeanne and me near Chatham, Massachusetts, on July 19. Ten years earlier to the day, Jeanne and I had been married in Nova Scotia, in a triple wedding with two other couples from our commune. The bride of one couple was sister to the groom of the other (Jeanne's ex-husband, incidentally), and they were originally from Chatham. So we stopped in to see how their parents were doing, and to pump them for news of our wedding mates, whom we had not seen in over eight years.

We found both couples *there*; their father was dying. He died later that night.

It was a strange, unplanned 10th anniversary reunion. These were people with whom we had weeded soybeans and chanted om, shared outhouses and thrown yarrow stalks. A *lot* of time had passed. Someone nervously suggested that we all go down to the beach and acquire an illegal smile, and after five minutes chatting under the moonlight someone said, diffidently, "Did anybody see that movie, *The Big Chill*?"— and we all laughed too long and too loud.

But do you know? It wasn't a *bit* like *The Big Chill*!

All six of us were still happily married—after ten years. Unlike Lawrence Kasdan's characters, we all had children, nice kids who weren't on crack. Each of us was doing what we had always wanted to do, enjoying it and surviving if not prospering at it. We had preserved most of our ideals, and found ways to pursue them in the real world. One couple had been teaching sanitation and erosion control and such in the country of Lesotho, which is the size of a picnic table and entirely surrounded by South Africa. The other couple had helped build the Ontario branch of a worldwide disaster-relief agency called Plenty, which has measurably reduced the amount of agony on this planet. I had managed to earn a precarious living by dreaming happy futures; Jeanne had kept one of the finest modern dance companies in Canada, Nova Dance Theatre, alive in Halifax for eight years, without federal subsidy. None of us had sold out to *People* magazine, or gone Hollywood; none of us had become a burnout or drug addict. We all happened to use the same computer—the one that global visionary created, the Mac. We were *not* brought together by the inexplicable suicide of one of the best of us, but by something more like white magic. Our being there helped them to help their father die, to help their mother through her time of sorrow.

Two days later—in the presence of our own families, who had missed the last one—Jeanne and I got married again on Cape Cod.

All this took place nine and a half years ago, and at last report all three couples are still married, still doing just fine. One of those folks is running for office! I'm still creating futures I'd like to live in, Jeanne is a lay-ordained Zen student, choreographer and part-time Hugo-winning novelist. Through my marriage to her I have come to learn that "faith" is not a dirty word after all. I "keep faith" with her. So I've been trying to make my life a kind of on-going act of faith, to keep looking for reasons to hope, and to keep hoping anyway while I search.

It hasn't been easy lately. It's been a brutal year, hasn't it? Bombs flying, people dying, cresting waves of witch-hunt hysteria producing cults of mass self-hypnosis (Facilitated Communication, Recovered Memory Syndrome, etc) . . . even the Right-to-Life extremists seem to have decided abortion is okay—if the fetus is in its 200th trimester. Personally, Jeanne and I have had some severe financial and artistic and personal setbacks, excellent temptations to gloom.

But we're still married, after twenty years, more in love than when we started. We just finished our third novel and thus our trilogy. I've had a miraculous, inexplicable total remission of seven years of devastating chronic belly trouble: my guts have literally stopped churning.

We're hanging on to hope—by our fingers and toes, sometimes, by reflex or habit, sometimes, but hanging on. It is not merely desirable to keep morale up— it seems to me it is *necessary*.

If anyone had told *you*, ten years ago, that shortly the Berlin Wall would come down, Mr. Mandela would walk free, the Soviet Union would come apart, nuclear apocalypse would recede, *perfect* music reproduction would become trivially cheap and simple, and Geraldo Rivera would have his nose broken on camera . . . would you have believed them?

Cousin, hang on to your eyebrows! The *next* ten years might just lift them into orbit . . .

Neils Bohr, one of the founders of quantum mechanics, once said, "The opposite of an ordinary truth is a non-truth; but the opposite of a profound truth is *another profound truth*." Yes: sometimes Life sucks—that's a profound truth. The flip side is: sometimes it sucks rather well . . .

Belief in the possibility of change is what's at the center of this. If you lose belief in the possibility of change for the better, you stop trying, and become part of the problem, part of humanity's dead weight. We'll solve the problems anyway—we always do, eventually—but right now people are dying while the wealthiest and luckiest of us piss and moan about existential angst.

Anything is possible. I once saw a man ski through a revolving door. There is going to be a future: let's chase it until it kills us.

I know a man named Keith Henson. He assumes (believes) he will probably live forever and become infinitely rich. Don't laugh: he's one of the co-founders of cryogenics, so he has a better shot than you do. Therefore the urgent question on his mind is, *assuming lightspeed is an absolute limit, will there be time to closely inspect the entire universe, before it burns out?* Careful calculation persuades him the trick is possible: an army of tourists (perhaps .01% of humanity) setting out in all directions at once at lightspeed within the next few centuries *should* have time to see everything, and still meet at the far end for a Grand Memory-Merge download, before the cosmic candle gutters. So Henson has already struck the Party Committee, and is busy planning the Party at the End of Space and Time. After all, you wouldn't want to get there and find no one remembered the beer, right? Using nanotechnological transmutation (less than a hundred years away, he says; maybe less than fifty), he intends to convert an entire solar system into beer cans alone—and several more into beer. Which will, of course, be recycled many times.

He's a bit stressed; he describes it as a "nontrivial problem." Hope costs. Once you concede that problems can be solved, you have to get up off your ass. Despair, by contrast, is cheap, self-powering, eliminates unwanted guilt, and requires—permits!—no effort. But you die young, and you're no fun to be around in the meantime. Keith Henson is fun to be around. Pay your money; take your choice.

Me, I think we are on the verge of cascading breakthroughs that will make everything we've seen in our lifetimes seem prosaic. Nearly unimaginable wonders and marvels are just around the corner; if half of the things on the drawing boards pan out, war, hunger, disease and loneliness really could all be eliminated within a century or less. Even fear (and its cover identity, hate) might conceivably be brought under control within our children's lifetimes . . . ours, if we get lucky.

You may well think I'm crazy. I remember when I was six years old, a seasoned sf reader, trying to explain to my father that one day there would be rockets to the Moon and computers in peoples' houses and robots and so forth. Sure, kid. A few years ago I bought Dad a robot; answers to voice commands, navigates, fetches your drink, US$48. They've just started selling a Mac that obeys voice commands, reads text aloud, doubles as a hands-free phone, answering machine, rolodex, fax, CD player *and recorder*, and VCR/video editor . . . and costs exactly what a 128K Mac did in 1984: US$2,500. The new one can be expanded to 128 *megabytes* of RAM. Ten years of progress.

I think human beings can do anything they Goddamn well want to. Remember what Robert Heinlein said: the last item to come fluttering from Pandora's Box was Hope . . .

"—AND SUBSEQUENT CONSTRUCTION"

God gets away with things no one else could. Want proof?

The greatest comedians of the last century, the ones who lasted longest commercially and physically, were named *hope* (who always looked young), *burns* (who always looked old), and *miltin' b[oy/g]irl* (remembered for his drag routines). Then there were *skel[e]ton*, who slumped when he got tired; *'kay*, who was absurdly agreeable; and *Cid Caesar*, who returned from the dead when he slowed down, slimmed down, and got control of his ego. The only woman one can call to mind from that generation was named *ball*, whom they loved loose, see?; enough said there. Not many would accept irony that heavy-handed from an author . . . yet the twentieth century swallowed it from God without comment, laughing their heads off. Today, in 2010, I'm the only one who seems to have noticed.

Remember that: it may help you with what follows.

I'm a mathematician by training, and I've been a relativist. I've logged trips to six different star systems. I pray not to a god, but to the Nameless; and I don't try to send my prayers anywhere—I just try to *be* them. I remember well the prayer I was being that night as I drove from home to my lab . . .

Thank you, Nameless!

For all my life, the statement [(good luck) > (bad luck)] has tended to obtain—consistently enough to compensate for my basic tragedy: having been born a supergenius. Want proof? The foster parents who have always sworn they picked their little Iris on the basis of my toothless smile happened to be a NASA image specialist and a chaoticist: experts in, respectively, the universe's surface appearance and its underlying causes. They tutored me at home until I passed their competence at age ten and was admitted to UCLA. Mom was a Buddhist and Dad a Taoist. No other sort of background could have prepared me so well to be a relativist— that's why there are so few of us, which is why we're so absurdly well paid—and if I hadn't been a relativist I would not have met my beloved husband Teodor (whose name means "gift of God").

In case you missed it, I've just defined an ascending curve from First Luck to Best Luck

. . . because a good marriage is one of the most worthwhile things a human can make.

The proof of that statement lurks within the proximate cause of the prayer I was being as I hurtled down the highway that night. Just before I'd left our home to drive to work, Ted had given me a series of orgasms so exquisite and intense that it was a good thing the act of driving is these days essentially finished once you've defined your destination to the car . . . and furthermore, he had declined my offer to return the favor. ("Sometimes I just like to make my Iris dilate," he'd said.)

Do you see why that was so special? One of the hardest things a person can learn is to forgive herself for the massive extent of her own selfishness—and such selfishness is necessary, because you can't love anyone else until you love yourself utterly. I'd always had trouble in that area until I met Ted; thank the Nameless, he was able to persuade me that he enjoyed my sexual greediness as much as *I* did . . . which freed me to appreciate *his* sexual greediness, whenever the wind blew from that direction, and all the other kinds of delicious mutual greediness as well.

My smug contentment at owning a marriage so good that we didn't feel the need to keep books on each other was so pervasive that evening that there was no room left in my heart for frustration at how poorly my work was going—

—until my car, counting off broken white lines traversed, concluded it had reached its required coordinates, shut itself down, scanned the area for unfriendlies, and unlocked my door. At the sight of my lab, sitting amid endless hectares of cemetery like the millionaire's mausoleum it might yet become one day, I did an instant emotional one-eighty and became depressed.

What use, I asked myself, are genius, wealth, fame, and one of the great marriages of the Solar System . . . if your work won't work? I actually tried to slam the car door.

This funk persisted while I persuaded the lab door I was me, entered the building, stripped in the antechamber (unlike most people these days, I dislike driving in the nude), and entered the lab proper—whereupon sadness vanished.

Standing at the far end of the room was someone I recognized at once. I part my hair in the middle, so it was the breasts that confirmed the identification: right noticeably larger than the left. This was no mirror-reversed image.

My visitor was me.

"Thank the Nameless," I cried happily, and then, "What *took* me so long?"

Me grinned at I.

When Ikimono-roshi (whose name means "life," "living creatures," "farm products," or "uncooked food") discovered the star drive in 1995, he thereby also created the profession called "relativist." The best definition ever offered to the layman of what a relativist does is (naturally) the Roshi's: he said we meditate on and with the engine, in order to make it happy enough to function. He held back the part about how we dissuade the star drive from becoming a star . . . until humankind had become utterly economically dependent on star travel. Fortunately that took only a couple of decades: the Roshi's only significant character flaw was reluctance to keep a joke to himself. (A great pity: it finally killed him . . . a joke he must have loved.)

The profession he created was ideal for me. It paid the highest salary in human history—in return for which I was *required* to spend days at a time meditating on the imaginary distinctions between mathematics, physics, philosophy and religion. In itself, that should have contented any supergenius . . . but one relativistic "day," as I was contemplating the second of Ikimonoroshi's three splendid 4-D *jukugo*, drugged to the eyeballs with don't-sleep (somewhere between Sol and Sirius A/B—going to the dogs, that is), I achieved the insight that should have made time travel practical.

Which caused me to shut down the engine, forfeiting my pay for that trip, and go look up a passenger named Teodor I'd met during turnover and drag him off to bed with me, which helped us finish beginning to fall in love, which inspired him to write a song so good it forced us to get married—yes, he's *that* Teodor—but these are other stories. Another time.

It took Ted and me four agonizing years to force the government to let me retire—hell, I understand their position; there were only forty-six relativists alive and sane at that time—but finally I was free to chase my chimera full-time. Perhaps my motivation will seem inadequate to you, especially if you're one of the hundreds who debarked at the Sirius System two weeks later than you expected, but it was sufficient for me: I wanted to go backward in time and meet my biological (as opposed to my "real") mother. Emotional considerations aside, it would have been useful to know rather than deduce my medical and genetic history. But only a fool puts emotional considerations aside: above all, I needed to know whether I forgave her.

In any case, there finally came a time when I was able to enter my ideal laboratory/zendo and put my full attention on time travel for ten hours a night. (I wish the biophyzzle folks would buckle down and solve immortality; 200-odd years just isn't enough time for a person to get any serious thinking done. There's always *some*thing, you know?)

What ensued were two solid months of frustration . . . which got worse as time passed. The question that kept digging around under my skin like a burrowing parasite was: *where the hell was I?*

(Am I going too fast? Brunner tells the story of a prof scrawling equations on the lecture-hall blackboard who declaimed, "It is therefore obvious—" frowned, scratched his head, left the hall amid growing murmurs, and returned ten minutes later to announce triumphantly, "I was right: it *is* obvious!" I often have the same trouble communicating with those more fortunate than myself. Hyperintelligence is a very mixed blessing.)

My antinomy was this: if I were to succeed in inventing . . . oh, let's give in and call it a time machine . . . I was sure the first thing I would *do* with it (after testing it for safety) would be to come back and tell me I was going to succeed. Naturally I would not have told myself *how* I'd done it—don't you hate it when someone tells you how the book is going to come out?—but I'm so cocky I didn't see how it could hurt to have my cleverness confirmed in advance.

So the fact that I had not met me during my first two months of work had been unnerving. No—maddening!

And now, at last, here me was. The sense of relief was overwhelming.

"Eventually," me said, "we'll either have to restructure English, or speak math. But for now, let's try to keep this as simple as possible. You can call me Jay, eh?"

I believed I understood. Jay is what comes after Eye-for-Iris in the alphabet, and the way Jay phrased it raised resonances of another old-time comedian we both loved because he had only a single joke to his name. I forgot what sort of bird a jay is.

"I . . . Jay . . . 'kay," I said, and had the satisfaction of seeing my self smile at one of my own puns. No one else but Teodor ever does.

But there was something about that smile I recognized all too well, even without the usual mirror reversal.

Jay was *miserable*, through and through. So

saturated with sadness, I think even another person could have seen it.

"What's wrong?" I cried . . . and then remembered what had once made me look that sad, and what had cured me. My yo-yo heart plummeted again. "Oh, *no*! Ted's—"

"No," Jay said at once. "It's almost worse than that, Iris. He's still alive. But we're divorced. Bitterly."

I screamed. First time in my life. Then: "WHY?"

"Do you really want to know?"

"Hell. Of course not. Thank you. Any . . . any hope at all?"

"I don't think so," she said.

Despair. "Ah Jay, Jay—why did you *tell* . . . cancel, I asked you. Oh, damn me! And my cursed curiosity . . . "

I had never in my life wished more fervently that I'd been born a normal human being, able to *not* think things through if I chose. Can you imagine how fervently that is? I wasted ten whole silent seconds feeling sorry for myself—a lifetime record—before I was able to turn my attention to feeling sorry for my *other* self . . . who had been in this pain for much longer than I had. That selfishness I mentioned earlier. "Is there anything I can do to help you, Jay?"

"Yes."

"What?"

Jay didn't answer. In a second, I got it. If you'd lost your life's one love, wouldn't you give anything to be with him one last time if you could? "Here," I said, and gave her my key ring.

A fraction of her sadness seemed to lift from her. "Thank you, Iris!"

"He'll be pleasantly surprised," I told her, trying to make this sad consolation prize as happy as possible. "He's ready for some loving, and not expecting to get it sooner than dawn at the earliest. Just tell him your selfish need to hear him groan with joy overcame your need to work; it'll flatter the hell out of him. Uh . . . if you think of it, afterward, kiss him once for me."

"I will," she promised. "I should be back by dawn. If . . . if you could use some consolation yourself, then . . . "

The concept was horridly hilarious, mind-boggling; I groped in vain for a response.

She turned and left hastily.

My pain was so great that I could not contemplate it. Greater, in other words, than the fire at the heart of a star drive. My choices were to go mad, or to drown myself in my work.

After all, I knew now that I could succeed. That I had . . . would have had . . . done so.

First invent the time machine, Iris. Then revamp English to fit the new facts.

I booted up my computer and got started. Somewhere in the back of my mind as I worked was the mad, less-than-half-believed hope that somehow I might employ a completed time machine to avert the disaster in my future, to use an "undo" key on reality. It was illogical, but so is all hope.

An hour later I roared with frustrated rage and pounded on my keyboard. Zero progress.

No. Less than zero. I had succeeded in *proving* that the line of attack I'd been using was a dead end. And I could see no other.

I wished I'd cheated, and pumped Jay for hints before letting her go.

Why hadn't I? In too much of a hurry, yes . . . but *why*?

It hit me like a slap. One small component of the eagerness with which I'd agreed to Jay's pitiful request has been . . . oh, shit . . . relief. Relief from a minor nagging guilt. At having accepted Ted's gift of unreciprocated pleasure earlier that night.

I had welcomed Jay's intervention because it would help me balance a set of books I prided myself on not keeping.

Why? Because now that I knew I was going to be divorced from Ted some day, I was subconsciously operating in accordance with one of the basic principles of star travel: "When the ship lifts, all bills are paid." I had been able to live with unbalanced books because I'd believed the ship was never going to lift. But if Ted and I *were* going to separate, my selfish subconscious did not want to leave owing him any debt—even one as trivial as an unreciprocated orgasm.

. . . which implied that the separation was *imminent* . . .

The second insight hit with the force of a death blow, although my subconscious seemed to have known it for an hour.

Oh, Nameless! All she has to do, in the heat of passion, is to make the slightest slip, offer the most harmless of hints. Ted's quick: he'll pick

up on it at once, even in the heat of passion, and then he'll get the whole story out of her—
—*and what will he think of me then?*

What would you think? Suppose you learned that your spouse had conspired with her divorced future-self to take advantage of you . . . to steal from you love and affection *which you would have withheld if you'd been in possession of all the facts?*

Future-Ted presumably had what seemed to him good and sufficient reasons to withhold his love from Future-Iris, from Jay. Therefore Jay's actions constituted rape, seduction-by-guile. Ted would see that at once if he learned the truth—
—and I, present-I, Iris, his trusted wife, had collaborated in his rape—

Dear Nameless—had I destroyed my own marriage? No wonder he was going to divorce me: I had betrayed his trust. In order to do a favor for Jay, for my self. Without thinking . . .

Only a supergenius could have been so stupid!

To confirm the awful inevitable, I phoned home.

There was no answer—the answer I'd half-expected—so I punched in my override code to activate the home camera anyway. It showed our . . . what had been our . . . bedroom, empty, sheets snarled by illicit love. There was something visible on the floor; I zoomed in on it.

It was a sheet of paper, handwritten; dear Ted was so old-fashioned. At max magnification I could read what was written on it.

The best song he'd written in his life. So good that even the best melody could not have added much to it. More than a song: a poem. I can reproduce it from memory:

Afterglow (Iris's Song)
by Ted Rowe

Tending to tension by conscious intent,
declining declension, disdaining dissent,
into the dementia dimension we're sent:
we are our content, and we are content.

Incandescent invention and blessed event;
tumescent distention, tumultuous descent;
our bone of convention again being spent,
I am your contents, and I am content

to be living . . . to be trying . . .
to be crying . . . to be dying—I want
to be giving . . . to be making . . .
to be shaking . . .
to be taking all you have . . .

Assuming Ascension, Assumption, assent,
all of our nonsense
is finally non-sent . . .
with honorable mention
for whatever we meant;
you are my content, and I am content.

How glorious, to see such a song, with my name on it.

How terrible, to see that the sheet of paper

on which it was written had been torn nearly in half and flung to the floor.

Jay had made some slip; he had guessed.

I broke the connection and buried my head in my hands.

My next conscious thought, an indeterminate time later, was: *How could me do this to I?*

How could Jay, my very own self, have done this horrid thing—when she had to have known it would blow up in our face, that it would precipitate all our mutual misery?

With that thought, my brain woke up and began to think for the first time that night.

My line of work had required me to study a little astronomy—an interesting field for a mathematician—and one of the few anecdotes from the history of astronomy which had stuck in my mind was the story of Fritz Zwicky's "Method of Negation and Subsequent Construction." Zwicky said he *began* with the absolute certainty that dwarf galaxies must exist, *because Edwin Hubble said they could not* . . . and thus certain, was able to prove their existence. This form of reasoning had amused me, so I'd remembered it.

I employed it now.

I wanted so badly to believe that Jay could not be me—that not even time and sustained pain could make me so stupid as to cause that pain—that I *assumed* it.

And that single axiom made all anomalies disappear, caused things to fall into place with an almost audible click. I came close to shouting aloud the word, "Eureka!"

I'll take you through it step by step.

Postulate that my unknown biological mother was at least highly intelligent. Not a supergenius like me, necessarily, but I can't see her as a dummy. Even now, no one knows for sure how much of genius is hereditary and how much is environmental, but grant me the premise.

Admittedly, she lived most of her life during the dark ages just ended. Provisionally accept the current theory that genius and genius-plus children tend to be borne by mothers over 30, and say that Mother (as opposed to Mom, who raised me) was born around 1955. The Stone Age as far as women were concerned.

But even if you assume her luck was minimal, that she was a poverty-stricken, handicapped, ugly, single parent in an era which treated single parents barbarically . . . still and even so, it would *seem* that she ought to have been able to cope with parenthood, at least for longer than the week or two she stuck it out.

But suppose she birthed *twins* . . .

Suppose further that my hypothetical identical twin—let's call her, for the sake of the argument, "Jay"—had even fractionally less than my own good luck in foster parents. Not hard to believe.

Endless studies have uncovered cases in which identical twins raised separately, unaware that a twin existed, had astonishingly similar lives, down to their professions, IQs, favorite swear words and the names of their spouses and children.

But with even a slight wrinkle in the blueprint, Jay might have grown to maturity without ever having learned the most crucial life lesson I had learned: that it's okay to be selfish.

Supergeniuses who lack that realization cannot love themselves fully. This must surely inhibit, twist their intelligence. Such a crippled supergenius might well cause her own marriage to self-destruct, to drive away a loving husband because of her inevitable contempt for anyone stupid enough to give unconditional love to a monster like herself.

That list of great comedians I started with? One I left out was *marks*, who said, "I could never belong to a club that would have me as a member." He went through quite a few broken relationships before merciful death eased his magnificent, needless suffering.

How might such a self-contemptuous woman punish herself for hurting and driving away a good and loving man?

Well, if she knew or somehow learned that she had a twin, she might be moved to research her. And if that twin's life was turning out infuriatingly better than her own, she might just construct an elaborate and cruel hoax to wreck her sister's marriage too . . .

As far as I was concerned the thing was proved. Yet I turned to my terminal. I intended to finally use some of the awesome clout and access even an ex-relativist can command to smash through all the bureaucratic barriers against my learning the name of my mother and the circumstances of my birth and adoption. I had not planned to do so until I had a working time machine and could act on the information . . . but I was aware that Negation and Subsequent Construction is a ladder of dubious strength, and I wanted this nailed down.

But as my modem program came up on the screen, the door to the lab opened and Ted came in. He was pushing Jay along before him; she was swearing brilliantly in Russian, my own favorite language for cursing. He locked the door behind them with his coded card and stepped past her to face me.

"I'm sorry, darling," I blurted, springing to my feet. "I wasn't thinking clearly—"

"In your place I think I might have done the same thing," he interrupted. "It was a sweet, selfish, human thing to do. Nothing worth losing a mate like you over. Very few things warp your judgment, my love: I'm flattered that the prospect of losing me is one of them." He smiled, and burst into tears.

So I did too. We embraced fiercely.

"I know how *I* figured it out," I said when I could. "But how did *you* figure it out?"

"You'll like it," he promised. "Nothing I could think of could have suddenly made you so bad a lover."

One of many reasons I love my Ted: he keeps his promises. I tightened my embrace.

"You can't hold me," Jay snarled. "This can't be construed as a citizen's arrest: nothing I've done is a felony." She poked futilely at the locked door.

"You seem to know me pretty well, sister," I said. "How much do I care for law?"

She paled. "What are you going to do to me?" she asked us.

"Your privilege, love," Ted said to me.

I nodded. "The nastiest, most sadistic, most poetically appropriate thing I can think of," I told my twin. "We're going to try to heal you." She looked shocked. "You're crippled with self-hatred, and I think we're just the two people who can fix that."

"Without my consent? That's . . . immoral."

"If you were anyone else," I said, "I would agree with you. I believe people have a general right to keep their neuroses as long as they think they need them. But in this special case, I cannot accept the risk. You're damn near as clever as me, and as long as you remain damaged you will mean harm to Ted and me. I decline to spend the rest of my life burning energy to stay a step ahead of you. Out of raw self-interest, I propose to teach you things you don't want to learn, and keep you prisoner until you've learned them." I smiled wickedly. "And make you like it. You'll thank me when I'm done—isn't that *awful*? Just remember: you asked for it."

She tried to attack me, but my husband is very quick and very strong. She ended up with one arm wrenched up behind her.

"And if we can manage to fix the kink in your heart," he went on while she cursed and struggled, "we're all going to track down your ex-husband—Russian, like me, isn't he?—and try to heal your marriage."

She was struck speechless. She went limp in his grip.

"It's certainly worth thinking about," I agreed—and suddenly it was as if two continental plates had slipped inside my skull: a massive realignment that was over in an instant. "Now if the two of you will excuse me," I said dizzily, "I've got a time machine to invent. It just now came to me: *two* fields, almost but not quite identical, just out of phase. If it works, I'll be waiting for you both at home when you get there." I caught Ted's eye. "We'll lock her up in the guest room for the night, and make other arrangements tomorrow. I'm going to make you write that song to me retroactively, darling. Very retro, very actively."

"Yes, dear," he said mildly, and got the hell out of my lab, dragging Jay with him.

That's another reason I love him. He doesn't try to top my puns.

And as I turned back to my workstation, there was a small clap of thunder, and a pressure change that made my ears pop, and my *real* future-self winked into being a meter away, wearing a grid of wires, a headband, a plastic backpack that hummed softly, and a smile.

"Congratulations," me said.

After a moment's hesitation—it had been a *long* night—I returned my smile.

NOT FADE AWAY

I became aware of him five parsecs away.

He rode a nickel-iron asteroid of a hundred metric tons as if it were an unruly steed, and he broke off chunks of it and hurled them at the stars, and he howled.

I manifested at the outer periphery of his system and waited to be noticed. I'm sure he had been aware of me long before I detected him, but he affected not to see me for several days, until my light reached him.

I studied him while I waited. There was something distinctly odd about his morphology. After a while I recognized it: he was wearing the prototype—the body our ancestors wore! I looked closer, and realized that it was the only body he had ever worn.

Oh, it had been Balanced and spaceproofed and the skull shielded, of course. But he looked as if when Balancing was discovered, he had been just barely young enough for the process to take. He must have been one of the oldest of the Eldest.

But why keep that ridiculous body configuration? It was hopelessly inefficient, suited only to existence on the surface of planets, and rather poorly to that. For a normal environment, everything about it was wrong. I saw that he had had the original sensory equipment improved for space conditions, but it was still limited and poorly placed. Everything about the body was laid out bilaterally and unidirectionally, creating a blind side. The engineering was all wrong, the four limbs all severely limited in mobility. Many of the joints were essentially one-directional, simple hinges.

Stranger still, the body was grotesquely, comically overmuscled. Whenever his back happened to be turned to his star, the forty-kilo bits of rock he hurled achieved system escape velocity—yet he was able to keep that asteroid clamped between his great thighs. What individual ever— much less routinely—needs that much strength in free space?

Oddest of all, of course, his mind was sealed. Apparently totally. I could get no reading at all from him, and I am a very good reader. He must have been completely unplugged from the Bonding, and in all my three thousand years I have met only four such. He must have been as lonely as any of our ancestors ever was. Yet he knew that the Bonding exists, and refused it.

A number of objects were tethered or

strapped to his body, all worn but showing signs of superb maintenance. It took me several days to identify them all positively as utensils, several more to realize that each was a weapon. It takes time for things to percolate down out of the Race Memory, and the oldest things take the most time.

By then he was ready to notice me. He focused one of his howls and directed it to me. He carefully ignored all the part of me that is Bonded, addressing only my individual ego, with great force.

"GO AWAY!"

"Why?" I asked reasonably.

"GO AWAY AT ONCE OR I WILL END YOU!"

I radiated startled interest. "Really? Why would you do that?"

"OH, GAAAH . . . "

There was a silence of some hours.

"I will go away," I said at last, "if you will tell me why you want me to do so."

His volume was lower. "Do you know who I am?"

I laughed. "How could I know? Your mind is sealed."

"I am the last warrior."

"Warrior? Wait now . . . 'warrior.' Must be an old word. 'Warrior.' Oh—*oh*. You kill and destroy. Deliberately. How odd. Are you going to destroy me?"

"I may," he said darkly.

"I see. How might I dissuade you? I do not believe I am old enough to die competently yet, and I have at least one major obligation outstanding."

"Do you lack the courage to flee? Or the wit?"

"I shall attempt to flee if I find it necessary. But I would not expect to succeed."

"Ah. You fear me."

"'Fear'? No. I recognize the menace you represent. I repeat: how might I dissuade you from ending me? Is there something I can offer you? Access to the Bonding of Minds, perhaps?"

This reply was instant. "If I suspect you of *planning* to initiate the Bonding process with me, I will make your death a thing of unending and unspeakable agony."

I projected startlement, then masked it. "What *can* I do for you, then?"

He laughed. "That's easy. Find me a fair fight. Find me an enemy. If he or she or it is as strong as me, I will let you go unharmed. If stronger, I will give you all I own, and consecrate my death to you."

"I am not sure I understand."

"I am the *last* warrior."

"Yes?"

"When I chose my profession, warriors were common, and commonly admired. We killed or destroyed not for personal gain, but to protect a group of non-warriors, or to protect an idea or an ideal."

I emanated confusion. "Against what?"

His answer was days in coming. "Other warriors."

"How did the cycle get started?"

"Primitive men were all warriors."

"*Really?*"

"Then there came a time when the average man had to be forced to kill or destroy. One day, he could no longer be forced. A Balanced human in free space cannot be coerced—only slain. Can you visualize circumstances which would force you to kill?"

"Only with the greatest difficulty," I said. "But you enjoy it? You would find pleasure or value in killing me?"

A week passed. At last he smote his asteroid with his fist, sharply enough to cause rock to fly from its other side. "No. I lied. I will not kill you. What good is a fight you can't lose?"

"Why did you . . . 'lie'?"

"In order to frighten you."

"You failed."

"Yes, I know."

"Why did you wish to frighten me?"

"To compel you to my will."

"Hmmm. I believe I see. Then you do wish to locate an enemy. I am baffled. I should have thought a warrior's prime goal to be the elimination of all other warriors."

"No. A warrior's prime goal is to overcome other warriors. I am the greatest warrior our race has ever raised up. I have not worked in over five thousand years. There is no one to overcome."

"*Oh.*"

"Do you know what the R-brain is?"

"Wait. It's coming. Oh. I know what the R-brain *was*. The primitive reptile brain from which the human brain evolved."

"And do you know that for a considerable time, early humans—true humans—possessed, beneath their sentient brains, a vestigial but powerful R-complex, called 'the subconscious mind'?"

"Of course. The First Great Antinomy."

"I have an R-complex."

I registered shock. "You cannot possibly be old enough."

I could sense his bitter grin before the sight of it crawled to me at lightspeed. "Do you notice anything interesting about this particular star system?"

I glanced around. "Barring your presence in it, no."

"Consider that planet there. The third."

At first glance it was an utterly ordinary planet, like a myriad of others in this out-of-the-way sector. It was wet and therefore alive, and even showed signs that it had evolved intelligent life at least once, but of course that was—by definition—long gone. None of its remaining lifeforms seemed anywhere near bright enough to leave it behind and enter the world yet. Its physical and ballistic properties appeared unremarkable.

But after only a few days of contemplation, I cried out in surprise. "Why . . . its period of rotation is almost *precisely* one standard day. And its period of revolution seems to approximate a standard year. And its surface acceleration is a standard gee. Do you mean to tell me that planet is . . . uh . . . is—"

"Dirt," he agreed. "And yonder star is Sol."

"And you imply that—"

"Yes. I was born here. On that planet, in fact. At a time when all the humans in the universe lived within the confines of this system—and used less than half the planets, at that."

"!!!"

"Do you still wonder that I shun your Bonding?"

"No. To you, with a reptile brain stem, it must be the ultimate obscenity."

"Defenselessness. Yes."

"A thing which can be neither dominated nor compelled. And which itself will not dominate or compel . . . you must hate us."

"Aye."

"You could be healed. The reptile part of your brain could—"

"I could be gelded too. And why not, since none will breed with me? Yet I choose to retain my gonads. And my R-complex. Call it habit."

"I see." I paused in thought. "What prevents you from physically attacking the Bond? I believe that at this point in history, you could harm it greatly . . . perhaps even destroy it."

"I repeat: what good is a fight you can't lose?"

"Oh."

"In the old days . . . there was glory. There was a galaxy to be tamed, empires to be carved out of the sky, mighty enemies to challenge. More than once I pulverized a star. With four allies I battled the Ten of Algol, and after two centuries broke them. Then were other sentient races found, in the inner neighboring arm of the galaxy, and I learned the ways of fighting them."

He paused. "I was honored in those days. I was one of mankind's saviors." A terrible chuckle. "Do you know anything sorrier than an unemployed savior?"

"And your fellows?"

"One day it was all changed. The brain had evolved. Man's enemies were broken or co-opted. It became clear that competition for unlimited wealth is insane. Peace broke out. The cursed Bonding began. At first we fought it as a plague swallowing our charges. But ere long we came to see that it was what they had freely chosen. Finally there came a day when we had only ourselves to fight."

"And?"

"We fought. Whole systems were laid to waste, alliances were made and betrayed, truly frightening energies were released. The rest of mankind withdrew from us and forgot us."

"I can see how this would be."

"Man had no need of us. Man was in harmony with himself, and his neighbors, and it was now plain that in all the galaxy there were no threatening races extant or imminent. For a long time we had hope that there might lie enemies beyond this galaxy—that we might yet be needed. And so we fought mock combats, preserving ourselves for our race. We dreamed of once again battling to save our species from harm; we dreamed of vindication."

A long pause.

"Then we heard of contact with Bondings of sentient beings from neighboring galaxies. The Unification began. In rage and despair we fell upon each other, and there was a mighty slaughter. There was one last false alarm of hope when the Malign Bonding of the Crab Nebula was found." His voice began to tremble with rage. "We waited for your summons. And you . . . you . . . " Suddenly he screamed. "YOU *CURED* THE BASTARDS!"

"Listen to me," I said. "A neuron is a wonderful thing. But when a billion neurons agree to work together, they become a thing a billion times more wonderful—a brain. A mind. There are as many stars in this galaxy as there are neurons in a single human mind. More than coincidence. This galaxy has *become* a single mind: the Bonding. There are as many galaxies in this universe as there are stars in the average galaxy. Each has, or is developing, its own Bonding. Each of these is to be a neuron in the Cosmic Mind. One day Unification will be complete, and the universe will be intelligent. You can be part of that mind, and share in it."

"*No*," he said emphatically. "If I am part of the Cosmic Mind, then I am part of its primitive subconscious mind. The subconscious is useful only for preservation from outside threat. As your brain evolved beyond your ancestors' subconscious mind, your universal mind has evolved beyond me. There is nothing in the plenum that you need fear." He leaned forward in sudden pain, embraced his asteroid with his arms as well as his legs. I began moving closer to him, not so rapidly as to alarm him if he should look up, but not slowly.

"When we understood this," he said, "we

warriors fell upon each other anew. Four centuries ago Jarl and I allied to defeat The One In Red. That left only each other. We made it last as long as we could. Perhaps it was the greatest battle ever fought. Jarl was very very good. That was why I saved him for last."

"And you overcame him?"

"Since then I have been alone." He lifted his head quickly and roared at the universe, "Jarl, you son of a bitch, *why didn't you kill me?*" He put his face again to the rock.

I could not tell if he had seen me approaching.

"And in all the years since, you have had no opponent?"

"I tried cloning myself once. Useless. No clone can have my experience and training; the environment which produced me no longer exists. What good is a fight you cannot lose?"

I was coming ever closer. "Why do you not suicide?"

"What good is a fight you cannot lose?"

I was near now. "Then all these years, you have prayed for an enemy?"

"Aye." His voice was despairing.

"Your prayer is answered."

He stiffened. His head came up and he saw me.

"I represent the Bonding of the Crab," I said then. "The cure was imperfect," and I did direct at him a laser.

I was near, but he was quick, and his mirror shield deflected my bolt even before he could have had time to absorb my words. I followed the laser with other energies, and he dodged, deflected or neutralized them as fast as they could be mounted.

There was an instant's pause then, and I saw a grin begin slowly and spread across his face. Carnivore's warning. He flung his own weapons into space.

"I am delivered," he cried, and then he shifted his mass, throwing his planetoid into a spin. When it lay between us, I thought he had struck it with both feet, for suddenly it was rushing toward me. Of course I avoided it easily—but as it passed, he darted around from behind it, where he had been hidden, and grappled with me physically. He had hurled the rock not with his feet, but with a reaction drive.

Then did I understand why he kept such an ancient body form, for it was admirably suited to single combat. I had more limbs, but weaker, and one by one my own weapons were torn from me and hurled into the void. Meanwhile mental energies surged against each other from both sides, and space began to writhe around us.

Mentally I was stronger than he, for he had been long alone, and mental muscles can be exercised only on another mind. But his physical power was awesome, and his ferocity a thing incomprehensible to me.

And now I see the end coming. Soon his terrible hands will reach my brain case and rip it asunder. When this occurs, my body will explode with great force, and we shall both die. He knows this, and in this instant of time before the end, I know what he is doing, beneath his shield where I cannot probe. He is composing his last message for transmission to you, his people, his Bonding. He is warning you of mortal danger. He is telling you where to find his hidden DNA samples, where to find the records he has made of everything he knows about combat, how to train his clones to be *almost* as good as he is. And he is feeling the satisfaction of vindication. *I could have told you!* he is saying. *Ye who knew not my worth, who had forgotten me, yet will I save you!*

This is my own last message to you, to the same people, to the same Bonding. It worked. He believes me. I have accomplished what you asked of me. He has the hero's death he craved.

We will die together, he and I. And that is meet and proper, for I am the last Healer in the cosmos, and now I too am unemployed.

SEDUCTION OF THE IGNORANT

Remarks delivered at "A Celebration of Literacy" on international Literacy Day, 8 September 1990 at the Trade and Convention Centre, Vancouver

Paul Simon once said that " . . . the words of the prophets are written on the subway walls/ and tenement halls . . . " I have myself recently seen the future writ large upon my own sidewalk.

Due to the recent construction of four megaboxes bracketing my own home in Point Grey, the sidewalk became so damaged as to require repair. The freshly poured cement naturally attracted *graffitisti* with popsicle sticks, determined to immortalize themselves. How few real opportunities there are these days for a writer to have his or her work literally graven in stone! Inevitably, one of these was an ardent young swain who wished to proclaim his undying love to the ages. His chilling masterpiece of . . . er . . . concrete poetry is located right at the foot of my walkway, where I must look at it every time I leave my home. It consists of a large heart, within which are inscribed the words:

TOOD + JANEY

Now, I don't know about you, but I decline to believe that even in this day and age, any set of parents elected to name their son "Tood." I am therefore forced to conclude that *young Todd is unable to spell his own goddam name* . . . despite having reached an age sufficiently advanced for him to find young Janey intriguing. As I make my living from literacy, I find this sign of the times demoralizing.

George Neavoll, an editor of the Wichita *Eagle & Beacon*, recently complained to Ann Landers that he could nearly always tell the age bracket of a correspondent by counting the errors in spelling, grammar and construction: the more there were, the younger the writer. We all know what he meant—our presence here today proves it. There is no point in my preaching to the converted. We are all, I hope, terrified at the growing prospect of a nation of illiterate voters attempting to make responsible decisions about complex and urgent issues of science and technology, issues whose cardinal points simply cannot be condensed into a ten-second sound bite.

He who cannot read, cannot reason. And we know that the trend is in that direction.

It is tempting to blame it all on the educational system. I am informed, to my horror, that the British Columbia school system is phasing in a policy discarding letter grades until Grade 11, in favor of vague assessments of a child's "intellectual and social growth." That is to say, no objective measure of their success or failure as teachers will even be attempted for the first decade of a child's education—so it certainly sounds as if *they* suspect it is all their fault. But for all of the English teachers in North America to have developed massive incompetence suddenly, simultaneously and at a constant rate would be a coincidence which beggars the imagination. The answer is too easy, and the only solution it suggests—shoot all the teachers—is perhaps hasty. By and large they are probably doing the best they can with the budgets we give them.

John D. MacDonald, in an essay he wrote for the Library of Congress just before his death, "Reading for Survival," put his finger on the problem: the complex code-system we call literacy—indeed, the very neural wiring that allows it—has existed for only the latest few heartbeats in the long history of human evolution. In competing with television and cinema and video games, books are competing with a system of information acquisition that predates them by several million years. Literacy is a very hard skill to acquire, and once acquired it brings endless heartache—for the more you read, the more you learn of life's intimidating complexity and confusion. But anyone who can learn to grunt is bright enough to watch TV . . . which teaches that life is simple, and happy endings come to those whose hearts are in the right place. If one picture is worth a thousand words, how much more valuable are the thousand changing pictures that go by at 20 frames per second to make up 50 seconds of a Walt Disney cartoon?

Literacy made its greatest inroads when it was the best escape possible from a world defined by the narrow parameters of a family farm or a small village, the only opening onto a larger and more interesting world. But the "mind's eye" has only been evolving for thousands of years, whereas the body's eye has been perfected for millions of them. The mind's eye can show you things that no Hollywood special effects department can simulate—but only at the cost of years of effort spent learning to decode ink stains on paper. Writing still remains the unchallenged best way—indeed, nearly the only way except for mathematics—to express a complicated thought . . . and it seems clear that this is precisely one of its *disadvantages* from the consumers' point of view. Plainly, recent generations of humans have begun to declare, voting with their eyes, that literacy is not worth the bother.

And things are about to get worse. A new technology called "virtual reality" is on the horizon, in which special goggles show you a three-dimensional holographic computer simulation of . . . whatever you choose . . . which you can manipulate using special gloves that let you "reach into" the simulation and "touch" imaginary objects. I submit that no book, however interesting, can compete for a child's attention.

What then can we do about the decline of literacy?

The educational system can do very little more than they are already doing—though I would suggest that they might give some passing thought to offering students something other than the most inexpressibly dull examples of the past millenium's worth of writing. You will not wean teenagers from *America's Funniest Home Videos* with the Brontë sisters.

Government can do even less. I have given up trying to get people to believe this—indeed, three times this year I have heard or seen it introduced as a "joke" by others—but ten years ago while I was in New York City researching a novel, I saw with my own eyes, swear to God, a U.S. government subway advertisement which read, and I quote, "ILLITERATE? WRITE FOR HELP!" . . . giving a box number to which one could write for a free pamphlet on how to learn to read. Your tax dollars at rest. This may be about the best we can expect from government, which has long been a last refuge for the terminally illiterate and innumerate.

We as a society can do little—because "we as a society" is a very rare lifeform, with over fifty million legs and no brain. Society does not make decisions; individuals make them, and the sum—rather, the product—of those decisions is what we, in hindsight, call society.

We as individuals, however, can do at least

some useful work as volunteer guerillas, one on one.

It will do no good merely to sing the praises of literacy to our children. We have done so all our lives, as our parents did before us, and it is not working any more . . . not working well enough, at any rate. We must be more devious than that: we must *con* our children into reading.

I can offer two stratagems in this regard. The first was devised by my mother, and used upon me; the second my wife Jeanne and I developed and field-tested on our daughter, who turns sixteen in October of 1990.

My mother's scheme was, I think, superior to my own, in that it required diabolical cleverness and fundamental dishonesty; it was however time- and labor-intensive. She would begin reading me a comic book—then, just as we had reached the point where the Lone Ranger was hanging by his fingertips from the cliff, buffalo stampede approaching, angry native peoples below . . . Mom would suddenly remember that she had to go sew the dishes, or vacuum the cat, or whatever—and leave me alone with the comic book.

I *had* to know how the story came out. There were pictures to assist me. Most of the words were ones I had just heard read aloud; I could go back and refer to them, again with visual aids. By the age of five, thanks to my mother's policy of well-timed neglect, I had taught myself to read sufficiently well that one day she presented me with a library card and sent me to the library with instructions to bring home a book.

The librarian, God bless her, gave me a copy of Robert A. Heinlein's novel for children, *Rocket Ship Galileo* . . . and from that day on there was never any serious danger that I would be forced to work for a living. Heinlein wrote stories so intrinsically interesting that it was worth the trouble to stop and look up the odd word I didn't know. By age six I was tested as reading at college Junior level.

The problem is that you cannot simply hand the child the comic book: you must read 80% of it to them, and *stop* reading with pinpoint timing. In this day and age, society has decided it can no longer afford the luxury of a full-time in-house child rearer in each family (opting instead to chase a chimera called "low-cost high-quality day care"), and with the best of intentions, you may not have that much time or energy to devote to the task of seducing your child.

In that case I recommend the system devised by my wife and myself. From the day our daughter was old enough to have a defined "bedtime," we made it our firm policy that bedtime was bedtime, no excuses or exceptions . . . unless she were reading, in which case she could stay up as late as she pleased. The most precious gift any child can attain is a few minutes' awareness past bedtime. She went for the bait like a hungry trout, and throughout her elementary school career was invariably chosen as The Narrator in school plays because of her fluency in reading.

Doubtless there are other schemes, and I urge you to give a little time to finding or inventing them. But one thing I promise you all: if you leave the problem to government, or the educational system, or a mythical animal called society—to anyone but yourself—you will effectively be surrendering the battle, and giving your children over into the hands of Geraldo Rivera. As Robert Heinlein said in 1960, in his immortal *Stranger in a Strange Land*, "Thou art God—and cannot decline the nomination." Your only options are to do a good job, or not.

And the consequences of a bad job will make the Dark Ages look good. . . .